the final piece

the final piece

MAGGI MYERS

amazon publishing

Published by Amazon Publishing

PO Box 400818
Las Vegas, NV 89140

ISBN-13: 9781477849217
ISBN-10: 1477849211

1

I place the needle down in the worn groove of the vinyl, my hand moving without any thought. The soft hiss of contact sends a wave of giddy anticipation through me. I clasp my hands together and eagerly wait. Music fills up the space in my tiny bedroom and it sends me spinning in circles with my arms cast wide. I smile at the ceiling and open my mouth to sing. Loneliness releases its grip on my heart with each note that flows through me.

This evening's audience is carefully lined up on my overly girly four-poster bed. Prue the Bear and Raggedy Ann are watching me like they have hundreds of times. I use my hairbrush as a microphone and dig my toes into the chocolate brown carpet, trying to ground the rogue butterflies in my stomach. By the time the first verse ends and the chorus begins, I am no longer timid as I start belting out the notes, conjuring the vision of Olivia Newton John roller-skating her way through Xanadu. Relief falls over me like a soft blanket as the loudness of the party is silenced and I can finally disappear into my daydreams. If I am really lucky, they will have forgotten that I am up here at all.

I turn to my reflection in the mirror above my dresser and attempt a pose that is supposed to be glamorous. I don't have my mother's stunning good looks or my father's charisma. Blinking my eyes really fast, I try to blur my reflection into a pretty girl with flowing blond hair and hazel eyes like my mom or wavy black hair and bright blue eyes like my dad. The room starts to tilt, so I slow down and my face comes back into focus—my long, straight brown hair framing wide brown eyes and a freckled face. I am as plain as they are spectacular.

Deep in critical thoughts of myself, I almost miss the faint sound of footsteps on the staircase. I lunge for the liquor cabinet that holds my record player, accidentally sending the needle screeching. The room goes silent and I pause to listen for the sound again. My heart begins to hammer a triplicate rhythm as I strain to hear movement in the hall.

No one is supposed to be up here.

Panic echoes in the empty space inside my ears as the commotion from downstairs finds its way to my bedroom door. I wish they would just leave me alone. My over-active imagination suggests flesh-eating zombies storming the staircase in search of fresh brains. It's not a far cry from the crowd downstairs because they're either drunk, high, or both; they might as well be zombies. There is a soft knock on my door followed by a quick shake of the doorknob, which is locked. I have learned the hard way that just closing the door doesn't keep people out. Another knock accompanies a voice.

"Mouse, are you awake?" I let out my breath and sag in relief. His voice drifts through the door again, "Mouse, sweetie, it's ok. Open up."

Jumping over my bed, I unlock the door, crack it open and look up into his familiar face.

"Hey there, beautiful, I brought you something." He cocks his head to the side and wiggles his eyebrows up and down. I try in vain not to giggle at his antics and attempt indifference.

I give him a calculated once over, noting his sandy hair is starting to silver at the temple and his clear blue eyes twinkle mischievously. I open the door a little wider and hear my mother's laughter among several other voices carrying up the stairs. He is holding out a record-shaped present wrapped in Strawberry Shortcake paper. It occurs to me that I shouldn't be letting down my guard just because he comes bearing gifts.

Yeah, right. Who am I kidding? I am not a hard sell. Bring me a new record and I'll be your best friend.

My stomach sours at that thought and I eye him warily.

"I missed your birthday last week. Ten is a big deal so I wanted to bring you something special."

He holds out the gift expectantly. I take it and he smiles at me—the kind of smile that softens his face but does nothing to hide the intensity of his assessment of me. I can feel my face flush so I drop my gaze to the gift in my hand, noting that all of the Strawberry Shortcakes are holding flags with the number ten above their heads.

"Happy Birthday, Mouse. Let's go open it."

His voice is gentle but his hands are firm as he places them against my shoulders and leads me back into my room. He turns to lock the door.

"My name is not Mouse." It comes out sounding petulant. I know this makes him mad. "My name is Beth, and besides, I hate Mouse."

I hate that nickname. My dad started calling me that because I reminded him of a timid little mouse. How he found that endearing is beyond my understanding. Mice are tiny, filthy pests that most everyone sets up traps to kill. It's not cute and I don't like the way it makes me feel when anyone calls me that. He turns back to face me with narrowed eyes that make me flinch.

"I'm not going to hurt you," he croons, "I'd never do that. Jeez, you think so little of me? I love you, Mouse. You know that."

His expression is wounded and sad as he sinks down on my bed. His sigh fills the room as he pats the space next to him, his body squishing the pink comforter's white clouds. He looks so out of sorts—this big man draped across my princess bed. It isn't lost on me that he is and I wonder if anyone knows he is here.

I continue to stare as I mull over his statement. Of course I know he loves me, doesn't he? He pays attention to me when no one else bothers. He dotes on me. Isn't that love? He listens to my records with me while my parents entertain all of their other yuppie friends. He'd rather sit with me than join the party downstairs. He chooses me, and that makes me feel loved. I should feel special. Instead, I feel my cheeks redden. I am ashamed and angry with myself for making him feel rejected. Climbing up beside him, I want to ask for his forgiveness. Before I can open my mouth, he pulls me onto his lap. I am stunned and don't have a moment to think before he tucks me against his big body in an embrace.

"You will always be my Mouse," he breathes into my ear.

My body goes rigid. I try to speak, but I cannot find my voice. An uncontrollable shaking starts in the center and spreads itself throughout my body.

Stupid! You let him in! Why did you let him in?

Tears overflow and saturate his shirt while he cradles me, murmuring soft words as he rubs my back in wide, languid circles.

"Shh, don't cry...." Each circle gets a little wider until his hands reach down far enough to cup my bottom. "Shh, sweet girl."

Stupid girl.

◌◌

Rays of sunshine warm my face, its light pulling me from a restless sleep. I open my eyes and stare at the ceiling fan going around in rhythmic circles, like a helicopter's blades. I pretend for a moment that the helicopter is here to sweep me away to a family where the mom and dad love and adore me and their friends don't love me so much.

Why? Why me? Why did I let this happen, again?

The answer is simple—he promised not to hurt me and I believed him. I am overcome with shame; my tears fall steady and silent down my temples and into my hair. I want to disappear. I want to die. I want this feeling to go away more than anything in the world. Mostly, I wish we could've just listened to the album he brought me. My wishes are worthless and there is no erasing the vividness of his hands on me, in me.

I scream into my pillow and pull the covers over my head as the evening comes back to me in detailed flashes. I remember the smell of alcohol on his breath as he panted against my neck. I can still hear the guttural moan vibrate against my back as he reached around and slipped his calloused finger between my legs, then inside of me. I still feel the pinch and sting of his finger. I still hear the Air Supply song keeping time with way he rubbed himself against my bottom.

My eyes focus in on Prue the Bear poking out between the pillows. Even his soft brown eyes are alight with sadness.

Stupid girl.

I struggle to reconnect my brain to my tattered body. Almost instantly, I am aware of my bladder and the need to use the bathroom overrides my need to hide. My legs swing over the side of the bed, making me wince at the soreness between my legs. There, on the floor are the remnants of the wrapping paper with the gift tag still visible "Happy Birthday, Mouse! We love you, Uncle Drew and Aunt Kristy."

2

"Elizabeth Bradshaw, you get back in here this instant!" My mother's face is purple with rage. I'm fourteen years old—doesn't she know I'm supposed to be uncooperative?

"No! Nothing you can say will make me stay and have dinner with those assholes!" My arms are folded across my chest, my hip jutting out to the side in defiance. There is no way I am backing down. I refuse to play nice when it comes to that cockroach. Anger, thick and acrid, is boiling up inside me. Cue the angry tears.

Crap!

I won't give her the satisfaction of seeing me cry so I stomp off to my room and slam the door shut. I flop down on my bed, face first, and reach for the power button on my stereo. It is a sweet solace from my mother's raging diatribe. I slip my headphones on, turn the volume up and close my eyes. Songs are my best friends and the only thing in my life that has never let me down. I flip onto my back and survey my room. As always, my stereo sits on top of the antique liquor cabinet with my records and cassettes tucked inside. The comforter has changed as I have grown but I'm in the same four-poster princess bed I have always been in. Even Prue the Bear is still around, although now he has an honorary position on my bookshelf. While I have been busy growing and changing, the space around me has remained oddly resistant.

It's been a year since "Uncle" Drew and "Aunt" Kristy moved over six hours away from us. An entire twelve months has passed, and yet in just an instant, he's back. When they first moved, I trashed every single record Drew gave me. I didn't have to hang on out of fear anymore. I purged him the only way I knew—by throwing away the things he used to bind me to him. I saved up my allowance to purchase new copies of the ones I especially loved. My copies. He took so much away from me, but the one thing he'd never touch is my music.

A tremor starts in my lip and my eyes fill up again, more wasted tears. I jump as my headphones are suddenly plucked from my ears and my mother's face comes within inches from mine.

"You will not use that potty mouth when speaking to me, do you understand?" Cussing, of all things, really gets under her skin. I pulled the trigger on that purposefully, just to get a rise out of her. She deserves it for inviting those assholes back into our home.

"Yes, ma'am." I mumble.

"Would you care to enlighten me, Beth?" sitting down next to my prone body. "What did Drew and Kristy ever do to you to deserve such ungratefulness?"

Is she shitting me?

I am almost disappointed that my thought didn't escape the confines of my rattled mind.

Tread carefully, Beth.

I sit up slowly, making sure that she stays in my sights. I don't trust her at all. I narrow my eyes in an effort to show her that I am not afraid, but, in truth, I am blown away that she's even opened up the door to this conversation. She always pretended not to see Drew's intent, but she had to know and then did nothing for eight years. She just let him and his airhead bimbo wife in and turned a blind eye. She is nervous; she has turned her attention to her wedding ring, spinning it on her finger. Afraid she will backpedal; I spill every thought at her feet.

"You know what he did! You pretend like you don't know—that you didn't see—but you know what he did!"

My stubborn, angsty teenage resolve shatters as memories slap at my face. I am swept up in a humiliating show of weakness, unable to control my sobs as they shake my body. Mom blanches, her mouth hanging slightly open.

"What did he do, Beth?"

Her voice is barely audible, but I can hear the fear she has for my answer. "He touched me, Mom! He did stuff to me...."

I hesitate, pulling my knees up against my chest and dropping my head down between them because I can't look at her when I say it. "From the time I was five," I whisper, "until they moved away last year...."

The second it comes out of my mouth I want to hit rewind and take it all back.

Oh my God, I don't want to talk about it. I really don't want to go there with her! Why did I have to open my big mouth?

This will not end well, of that I am certain. I hold my breath and steal a peek at her face. It's completely devoid of emotion. She speaks slowly, punctuating each syllable with her accusatory tone.

"What do you mean he touched you? Why haven't you said anything before?

She glares, the whites of her eyes getting larger as she waits for me to give her an answer. I don't have one.

"I don't know, I just couldn't," I cry.

She shakes her head, looking down at me with ill-concealed disgust. "Drew touched you? That is an awful thing to say about someone who has adored you from the moment he and Kristy met you."

My breath hitches, getting caught in my throat. I had adored him, too. I loved him and he spent the better part of seven years twisting my brain into believing that he loved me, too. At five years old, the attention was confusing but flattering. At first, he refrained from touching me, choosing instead to use words to confuse my mind and relax my boundaries.

"Mouse, I can see your underwear."

This is one of the first memories I have of hearing the subtle inflection change in his voice. The shift went from loud and jovial to soft and intimate.

He started speaking to me in these hushed tones like we were in on a secret no one else knew about. It felt good and I started seeking him out for more of the attention he was willing to give me. That day, I was sitting cross-legged on the kitchen floor, playing jacks. I had on a skirt. At my mother's insistence, my closet was full of them. I, on the other hand, would rather climb trees and catch lizards. The skirts did little to deter me, despite my mother's efforts. There I sat with my hands frozen in suspension, one holding the ball and the other my jacks. I looked at him wide-eyed, squirming where I sat. I moved to shift my legs underneath me, to allow my skirt to fall more modestly.

"Don't," Drew whispered, "you are beautiful just as you are." He winked at me. Confused, but giddy from his words, I smiled. I was a lonely little girl and he was an attentive friend.

My mother would never accept such tarnish on her perfect family picture. She is delusional, maniacal even, about keeping up appearances—to the point that she displays these Norman Rockwell plates in a display case in the dining room. I hate those ridiculous plates; each one depicts its own lie. My head feels like a dinghy being tossed around inside a hurricane.

Pitch. Lurch. I close my eyes and try to steady myself. This is going to blow up in my face. I desperately want to take each word back, but I know all I can do now is try to protect myself for the oncoming attack. I retreat into my defense strategies, systematically slowing my breathing and my heart rate as I have taught myself over the years.

Detach. Float away. I tell myself as I let my mind go numb, a skill I acquired when Drew's affections turned physical. If they can't get in, they can't wear you down.

I size up the enemy, scoping out a potential weakness. Even in her anger she is stunning, staring at me, daring me to defy her. This is my Achilles heel: I am a notorious people pleaser and she knows it. She is banking on my need to say what she wants to hear and end this standoff. As much as I need for her to be pleased with me, I just can't find it in me to concede. I look directly into her blazing eyes and simply state, "He did."

Her beautiful face is awash with anger as her shaking hand strikes my cheek. I don't know if it is the sting of her hand or the sting of rejection that sends the last steel shutter into place. All I know is the pain is fleeting. Numbness takes over in defense. I have secured the fortress. I'm checked out of this conversation, and she couldn't hurt me right now if she set me on fire.

"You are sick, Elizabeth! You don't accuse someone of something like that to get out of being at dinner! He is affectionate with you because he loves you. You are special to him and to Kristy! They don't have children of their own, they have always thought of you as theirs!"

Her words bounce off of my armor and I am grateful for the thick iron gates I have erected around my heart.

"He hugs you and what? Does he tickle you, Beth?" She mocks me. "Jesus Christ, Beth, everyone gets tickled at some point!"

I wonder if she can hear herself.

She takes my silence as defeat and adds, "You will be at dinner tonight with your family, or I will take every one of those records and toss them in the trash."

With that threat, my armor cracks and I panic.

She can't take away my music—it's all I have!

"They are NOT my family! You think because you make me call them Aunt and Uncle that makes a difference?" I spit.

With smug satisfaction she sneers at me, knowing I will choose my music over my pride. "No, Beth, they are not, but they are the best friends your father and I have. You will show them the respect they deserve."

Squaring her shoulders and straightening her spine, she walks out of my room and closes the door. Once again, I am alone. I was before she left, and I am now that she is gone. For once, I am grateful for the solitude. Seeking the only comfort I know, I place my headphones back over my head, close my eyes and let the music carry me away.

3

A knock on my door shakes me from my daydreaming and before I can react, the door swings wide and a man sticks in his head. I am treated to the Tommy Cantwell megawatt smile, which instantly brightens my mood. He is working his hands in some mad game of charades. Looking at him quizzically, he finally points to his ears. I laugh and sit up, removing my headphones.

"Hey, baby girl! Where you been? Uncle Rob and I got in about an hour ago...." His words trail off as my attention shifts to the clock on the stereo. Three hours have passed since my mom stormed out and it is now 5:30 P.M., thirty minutes until my hell is unleashed at the dinner table. I look back toward Tommy and find him standing in front of me.

"How long have you been plugged in?" He leans down and places an arm around my shoulders as he sits.

I can't fake anything around Tommy. He is one of few people I allow close enough to really know me. He scans my face with his warm brown eyes.

"What happened, Beth?" Tommy's tender concern stokes the smoldering remains of my relationship with my mom. My tired eyes leak a deluge of tears as I throw my arms around Tommy's neck.

"I got into a really bad fight with Mom and she hates me!"

He places his hand against the back of my head and an arm around my waist to pull me against him in a bear hug.

"Oh, honey, she doesn't hate you. She could never hate you. Sometimes we fight the hardest with the people we love the most. Your mama and your daddy adore you." He leans back, placing his hands on my arms and gently turning me to face him, as he looks me in the eye. "No one hates you, Beth. You are loved very much by me, your Uncle Rob and all of us hanyaks back home."

I laugh at the absurd term he uses. Hanyak, pronounced *hawn-yock*. It's a word assigned by my grandfather to his loved ones. He is old and ornery, so it's only fitting that he'd label us with an equally ornery title. Only Pops could generate a term of endearment from a phrase with synonyms like *hoodlum* and *hooligan*. I am comforted at the thought of my grandparents and my aunt and uncle back home in Iowa. I miss them so much and am so grateful to spend my summers with them. I think I might be the only kid alive who is happy that her parents ship her off to the Midwest every summer.

Tommy laughs with me, his mustache curling up on the ends as his smile widens. He is the definition of a family friend, not Drew. He has been my Uncle Rob's best friend since grade school. He's always been around, so he is as much my uncle as Rob. He and Rob attempted to teach me to water ski the first summer I spent in Des Moines. When that effort was proven futile, Tommy bought me a big yellow tube.

"You are not tying that thing to the back of my boat." Rob stood on the dock of the marina blocking Tommy from his beloved jet boat.

"Man, get over yourself, she is too little to pull herself up on skis yet. She can hang onto this just fine." Tommy chided.

Rob audibly scoffed and then looked at me. I stuck my tongue out at him for effect, which sent him into full belly guffaws.

"Fine, but teaching this squirrel, I mean girl, is on you, T."

I spent the rest of the summer on that tube behind Uncle Rob's boat.

The following summer, Tommy brought his nephew, Ryan, out to his dad's farm in Cumming to detassel corn.

"It's a rite of passage for every child in Iowa!" he said, staring at us in disbelief as we moaned about the heat and time wasted.

"I'm from Miami, Tommy. I should be exempt." I tried to keep a straight face, but Tommy's bug-eyed slack-jawed response sent me into fits of giggles.

"Baby girl, you cannot deny your heritage. I was there the day you were born at Iowa Methodist in the fine capital of our state." He placed his hand over his heart for dramatic effect. "It is inconsequential that your folks lost their collective mind and moved to Florida." He paused to make sure we were listening, which gave Ryan an opportunity to chime in.

"*Inconsequential?* When did you learn such big words, T?" Ryan was a smart ass by nature. He was two years older than me and reminded me of it every chance he got.

"Get over here, you hanyak!" Tommy teased, as he grabbed Ryan in a headlock and scrubbed his knuckles across the top of his skull.

"Ow, old man! Knock it off!" Ryan all but squealed, "I'm gonna tell Mom!"

"You're going to rat on me?" Tommy laughed in disbelief. "I'm not afraid of your mama. She might be my sister, but I can take her on."

For the rest of the day, random laughter could be heard throughout the rows of corn when one of us would think about Tommy and Ryan trying to best one another.

Recalling those memories makes me smile and immediately I start to count on the calendar in my head—just two more months until I can go home again.

I let go of Tommy, wipe my face on my shirtsleeve and brave a smile. "There are some fights that can't be fixed, though."

I try my best to shrug and act nonchalant but I can see my sadness reflecting in Tommy's expression. He knows me so well and right now, he can see that something is different.

The doorbell rings and I am slammed back into reality. My eyes search the clock on the stereo, 5:55 P.M.

Great, the assholes are punctual.

Though a year has passed since I've had to be in the same room with Drew, the same sense of panic mixed with dread spreads inside me, infecting every fiber of self worth and esteem. I can't see it; I only feel it as the happiness leaves my body in a dizzying rush. It bleeds out of me like I've been gutted with a dull knife. My spiral into despair feels like slow motion, but in reality, it's just a matter of seconds. That is all it takes for Tommy to see past the breach, I don't know what clued him into my distress, but suddenly Tommy freezes and the air around us grows thick with tension. I try to ignore it. His brow creases and his eyes narrow in suspicion or contemplation— I am too nervous to get a good look at him to know. The sound of his voice makes me jump.

"Is this about Drew and Kristy?" The question hangs in the air, stealing the last of my ability to breathe. In an attempt to deflect the situation, I force a grin-shrug combination, stand and head for the door.

Beth! Could you be more unconvincing?

I glance back when I realize that Tommy is not following, he is looking out the window blankly. He seems lost, the light gone from his eyes, his face stoic. For the first time in my life, I feel uneasiness separating us. He is the glue that holds me together. I can't stand the thought of anything coming between us. This awkwardness is like the death knell of Drew's toxic effect on everything in my life.

The mere idea that my friendship with Tommy could change turns my blood to ice water.

"Tommy?" My voice breaks the strange spell and he faces me, pinning me with compassionate eyes. I cannot disguise the look of horror that crosses my face, and Tommy's expression turns soft with sympathy. I must be getting paranoid because there is no way he can possibly know a thing. I don't know what the hell he thinks he might know. He doesn't even live here. He's only here once a year with Uncle Rob for their annual trip to the Daytona 500.

I struggle to retain composure but my head feels faint, my lungs cease to expand and contract. I refuse to look away from his stare, certain that this will prove I am perfectly unaffected by whatever assumptions he has floating around his head. He looks away from me when he stands and says nothing while he moves to joins me in the hallway. As we move forward toward the jubilant reunion in the living room, Tommy's arm comes to rest across my back in a protective gesture. Sweat starts to collect on my top lip.

Take a deep breath, Beth.

As we reach the living room where the guests await, he finally speaks. "Is it cool if I sit next to you at the table?" his casual question bears no lingering traces from his mood just a moment before.

"Sure," I say, "but first you have to clear it with Attila the Hun."

With that, he smiles and I relax.

We step into the fray of meaningless chatter and "air kiss" greetings. Tommy's arm is still draped across my back. His gesture is meant to reassure, but it is skyrocketing my anxiety. I need to find a way to get Tommy off the scent of my blood in the water. I find the one person I want and am instantly at ease.

"Hi, Uncle Rob! I am so glad you're here." I embrace Uncle Rob as he wraps me up in his big beefy arms and peppers the top of my head with kisses.

"How's my squirrel? I mean, girl?" His greeting never gets old. I feel momentarily guilty for the lie I am about to deliver but remind myself of the mess that honesty made earlier with my mom.

Lay it on thick, Beth.

"I'm good!" I cringe, hearing the unconvincing words squeak from my mouth.

"Uh-huh," Uncle Rob mumbles. "'Never mind if the cart's on fire, just keep loading the wagon.'" My head bounces lightly against his chest as he starts to laugh. I hear Tommy sniggering behind me and I immediately feel defensive.

"What is that supposed to mean? I don't speak Rob, Tommy." I lean back to gauge Rob's face and frown at him in disapproval.

"Quit lying to me, kid. You're not fooling me into thinking that everything is fine when I could tell you were about to come out of your skin the second you came through the door." He sighs heavily, rolling his eyes dramatically. "Did you forget your decoder ring or has it been too long, baby girl? You are the cart. You are on fire but you're pretending like everything is fine. So you keep loading it up, pretending your shit's not going up in flames. You feel me, Tommy?"

When Tommy doesn't answer, I glance over my shoulder at him. He meets my gaze, raising a curious eyebrow. Great, I hate being put on the spot.

"How's Aunt Melissa?" I attempt to change the subject.

Uncle Rob laughs. "Nice try. She's good. She sends her love, wishes she could see you—you know, the usual. Now, back to the issue at hand. . . ."

"It's just been a crappy day, Uncle Rob. Things have been really hard with my mom today. She will flip if I am not welcoming to Drew and Kristy." I plead, nodding toward the guests of honor.

"Later, then?" Giving me one last squeeze, he lets me go and greets the others. I am so grateful to have dodged the rest of his questions that I forget Tommy is still standing with me.

"Why wouldn't you be welcoming, Beth?" Tommy's voice is concerned but far from gentle, "What's going on with you and them?"

Damn.

"Do I have to like everybody?" I laugh. It's honest enough.

"Uh-oh, do I have to kick someone's ass?" Tommy teases. Little does he know how close he is to unraveling all of my dirty little secrets.

"No, Tommy. I can do my own ass kicking when necessary. Thank you." My smile is genuine because I know the sincerity of his statement.

Before he can argue, I turn to face the rest of the crowd. An instant later I feel Tommy stiffen beside me. I look over my shoulder at him, but he isn't looking at me. He's looking at Drew, who is schmoozing Uncle Rob. Tommy replaces his arm across my back as he watches Drew work Uncle Rob over like a used car salesman. So much for relaxing.

When Uncle Rob moves on to speak with my father, Drew turns my way. His eyes are deceptively warm and kind. He grabs hold of Kristy's hand and heads toward Tommy and me.

"Mouse! I can't believe how much you've grown up!" Kristy squeals, kissing me on the cheek, leaving a smeared orange lip imprint.

I think I'm smiling.

I'm definitely nodding.

This is so messed up.

"Tommy," Drew says, offering his hand to shake.

"Mouse? How long have you two been gone? No one's called Beth that since she was knob-kneed and toothless," Tommy chuckles as he pumps Drew's hand.

"I guess she'll always be Mouse to me." I can hear the subtle chill in Drew's voice, giving away his irritation. No one else seems to notice, but it sets me on edge.

"Beautiful Mouse," Drew shifts his attention to me, "you have grown up to be quite a young lady."

He's giving an Oscar-worthy performance as the doting family friend when he leans in to kiss my cheek. He gives me a quick wink and a wry smile. I want to scream.

"Okay, everyone!" My mother is raising her wine glass, demanding our attention. "Dinner is ready! Let's have a seat."

4

I eye my plate and wonder how I am ever going to be able to eat beef tenderloin and new potatoes ever again. The thought of taking another bite sends the contents of my stomach surging into my mouth. My fork clangs loudly on the plate as I force the food down my esophagus. I reach for my water. I am about to take a sip when I feel a hand settle on my thigh from under the table. I whip my head to the left while the water in my goblet splashes onto my hand and onto my mother's perfect table setting.

"Oh, no! Mom, I am so sorry! Let me grab some napkins."

I jump up from my seat, ready to head for the kitchen. Drew's hand drops from my lap and I shoot him the nastiest sneer I can muster.

"Sit. Down."

I turn toward the sound of my mother's angry voice.

"Don't be ridiculous, Beth. It's only a few drops. Stop making a scene!" she spits.

I slump back down in my seat, trying to rein in tears of rage. Tommy puts his hand on the back of my chair and discreetly leans his head toward mine. Before he has a chance to instigate the Spanish Inquisition, I clear my throat.

"Excuse me, please," I mumble. Without waiting for a response, I push back from the table, scraping the chair legs across the floor in loud protest.

Run.

Bolting toward the living room, I don't look at any of the surely shocked faces left in my wake. When I reach the couch, I flop down and place my head between my knees. I am concentrating on breathing in and out with deep, controlled breaths when I feel the cushion next to me dip with the weight of someone's body.

Tommy.

Of course he would follow me in here and check on me. Now I won't have to go back into the dining room alone. I lift my head, a smile already playing at my lips to greet my friend, when I realize my error. Shifting so his leg is pressed against the length of mine, Drew is watching me with predatory precision.

No, no, no.

I can hear Tommy's voice from the next room. "What the hell, Casey? What is going on with you two?" he angrily questions my mother.

My thoughts refocus on Drew as he leans his head in so close to me that his lips brush against my ear.

"Mouse, you have grown up so much. God, you are gorgeous," he whispers against my ear, kissing it.

I squeeze my eyes shut and try to shift away from him. He grabs hold of my arms and keeps me still. Slowly moving his hands up and down my arms, he rubs the back of his knuckles against the sides of my breasts.

"You are really starting to fill out." His voice is breathy with arousal. It is all I can take.

"NO!" I shout into his face. I leap from the couch and am about to run for my room when Drew grabs my wrist, jerking me backwards. I stumble and land in Drew's lap. His smug, satisfied face enrages me.

"I didn't think you'd like me rough, Mouse," he whispers. I yank as hard as I can to get him to release my wrist, but that only shimmies my lower body across his erection.

"You know you like me, Beth. Why fight me?" He moans.

With all the anger and hatred I can muster, I wrench my hand free from Drew's grasp and tumble to the floor. I scramble backwards on my hands and feet to put as much distance between us as I can.

Drew's face registers shock. He is used to having the upper hand, and I am not afraid of him anymore. Quickly, his confusion morphs into rage as he dives off the couch after me. I prepare for his impact by curling my body into itself in the smallest ball I can, but the impact never comes. My eyes are squeezed shut, my hands are over my ears but I can still hear the shrill war cry erupt from Tommy's mouth.

"*YOU MOTHERFUCKER!*"

My head pops up from the floor in time to see that Tommy has Drew by the back of his shirt, keeping his body from propelling forward onto mine. I unfold myself, stand and wobble to the corner of the room. I sink slowly along the wall, down to the floor.

"*You sick fuck!*" Tommy wails as he pushes Drew to the floor and kicks him in his side.

"*You bastard!*" He kicks him again and again.

"*How long, you motherfucker? How long have you been touching her?*"

5

"Beth?" Uncle Rob urges, "Beth? Baby girl, look at me."

The words blow through me like a soft breeze, but I am not able to latch on to any of them.

"She is in shock, let the paramedics look at her." An unfamiliar voice answers Uncle Rob's plea.

Blue. Red. Blue. Red.

The colors shift and undulate in abstract patterns across the front yard. I am vaguely aware that I am sitting on the front step.

"Excuse me, miss, can you tell me your name?" a piercing light shines in my eyes, making them water. I don't answer. Unfamiliar hands grip my wrist at its pulse point. I wonder if they can find a pulse. I am positive my heart ceased to beat since the moment the police arrived and took Drew away. "Miss, are you in any pain?"

Everything hurts. Angry purple fingerprints wrap around my arm, my knees are raw and bloody. These physical markers are a poor reflection of the riptide of emotion coursing through me. There is no steel shutter or iron gate to hide behind. I am completely exposed.

How am I going to look anyone in the eye ever again?

The EMT asks me more questions that I don't answer. I just want to close my eyes and sleep. Exhaustion wraps around me in a vice grip, lulling me away from the fray.

"Her vital signs are good, she's just suffering a little post-trauma stress," the EMT encourages.

My humiliation is suffocating me. I squeeze my eyes shut, forcing my mind to take aim at the one place that will provide refuge.

A white stucco house with red siding shines like a beacon across the darkness. I am walking up grey cement steps onto the front porch. Passing potted herbs and geraniums, my feet shuffle across the chipped green floorboards until I reach my destination. I run my fingers across the smooth, worn wood as I sit. The wind plays with my hair, sweeping the scent of honeysuckle into my senses. I let go and let the gentle rocking of the porch swing have its calming effect....

"I want to go home." My voice is flat, lifeless.

"Beth? Oh, thank God. Honey you are home. Do you remember what happened?" Uncle Rob grabs my hand and gives it a comforting squeeze.

"Where are my mom and dad?"

His hesitation answers before he can form the words. They aren't here. Why would they be? I have made a mockery of their perfect life. Nothing will ever be the same again and it is my fault.

Uncle Rob lets out a heavy sigh before he answers, "They took Kristy to the police station."

Of course they did, why would they stay to comfort their lying daughter? That's what they think. If my own mother doesn't believe me, no one else will. I am entirely alone on my side of the battlefield. My parents, Drew and Kristy are all lined up on the other side, ready to finish me.

Except for Tommy, he protected me.

"I want to go home, Uncle Rob," I sob.

"Baby girl," he starts, his voice full of sorrow. I cut him off.

"No! I want to go home! This isn't home!" I wail, "I want to go home, please!"

Tommy lifts me into his strong arms and walks into the house. He sits me on the edge of my bed and begins to idly survey the room.

"What do you want to bring with?" he asks. When I don't answer him, he squats in front of me. "Look at me, Beth," he pleads with me, but I can't. My breath comes short and shallow as the panic starts its ascent to the surface. An unfamiliar wail escapes from my lips and I bring my knees to my chest.

Hide.

"Beth, please let me in. You're breaking my heart, baby girl," Tommy's voice cracks. My panic ebbs at the sound of his pain, and I lift my head to meet the gaze of a strung out man. Tommy's eyes are red and puffy with tears. Hair is sticking out in a million directions from running his hands through it again and again. His shirt is torn at the seam of his shoulder and there is a bruise darkening its away across his jawline. My hand is drawn to that spot.

"I'm sorry," I barely whisper.

"No, Beth. I don't ever want to hear you say that again," he says with ferocity. "There isn't a single reason for you to be sorry. I'm sorry that I didn't know to protect you sooner." Tears spill from his bloodshot eyes.

There is a palpable sadness that fills the space between us, stealing words from my mouth. I don't know what to say to comfort him; I am completely helpless. Desperate to push away the sorrow, I assign us a task.

"The records. I want to bring my music."

"You got it," his mustache tips in a weak smile, "I will load them up. You pack some of your clothes while I call Pops and Ellen." He pats my knee as he rises and walks out the door.

Mechanically, I grab my suitcase from the closet and reach blindly for things to fill it.

Pops and Gran.

My hand rubs the burrowing ache in my chest but it brings no relief. I silently pray they will still welcome me home after they find out I have broken our family. A fresh wave of panic threatens and just as I am sure it will sweep me away, Tommy reappears in my doorway.

"All set, baby girl. They can't wait to see you, Ellen is making up your room right now." He takes a tentative step towards the suitcase, peering inside, "Let me help." Soft, sympathetic eyes convey deeper meaning.

Together, we pack my clothes and records into the back of the car. Uncle Rob is finishing with the last police officer when my parents pull into the driveway. Instinctively, I take a step behind Tommy. My mom is quick to get out of the car and confront us.

"What is going on?" Confusion creases her brow. "Where do you think you are taking my daughter?"

Uncle Rob steps forward and holds his hand out to my mom, stopping her. "Casey, Mom and Dad are going to take Beth early." He is stern. This is not a request.

"You can't just take her! She has two months left of school!" The evening's events are showing on my mom's beautiful face. Her eyes are shadowed with dark circles and her face is pale. "We need to talk as a family—there are things we need to discuss that don't involve either of you." She waves her hand at Tommy and Uncle Rob. My father walks up to join my mother.

"You chose them." A fragile voice adds. It takes me a moment to realize that it is me who has spoken. My mother jerks back like I have hit her, bringing her hand to mouth. A tear rolls down her cheek, leaving a trail of runny makeup in its wake.

"I didn't know," she sobs. If I weren't so enraged by her declaration I would've been struck dumb at her show of emotion. "I know you tried to tell me, I just couldn't believe that Drew...."

she stammers. "How did this happen without me knowing?" she sobs. "Help me understand, Beth."

My father takes her into his arms, trying to soothe her. Soothe her. There are no condolences for me, not even a look in my direction. This is codependence at its finest. With a hiccup she adds, "We dropped Kristy off at their place. She is going to divorce him."

Hooray for Kristy! Does she want a medal?

I'm unsure of where any of this is leading and shift nervously behind him.

Please don't leave me here.

"That's great, Casey. Do you think she gives a shit about Kristy right now? Is that all you can think about?" The vein in Uncle Rob's neck punctuates his angry questions. My mother is about to defend herself to Uncle Rob when Tommy intercedes.

"Don't you think Beth deserves a little space from all of this?" Tommy sounds incredulous. "You owe her that."

She stops and looks at me, regret pooling in her eyes.

"Case, Mom will homeschool Beth the last quarter of ninth grade. Don't let that be an issue here. We all want what is best for her—time and space is a good start." Uncle Rob moves to stand in front of my mom and dad. "It's a good start for you, too. You need to get your shit straight and get some help." His tone is biting.

"Rob, you don't speak to your sister that way," my father chimes in. "I won't tolerate it!"

"But you will *tolerate* a pedophile molesting your daughter while you do BLOW with Miami's upper echelon?" Rob spits. "You two get your asses into a rehab program or, so help me God, I will sue you for custody."

My parents stand in statuesque unison, gaping at Uncle Rob. They don't appear so perfect to me now. Their pupils are slightly dilated, accentuating their glassy eyes along with tiny broken blood vessels around their noses. Tell tale.

Tommy senses me cowering behind him and grabs my hand. Without missing a beat, he pulls me forward and into a reassuring hug. "I got you, baby girl."

"Get in the car." Uncle Rob commands and I obey.

As I pull my seatbelt over my shoulder, I steal one last glance at my parents. They are holding each other in a tight embrace; neither of them looks my way.

6

It's been a month since I left Miami. I haven't spoken to my parents since that night. My grandparents tell me that they are in an outpatient program, but I have my doubts about that. It's just one more thing I don't want to talk about. Truth is, I don't talk to anyone about anything. Silence is my refuge, besides, what can I possibly say? "Hey, sorry I ripped our family in half. Want to play gin rummy?"

Every time I open my mouth to speak, an overwhelming fear of what I will be expected to say stops me. I realize I'm digging myself a deeper hole to bury myself in, but my fear is a powerful and all-encompassing force. With my head rested against the cool wall, I listen to them anxiously discuss what they should do for me. I don't want to interrupt their heart to heart but I wish they would just move on. I can't take much more of everyone's well-meaning intentions. I am a kind of broken they can't fix. I am no longer the same little girl they loved.

The more Pops and Gran hover, the more alien I feel. I've been hiding out in my room avoiding "the look" they give each other. Their faces reflect the helpless horror that follows when you happen on a bad car accident. Well, Gran and Pops have been looking at me like I am a fifteen-car pile up on I-80. It breaks my heart that I am responsible for the lines that furrow Pops' brow and for the shadows under Gran's eyes. The infinitely strong made weak by my mess. I am tempted to retreat back to my room and to the security of my music when Tommy's voice breaks in.

"Pops, she is going to have to talk to someone at some point." He sounds tired and frustrated.

"Don't you think I know it?" Pops harrumphs. "Forcing her to ain't gonna do nothin' but push her further away."

"She'll come around. You boys need to give her some room to blossom," Gran adds in.

"I don't know, Ellen. I just don't know." Pops sighs with defeat.

My heart sinks with guilt. I don't want them to worry over me but I can't talk to them. They are better off not knowing certain things, or next time Tommy won't stop at breaking Drew's ribs.

Drew.

Drew, who walked away scot-free in a bargain not to press charges against Tommy for assault. The violent thud of my heart punches hard against my chest at the thought. Who said life was fair?

I will myself to focus on Tommy and what he risked that night. The more I think about how he beat Drew senseless, without regard for the consequences, the less it hurts. Tommy came to my rescue when no one else bothered. He will always be worth more than vengeance.

"Psst. Snoop much, Beth?"

My eyes dart toward the source of the sound.

In the shadow of the front door is Ryan, Tommy's nephew. He is grinning his cocky "caught you" smile, which sends waves of red to my cheeks. He is the one person who will take the most joy out of taking me down a peg. For as long as I have spent my summers here with Gran and Pops, Ryan has been spending his with Tommy. At the beginning, Ryan treated me with cool indifference. When he realized that Tommy had a soft spot for me, all bets were off. A primordial need to beat his chest and get territorial manifested into an unrelenting need to torment me. Catching me eavesdropping is like reaching the summit of Mt. Everest.

I square my shoulders and hold my chin up to shake off the embarrassment of being caught. Ryan cocks an eyebrow at me and nods toward the next room where Pops, Tommy, and Gran are still talking. He's baiting me and I don't bite. Pushing off the wall, I march toward the front door, stopping momentarily to shoot Ryan the stink eye. Bewildered, Ryan steps out of my way just in time for me to storm out the front door.

That's right, jerk. Get out of my way.

Hot humid air hits me the moment I set foot outside. The soles of my flip-flops slap the sidewalk with purpose as I make my way around the side of the house and into the back yard. My body moves forward, already knowing where it is going, as I grab a basket and move into the shade of the cherry tree.

Muscle memory propels me upward and I disappear into the thick green canopy of leaves. Settling into my nook between the tree trunk and a low branch that faces the deck, I take a quick scan of the yard. I seem to have shaken Ryan.

"Thank God," I whisper to myself.

I need a few moments of peace without Ryan waiting in the shadows to judge me or condescend to me. He is two years older than I am and has an uncanny ability to make me feel like a total dork with one look. I never expected us to be best buds, but I never thought he would take such a keen interest in torturing me either. I groan to myself thinking about Ryan's hijinks last summer.

൭ം

"Hey girls, can you keep a secret?" I pop my eye open at the promise of gossip. Ryan is smiling down at my cousin and me as we're sunbathing on the dock.

"What?" I stutter, caught off guard, trying to recall the last time Ryan acknowledged my presence.

"A secret, dummy. Can you keep a secret?" His eyes twinkle with a kind of mischief that smacks of no good. I look over at my cousin who is pretending she is asleep, rather unconvincingly. Coward.

"I guess so. What is it?" I sit up.

"You two are going into ninth grade this year, right?" he leads.

I nod my head and try to hide my sheepish grin. He knows what grade I am entering. The thought makes me giddy.

"And I assume there is a boy crush worthy of your attention."

He winks. I flush.

Shaking my head and sputtering nonsense, I finally eek out, "No! Psshhaw. Whatever." I am tempted to dive off the dock and into the water. Ryan's laughter only enhances my desire to jump overboard.

"On the off chance a pimple-faced, metal-mouthed loon wants to ask you out, you want to be ready." His laughter has simmered to a condescending chuckle. "Don't you?"

"I don't need to know your secret, Ryan. You are a jerk." I start to stand up when my cousin rouses from her fake slumber.

"Wait. I want to be ready. What's the secret?" she asks. I try to slink off to the side and into the inviting water, but she grabs my foot. "Come on, Beth. It can't be that bad."

Ryan wastes no time waiting for my answer. He gleefully continues, "All the popular girls already know this trick, but I am sharing it with you two as a charitable act."

I fold my arms over my chest and stick my chin out in defiance. He ignores me and keeps talking.

"To get the boys to notice you, you have to do this one thing every night before you go to bed."

My cousin's eyes widen; she is so gullible.

"What? What do we need to do?" she urges.

Ryan leans his head toward us, his blond hair falling into his green eyes.

"Tweak your nipples," he whispers, "it makes your boobs grow bigger."
He is biting the inside of his cheek, trying not to burst at the seams.

My cousin is seriously mulling this over. Idiot. I can't stand the
embarrassment another minute. I turn to face Ryan.

"You. Are. A. Moron."

To punctuate my statement, I take a running leap off the end of the
dock and let the cool water take me under. When I surface a moment
later, Ryan is peering down from the edge.

"I was only trying to help, Beth."

For the rest of the summer, I did my best to ignore Ryan. It didn't
work. Wherever I turned, there he was tweaking his nipples and wink-
ing conspiratorially at me.

✑

I wanted to hate him, I really did.

I grab my basket from the branch below and get down to business.

One for you. I toss a cherry into my basket.

One for me. I smile in satisfaction as the sweet red fruit bursts on my tongue. I repeat the process until the basket is full, my face and hands stained.

This is the best part of summer, right here.

"You going to save some of those for Gran's cobbler?"

I jump at the sound of his voice, sending the basket tumbling to the ground.

"*RYAN!*" I yell.

Horrified, I scramble down the tree to refill my basket.

"Aha! She speaks, after all." His tone is suspiciously gentle. I cock my head and look at him quizzically.

"Yes," I offer hesitantly. "I speak. I just don't have much to say."

"Oh, I doubt that," he sighs, lowering to his knees to help.

The hair on the back of my neck rises in defensive awareness. This is why I don't talk. Every time I open my mouth, someone takes it as an invitation to get me to "open up."

"I don't need this crap from you, Ryan. You don't know a thing about me," my words bite.

Ryan looks at me wearily but continues like I didn't just rip off his head.

"I hear you are a big music fan." He turns his attention back to our task. "There are some great bands coming to the Iowa State Fair this summer."

Sitting back on my haunches, I watch him place the last of the cherries back in the basket. Where is the sharp-tongued tormentor I am accustomed to? He catches me sizing him up, trying to figure out his angle.

"I'm not going to talk about anything else, Beth." He reaches over and I flinch as he pulls a leaf from my hair. "We will only talk about the things you want to talk about, okay?"

I cast my eyes down, unable to look at him. I don't want him to see tears and almost make a run for the house.

"Why?" my voice is small and pitiful.

"Because, you could clearly use a friend. If we can convince the masses that you aren't as fragile as they're thinking, we may just see the shore of Lake Panorama sometime this year." He rolls his eyes dramatically and it makes me laugh. It feels so good to laugh I don't bother with a defensive retort.

"Trust me," he pleads, and there is sincerity in his tone that has me believing him. With a faith I didn't know I still possessed, I lift my head and smile.

"Ok, Ryan. I'll trust you."

7

We enter the house through the kitchen door with our cherries, carrying on about the Iowa State Fair concert series. As I make my way to the kitchen sink, a trio appears in the doorway. I know it's Tommy with Pops and Gran, but I ignore them and keep talking to Ryan.

"Don't you think they should have stopped at the last tour?" I ask while I busy myself with washing cherries. "What's that line? *It's better to burn out than to fade away.*"

"Go Beth! Way to quote one of the greatest hair bands of the '80s," Ryan shoots his hand up and down invisible frets, while strumming his fingers across his stomach. Air guitar quickly turns into head banging. I watch him thrash around the tiny kitchen.

"Oh my God, you are such a tool!" I giggle, throwing my dishtowel at him. It lands with precision on top of his head, covering his face. Howls of maniacal laughter rip from me, and I grip the countertop to keep from keeling over.

"What in hell are you hanyaks doing?" The emotion in Pops' voice silences the room. He looks at me with disbelief and wonder playing across his wrinkled face. Before I can overanalyze every possible answer to his question, I blurt out the first thing that pops into my head.

"We picked cherries, Pops."

It takes two steps for him to cross the kitchen and grab me in a fierce hug. My arms don't reach all the way around him, but I squeeze him as tight as I can, inhaling his scent of tobacco and Irish Spring. I have to will myself not to cry, to allow my grandpa to savor this moment after all the pain I have caused him.

"Baby girl, it is so good to hear your voice," he whispers, his breath catching.

"It's ok, Pops. I am ok, Pops." I can't hold back my tears any longer. "Everything will be ok." Delicate hands grip my shoulders and I feel the gentle pressure of a kiss on the top of my head.

"There's my blossom." Gran whispers.

I peel open an eye and find Tommy and Ryan leaning against the chipped red linoleum countertop staring. My eyes lock with Ryan's and I am surprised to find affection in his gaze.

"Thank you," I mouth to him silently.

He crinkles his brow and shrugs, confused. I give him a watery smile and wonder how foolish it is, thanking him for caring.

"She's something else, isn't she?" Tommy nods his head toward me.

"She sure is." Ryan shakes his head and returns my smile.

"Def Leppard, right?" Tommy queries.

"What?" Ryan asks, turning to Tommy.

"'It's better to burn out than fade away,' that's Leppard, right?" Tommy's mustache twitches under the scrutiny of Ryan's disbelieving look. "What?"

"Yeah, it's Leppard," Ryan chuckles. "Your timing is impeccable."

"*Impeccable*? Are we busting out the SAT words, now?" Tommy teases.

"Don't you two start that again!" I laugh as I let go of Pops.

"I guess I am making cobbler." Gran tries to act put out but she is beaming.

"I'll pit the cherries." I offer.

"Not by yourself, you won't. You two," she points to Tommy and Ryan, "help carry these to the front porch, I don't want cherry juice all over my kitchen." She's trying hard to sound stern, but I can see the smile tugging at her lips.

8

I scoop the last bite of cobbler in my bowl and steal a look around the table. It's quiet, but, for once, my shoulders aren't hitched up to my ears. There is an ease to the silence as we stuff our bellies full of Gran's dessert. My spoon is about to cross my lips when a foot comes into contact with my shin.

"Ow!" I yelp, dropping the spoon back into my bowl. My eyes meet Ryan's mischievous smirk. I reach down to rub my singing leg and am about to give him a piece of my mind when he lunges for my bowl. "What are you doing? Hey!" I cry as he scrapes the last of my cobbler into his greedy mouth.

"Mmm," he moans in satisfaction. "You weren't going to eat that were you?"

"You pig!" I laugh as I throw my napkin at him.

"All right, you two," Pops scolds, "not at the table."

I bite the inside of my lips together to keep from smiling, but an unladylike snort escapes before I can tamp it back down.

"Oh, I'm a pig?" Ryan's voice raises an octave with his laughter and I gasp for air between guffaws.

Gran reaches for Pops' hand and rubs her thumb across his knuckles. Joy is radiating off her, filling up the space between each of us. It pulses through our veins, connecting us to one another. This is family. This is my family, a menagerie of blood and friendship. Both equal, both vital.

"Remember when Casey and Rob were like that?" Gran sighs, leaning her head on Pops' broad shoulder.

A shudder runs down my spine at the mention of my mom's name. My eyes fall to the table and I run my fingers over a bubble in the lacquer finish. I don't expect them to avoid talking about her, but I don't know what I am supposed to say when they do.

"Beth?" Gran's gentle tone halts my inward retreat. "I didn't mean to upset you." Guilt and frustration beat down on me with angry fists, each blow punctuated with my thoughts: *You. Are. So. Selfish.*

They wait me out with patience and understanding, giving me what Uncle Rob promised—space and time. Gran's hazel eyes swirl with worry as my shame creeps into my cheeks. I owe them so much more than a fast retreat at the first mention of her name.

"I don't know what you want me to say." I whisper, deciding honesty is the best I can give her.

"Blossom, I don't care what you say. Just don't stop talking to us, okay?" She places her free hand over mine, and squeezes. Her new nickname makes my heart hurt. She's so full of hope. The laugh lines on her face tilt upward with it, igniting my fear of saying the wrong thing.

"What was she like," I readdress the table's lacquer finish. "You know, when she was my age?"

The chair squeaks as Uncle Rob turns to me. "She was a spitfire, she knew how to have fun. We spent a ton of time in the basement with our friends, playing music. We had a makeshift dance floor down there that we kept waxed and everything." Surprised, my head pops up at his statement. "That's right, your mama was a music fanatic."

"What happened?" The words escape before I can filter the astonishment out of them.

Uncle Rob barks with laughter and continues his story, "Well, I suppose people grow and interests change. What makes you think that she doesn't still love it? She has a beautiful singing voice and that girl could cut a rug!" My face reflects my complete shock. Uncle Rob's smile stretches to the furthest corners of his face.

"Your mom, Uncle Rob, and I used to go down to the Val Air Ballroom and listen to the bands that played there. There were dances, concerts, all kinds of different music." When Tommy chimes in with his memory it reminds me of how long he has known my mom, too. "She always had them lined up to dance with her. We would spend half our night beating the boys off your mama with a stick."

Uncle Rob is nodding his head in agreement as he chuckles, "Good times."

"What happened? What made you grow apart?" At this point, my curiosity has bested my anxiety. I plop my elbows on the table and lean my face into my hands.

"Well, when your folks moved to Florida, it was hard to stay close," Uncle Rob murmurs. "Our lives changed and the miles just made it that much harder." The vein in Uncle Rob's neck flutters as he stammers over his lame excuse.

"You mean when they started to do drugs." I correct.

Uncle Rob's blue eyes swim with sadness—this is harder on him than I thought.

"I'm sorry, that was harsh," I mutter.

"It's okay, Beth," his face softens with sympathy, "I'm just not sure how to answer that. I don't know when the drugs started. You probably know better than anyone."

My breathing quickens as I think about the countless times my parents left me to fend for myself while they went off on one of their benders. I choke on angry words and consider my answer more carefully as I focus on the pain in Uncle Rob's voice.

Drawing in a deep breath, I compel myself to speak. "I don't remember a time when there wasn't drugs. For a long time, I just thought everyone's family was like that. It was at least two years before I realized I was wrong." My answer is a pained whisper.

Gran's arms wrap around me from behind; I never even noticed her leave her chair to stand by me. "Blossom, I am so sorry," she coos, kissing the top of my head, cradling me against her chest.

I have never told anyone about this part of my life. Keeping it secret gave me a sense of control over the uncontrollable; unveiling the lies leaves me painfully exposed. I close my eyes to try and pare back the panic attack creeping its way through my body when I feel Ryan interlace his foot with mine. A weak grin tugs at my lips as his simple gesture grounds me.

"Blossom? I like it!" Ryan encourages a not so subtle change of topic.

I tap my foot against his where they are still connected. I open my eyes to find the concerned faces of my family all accounted for. I want so badly to make them stop looking at me like I am going to shatter at any moment. It makes me want to try harder, be better for them. I direct my attention back to Ryan and his comment.

"Don't you dare," I say, raising my eyebrow in warning.

"That one belongs to me, Ry," Gran chuckles, "she is my blossom." Her hand drifts up to cup my face as her eyes sparkle with adoration. I am so lucky to have her. She gives me a quick kiss on my forehead before she stands. "Pops, you help me clear the table. These hanyaks did the dirty work."

9

The weeks pass quickly as I fall into a comfortable routine of schoolwork and family. Gran and I finished my last assessment test of ninth grade this morning; I am officially on summer break. This afternoon we are cruising up the river for a bonfire to celebrate. There's peacefulness, being on the water that is undeniably appealing. There are no pressing demands, just the lull of the water slapping against the sides of Pops' pontoon boat as we drift along the current. My favorite river pastime is admiring the stately houses that are perched on the jagged shore and daydreaming about the people who live there.

My favorite is about a family I call "The Browns." Mr. Brown is a tall dapper man with blond wavy hair and clear green eyes that twinkle when he laughs. He is a partner at a law firm downtown and an avid tennis player. Mrs. Brown is a curvy redhead with milk chocolate eyes and a warm smile. She's a stay-at-home mom to their only child, volunteers with the Humane Society, and is a yoga enthusiast. Life inside this daydream is a flawless rhythm of give and take, ebb and flow with each family member in perfect unison with the next. Their happiness is intoxicating and I find myself wishing that my own life could be that way.

My parents' faces dance across the back of my eyelids, bringing me back from my fantasy. For the last month I have tried envisioning my mother as a teenager with Uncle Rob and Tommy. It's hard to reconcile the carefree girl they describe to the version of her

I know. Regardless, I am starting to understand her through their old stories and records. Tommy's even teaching me how to dance like they did—he says my Pony is impressive. It gives me hope to know my mother wasn't always so lost. All I really want is to understand her so I can start to forgive her.

∽

"Beth, I am so sorry," mom cries into the phone, "I will never forgive myself. Never."

"Mom, don't," I breathe out on a frustrated sigh, "I can't make you feel better."

"I don't want you to, honey. I just need you to know that I ache every day in my heart for what happened." Her voice breaks on the last word and I listen silently while she sniffles and collects herself, "Gran tells me that you are finally opening up," her voice instantly brightens.

I twist the telephone cord around my fingers and tap my foot against the floorboard. "Yea, well it is the least I can do after everything," I mutter.

"That's not how they see it. They want to be there for you more than anything. You are their heart, Beth. All Pops talks about is how you are his little kindred spirit and Gran can't stop herself from bragging about how smart you are. You are so special, Beth." Her words surprise me.

"Thank you, Mom," I whisper as tears spill, relentlessly down my chin.

"All they want, all I want, is to find a way to make things right." I hear the emotion in her voice and can feel the sincerity behind what she is saying but she is wishing for impossible things.

"I know that is what you want but this can't be made right. Everything is ruined. I am ruined!" I sob.

"No, baby girl. You aren't ruined, you are magnificent." Her voice is a soft caress, *"We are all broken in one way or another. It's how we put those pieces back together that matters. You, my darling, are going to fit the pieces back together again, you'll see."* My shoulders slump, my chest heaves but hope grips my heart at my mother's words.

"Mom?" Cautious, I reach out to her, my first piece. *"Sobriety really suits you."*

10

A loud whistle rings across the water, snapping me out of my reverie. "Here, take the line!" Pops shouts as he cuts off the engine. A little dazed from my daydream, it takes me a minute to soak in the sight. We're drifting onto a sandy patch of shore where Uncle Rob's boat is already anchored. In the water, Tommy and Ryan have secured the line and are pulling us in. Uncle Rob and Aunt Melissa are lounging in a couple of beach chairs set around the makings of a fire pit.

"Hey squirrel, I mean girl!" Rob hollers. Melissa swats him on the back of his head. "Easy, babe, I am just teasing." His boyish, goofy grin makes an appearance as he leans to kiss her cheek. I smile and wave to them but they are already nose-to-nose cooing over one another. The ease at which they show affection makes me fidgety but it is as natural to them as breathing. I don't like shows of affection; it confuses me. It's hard to get much out of such things when you are constantly wondering about ulterior motive. Somebody always wants something in return. Nothing comes free.

As I study the rest of the beach set-up, my attention is drawn to the water. Eyes popping wide, I am dumbstruck at the sight of a shirtless Ryan guiding the boat to shore. His shaggy blond hair is raining drops of water down his chest, making my heart somersault. I dip my head as my face flames, I have seen him in his board shorts millions of times, but there is something about the way his lean muscles strain against his skin that makes me giggle nervously. I peek without lifting my head to find Ryan eyeing me curiously.

I want to die.

"Blossom, you want to help me carry some of this?" Gran interrupts.

Thank you, Gran! I jump up to grab a cooler and work my way toward the back of the boat. If I busy myself, maybe my face will return to its normal shade of pale and freckled. I give Tommy and Ryan a curt nod as I wiggle off the end of the boat and wade through shallow water toward camp. I'm just beyond Ryan when water hits my back so hard it sprays over the top of my head. Still gripping the cooler, I spin toward the culprit. Ryan is crouched down with his hands spread out along his sides, sluicing the water between his fingers, and his green eyes glow with mischief.

"You looked a little warm under the collar there, Beth," he smirks.

I swallow the lump in my throat and try to feign indifference, but I am mortified. I roll my eyes at him, give a disdainful, "Whatever," and proceed to drag my humiliation to shore.

"That was mean, Ry!" Aunt Melissa is wagging her finger at him "That boy is such a teaser," she tsks.

"How is my tenth grader? Come here, you sweet thing," she chirps as she wraps me in a towel. "How does it feel?"

I pretend to adjust my towel and glance over my shoulder. Ryan is still in the water, unloading a bag of charcoal from the boat when he turns my way.

"Wet." I deadpan, shooting Ryan the stink eye. His face lights up with laughter as he hands Tommy the charcoal and dunks himself in the river. He pops up out of the water with his arms cast wide in a "ta-da" gesture. Right, like that makes us even. I shake my head at him and turn my attention back to Aunt Melissa. She is looking at me with narrowed eyes and pursed lips.

"What?" I ask, sheepish.

"Listen up, Stinkerbell, I get enough sarcasm from your uncle. Don't you dare blow me off, I want deets!" she nudges. I feel bad for Aunt Melissa. Uncle Rob tends to speak in phrases, particularly his arsenal of idiom originals. It's hard enough to decipher what he means when he busts out with "Never mind the cart's on fire, keep loading the wagon!" When you couple that with his sarcasm, it's almost impossible to decode his lingo.

"It should feel like a huge relief," I breathe out on a long sigh, "but it hasn't really sunk in yet, ya know?"

She nods her head and starts shucking ears of corn. "I can see that. Once you have a couple of days of freedom, I bet you'll feel different. Have any big plans?"

"I am spending my freedom on the porch swing with a book," I say wistfully.

"Mmm. That sounds wonderful. What are you reading?" Aunt Melissa and I fall into easy chatter about the books I have waiting to read while we set up for dinner. I am engrossed in the task and the conversation, making it easier to push Ryan from my thoughts. By the time the food is ready, the fire in my cheeks has cooled to smoking ash.

After dinner, Tommy grabs his guitar case and plops in sand by the fire. As he starts tuning the strings, I am unable to resist the pull of the notes and move to sit closer to him. He looks up at my approach, giving me a brilliant smile and begins strumming the chords to "Beth" by Kiss.

I groan in mock misery and throw my hand up to my forehead, "Doesn't that ever get old?" I whine.

He stops strumming and kicks my foot. "Kiss hater," he laughs, "have any requests?"

I shake my head and wait for him to start again. This time he chooses an upbeat song, laced with a little reggae.

"I like this," I encourage as I subconsciously begin swaying to the rhythm. He starts singing about how short life is and how we shouldn't hesitate to grab it before it goes by. Slick move, tricking me with a carefree island beat that carries hidden philosophical words.

"I'm yours-ah," he exaggerates the last line and chord. His enthusiasm is charming my suspicious nature into submission. As if he can sense a shift in my demeanor, he starts to play one of my favorite songs.

Brown noser.

I lean back on my elbows and close my eyes as the sound of the notes moving across the fret board flow through me. Tommy starts to sing the first verse and I join him on harmony during the chorus. We drift along, singing in sync together like we have a hundred times before. I open my eyes when the song ends and find Tommy's eyes swimming with unspoken emotion. "You sound just like your mama."

The praise makes my heart full. "I do? Thanks, Tommy!" No one has ever said that I remind them of Mom in any way. Mostly I hear about how I'm not like her at all.

"You are more alike than you know, baby girl." He chuckles.

When I sit up and brush the sand from my elbows, I see Ryan sitting across the fire, watching us. I hold my breath, waiting for him to start making fun of me. One side of his mouth tilts into a lopsided grin that starts my heart tripping again.

"Pretty." He says.

My mouth drops open in cartoonish fashion at that one word. Tommy's barking laughter reverberates in my ears and my entire body turns beet red.

"Your voice, Beth!" Ryan stammers, glancing back and forth between Tommy's amused face and my shocked one.

"I know what you meant," I lie. For a moment, I had been soaring at the thought of him calling me pretty. I stand and brush the rest of the sand off me, not wanting to stick around for round two of *Awkward Conversations With Beth and Ryan.*

"No! I mean, you are pretty and all," he is stuttering now. "I just meant...I mean, you have a great voice but...you're fourteen!" He's rambling, which has Tommy howling. This only sends Ryan deeper into his despair when he blurts out, "Knock it off, Tommy! It's not like that, I am not a pedophile!"

There it is. I can never get too comfortable without something dredging it back to the surface. I picture a neon pink sign flashing bright cursive letters above my head, "Pedophile Plaything." My subconscious is cruel enough, but Ryan's words sting like I have been slapped. My eyes blur with my hurt. It is a direct contradiction to the practiced smile I have cemented on my face. Before the tears can spill over, I spin on my heel to scurry out of there.

Within a few quick steps, warm hands grip my shoulders and spin me around. Tommy squeezes me against his chest whispering into my hair so no one else can hear, "He doesn't know, Beth. He has no idea. He just thinks you're embarrassed because he said you're pretty. Shoot, he can hardly see past his own verbal diarrhea. He's squirming over there." Tommy's words rumble deep in his chest, against my ear.

"It doesn't matter," I whisper back. Who cares whether he's figured it out or not, it doesn't change what I am or what's been done.

"It *does* matter because it is *your* story to tell to whomever, whenever *you* want to tell it."

Tommy's words are reassuring, but I still want to find a big hole to climb inside. I let go of him and peek around his back at Ryan.

He is sitting with his arms draped across his bent knees. He is shaking his head at the sand, and I wonder if he is replaying the scene in his head, like I am. He lifts his hand to run his fingers through his hair while he scans the beach.

"It's better if I just scoot. Pops and Gran are packing up, anyway." I wipe my face and smile at Tommy's concerned expression. "I love you, Tommy. What would I do without you?"

"You've never got to worry about it, baby girl. I am always here. Always," he promises with a kiss to the top of my head.

"Beth, wait!" I cringe when I hear Ryan call out. Tommy raises an eyebrow at my reaction but stays quiet as Ryan catches up to us. "Hang on a minute. I'm sorry that got so weird," he sounds unsure, nothing like the cocky boy who doused me with river water. "We're good, right?" He squats a little to get level with my eyes, but I turn my head away. He catches my chin with his thumb and index finger and brings my face back to his. "Please don't be mad at me." His brows pinch together and his expression is so pathetic, it tugs at my heart.

"I'm not mad, just embarrassed. Okay?" I shift nervously under his scrutiny. I bat his hand away from my face.

"*Now go away or I shall taunt you a second time.*" Nothing breaks awkward like Monty Python.

"*Fetch le vache!*" he drawls out in a terrible French accent. His relief shows through his smile and all is set right again. We snicker at Tommy who is shaking his head muttering about "kids these days."

On the ride back to the marina, I can't help but replay Ryan's voice in my head over and over.

"*Pretty.*"

Pretty messed up.

Pretty stupid.

Pretty ridiculous.

Pretty pathetic I thought he meant me.

11

The week passes by in a blur and my lament over Ryan is forced to the back burner. To appease my worrywart grandparents, I've agreed to see a family therapist. For all my complaining, I am really glad that I am going. Despite myself, I am relieved to have a place to talk freely without having to freak out over the reaction I will get.

Dr. Warren is my therapist. She's my mother's age with long russet hair and chocolate eyes. She has freckles that skim her nose and cheeks like me, but they look good on her. She is beautiful in a classic Hollywood kind of way and has a Judy Garland quality to her—pretty and approachable. The best thing about Dr. Warren is that she doesn't cringe, sigh or otherwise when we talk about Drew or home. She always considers me with the same warm smile-and-nod encouragement.

I don't feel embarrassed talking to her and I don't have to hide anything, so I bear it. All of it.

"Tell me about your phone calls with your mom. How are things going?" Dr. Warren and I are sitting on the floor playing checkers. Keeping myself busy while we talk helps, I'm a lot more candid and relaxed if I'm not the center of attention.

"Strange," I mutter as I contemplate my next move. "I feel bad for not being more open with her, she is trying really hard."

Dr. Warren regards me with her warm eyes. "Beth, we have talked about this. You are not responsible for absolving your parents," she notes, reaching over to rub my knee. "They are working on their own set of issues, you need to do the same. Focus on forgiving yourself if you want to start to forgive them."

"I'm not taking any blame for what happened, but it pisses me off that it did." I'm irritated she's bringing this up again. "I thought we were moving on."

She raises an eyebrow at my tone, "Well, Beth, you are very good at saying what you think I want to hear, and I am very good at reading between the lines. We keep coming back to this because it's not resolved, sweetie. You can't move on with your life until it is."

"So you think I'm lying?" my voice cracks over my surging panic. "You are the only person I don't have to lie to!"

"No, Beth, I don't think you are lying to me. I think you are lying to yourself. You did not invite Drew to molest you but when you talk about him, you insinuate blame."

"I didn't invite it, but I didn't stop it, either." I flip a black checker between my thumb and index finger. "It goes both ways."

She is starting to question me, too. What is it about me that is so untrustworthy? My mother didn't believe me when I told her what Drew was doing to me, and now Dr. Warren is basically calling me a manipulative liar. Silent tears drop into my lap, bringing a fresh wave of shame with them. My biggest fear is to trust someone with the details of what Drew did to me, only to have them walk away. Could I really blame them? Of course not, but there is a part of me that wants to believe I deserve the kind of love that would stand up to my past.

"That is what I am talking about, Beth. There are no 'buts' here. You aren't responsible for Drew's actions and you didn't perpetuate them. He molded you into someone he could take advantage of, got you to trust him completely and question yourself. It is a tried and true formula that pedophiles have been using since the age of time."

Dr. Warren means to be reassuring but now I just feel like a chump. I can't even relish that she hasn't given up on me yet because I know it's only a matter of time.

"If that's true and Drew did such a number on me, making me believe all of his bullshit, then how will I ever know what's real and what isn't?" I whimper, "How do I trust myself to know the difference?"

"Oh, Beth." Dr. Warren sighs as she moves to sit next to me, "let's look at this in two pieces, okay? First, we will work on those boundaries so you know what is safe and comfortable. Second, you have already taken steps to open up and trust again."

My eyes dart from the floor to her face. As if she can read where my thoughts have taken me, she grabs both of my hands, squeezing them, "I am not giving up on you, Beth. I am only trying to encourage you not to give up on yourself. You can trust me. Speaking of that, let's focus on the progress you're making. Tommy? Ryan? How is that going?" Hearing Ryan's name makes me fidgety, and Dr. Warren notes my demeanor with an amused smirk.

"Don't look at me like that, okay? It's bad enough, already," I mumble, wiping my face with a tissue. "Tommy just feels safe, I can't explain it. I just know I can trust him. Ryan is..." I let out a frustrated breath, "...he confuses me. One minute he is my friend, and the next minute I am getting dunked in the river." I tell Dr. Warren the whole sordid tale of the bonfire night.

She regards me carefully before she speaks. "Well, it sounds to me like you don't have a problem trusting yourself or your instincts with Tommy. You are learning to listen to your intuition and that is great, great progress! He is a solid choice. He loves you very much and wants what's best for you. You couldn't ask for a better champion." She shifts her weight forward on her hips, leaning closer to me, indicating an even more serious conversation. "Ryan on the other hand, he is a little more complicated. He isn't a grown up, he's your peer. Your willingness to trust him says a lot about how you feel about him," she pauses to ensure she's eye to eye with me. "It's okay to be attracted to boys, Beth." My face pulses with a hundred different reds, each one mingling with my insecurities.

Attraction is complicated for anyone but for me...well, complicated would be a breeze in comparison. I don't even know if there is a word to describe how it feels. When I think about him, my body goes into a hormonal overdrive—my heart pounds, I can't breathe, my stomach flutters. I am a Judy Blume cliché, for crying out loud! No matter how far I push Drew from my thoughts, everything comes back to him. There are things he taught me that I wish I could unlearn.

God, I wish I could be sitting here talking about having my first crush and not feel ashamed. The whole point of first crushes is the emphasis on first. First kiss, first touch, first everything. Drew was a thief. He stole all of my firsts. He taught me things about my body that should have been reserved for someone I love.

⌒○

"Do you trust me, Mouse?" Drew is splayed across my bed on his back and I am curled into the nook of his arm with my head on his chest.

"Yes?" It comes out as a question, but I do. I trust him. I love him.

"I want to show you something," he whispers into my hair, running a hand up my ribcage under my shirt. I suck in my breath and tense at his touch. "Relax, Mouse, this is going to make you feel good." His hand drifts to the back of my training bra and effortlessly releases the clasp.

Self-preservation takes over as my mind starts flooding my veins with adrenaline. Rolling away from Drew, I fold my hands over my chest where my bra is hanging worthlessly.

"No, I don't want to." My voice betrays me. It is small and weak, whereas my mind is screaming, "NO! I DON'T WANT TO!"

"You always say that, does it make you feel better? Don't kid yourself, Beth. You want me as much as I want you. Let me show you." He sits up and scoots back to lean on my headboard. "Come here," he commands, holding his hand out for me. I know better than to disobey, his touches are harsh and punishing when I am resistant. It's better if I am obedient; he is tender with me when I am.

I crawl into his lap and Drew turns me away from him, placing my back against his chest. He runs his fingers lightly across my arms, spreading goosebumps along my skin. "See, doesn't that feel good?" he whispers against my ear, kissing it lightly.

"Yes." I sigh and relax back against his chest, melting into the pleasant feeling. Drew's hands continue to float up my arms, along my shoulders. That is when it happens for the first time, my nipples harden as his hand brushes across my collarbone. I don't understand what is happening, my body has never responded like this before. I jerk my arms to cover my breasts, but Drew catches me by the wrists.

"Trust me." His breath against my skin stokes a treacherous tingling I don't recognize. Without hesitating, he runs his hands beneath my shirt to cup my budding breasts. I lean my head back against him and arch my back involuntarily while he pulls gently at my nipples.

"That's it," he encourages.

I start to cry. My mind is warring with what Drew tells me and what my heart knows. He wants me to believe that what we are doing is special, but I know it's wrong. Still, here I am with his hands all over me, crying over something I have failed to stop. I jerk at Drew's sudden movement behind me, he's pulled his shirt off. He grips the hem of *mine and pulls up, taking my bra with it. I curl forward, hiding myself from him.*

"Uh-uh," he scolds, gripping me around the waist and tossing me off his lap. I land with a bounce on my back, and Drew is already on me, pulling my shorts and panties down in one violent motion. I am sobbing uncontrollably, tears and snot running down my face. Drew pushes the insides of my knees apart, exposing me in the most intimate way possible. I writhe and kick at him, but he laughs at my weak attempt.

"You disappoint me, Mouse. Crocodile tears, really?" His stare is drawn to where he has boldly exposed me. His focus is predatory. "I am still going to teach you to come." I don't know what that means, but my mind races as he releases one of my legs to unzip his pants, unveiling his angry erection.

I suck in a deep breath to scream. Anticipating my reaction, Drew slaps his hand over on my mouth, "Don't you scream, you fucking little liar! I know you want this, you goddamn tease!" Panting with exertion, his eyes are ablaze with fury. I don't dare move. Sensing my submission, he releases my mouth to run his hand down the length of my torso, stopping at the entrance of my body.

"This right here," he takes a more gentle tone as he rubs a finger against my opening, "this is mine. I am going to fuck you, Beth. I am going to fuck your tight little pussy and you're going to love it because I'm going to make you." He takes my hand, running my fingers through my folds. At the very front he pauses, "Do you feel that bump? That is where I want you to touch yourself, like this." Entwining our fingers, he strokes the tender spot. After several minutes, I start to panic because nothing is happening and I am getting sore. "Do NOT defy me," he growls, shoving my hand away. To teach me a lesson he pinches my nipple hard, making me cry out in pain. I realize my mistake a second before he slaps me across the face.

"You did this to yourself, you don't get to cry," he spits. My face is hot where his hand connected. It stings, but it is a welcome distraction from the assault on the rest of my body. Drew plunges his finger into my body as he stares into my eyes, daring me to cry out again. I don't. My only protest is the tears that won't stop spilling. I close my eyes and pray for God to make me numb.

His finger probes my body, in cruel hard thrusts. When I think I can't endure anymore, he pulls out and positions himself between my legs.

"Look at me," he demands. I force my eyes open and find Drew stroking his erection with force. "This is going to hurt, but I promise I'll make it good for you, Mouse." He grabs my hips and lunges forward, covering my mouth with his as he slams into me. I scream in agony but the sound is absorbed by Drew's bruising kisses. I am being ripped in half—the pain is unbearable.

Drew is pumping himself into me with brutal force when he reaches down to where we are connected. He finds the bump from earlier, pressing it against our joined bodies. The searing pain between my legs slowly shifts to an uncomfortable tension, stirring deep within me.

I squirm beneath him, attempting to get away from the pressure building inside of me. Without warning, my back arches and a moan escapes my lips as I begin to pant and shake beneath Drew. Terrified, I search his face for some clue to what is happening to me. His eyes shine with tenderness a moment before he throws his head back, pulling my hips flush against his. He moans my name over and over as he spills himself into me.

◌◌

I moan, hiding my face in my hands. No, there are certain things I can never ever tell anyone.

"Beth, look at me," Dr. Warren encourages. My hands drop away, revealing an exaggerated grimace. "You are a beautiful girl, there is no reason for you to assume that Ryan didn't use 'pretty' to mean several things. Pretty voice, pretty smile, pretty heart and soul. You, my dear, are the whole 'pretty' package." I blink slowly, trying to absorb each word. Dr. Warren grabs my hand and stands, dragging me with her. She spins me to face the mirror hanging above the couch. "What do you see?"

"I see a lot of brown and freckles," I grumble.

"Do you know what I see?" she whispers. "I see a young woman with beautiful brown hair that catches warm red tones when the light hits it. I see a girl whose big brown eyes are soulful and mesmerizing and a smile so contagious it can light up the whole room. I see an incredible young lady who has been through hell and is coming out of that with a grace and strength that most women twice her age couldn't muster."

"I wish I could see that." I sniffle between tears.

"You will, Beth. You will," she insists.

12

My conversation with Dr. Warren plagues every thought I have. Giving me permission to be attracted to Ryan opens up all kinds of mixed emotions in me, each confusing and conflicting. No matter how hard I try to focus on our trip to the lake this weekend, my thoughts are consumed with Ryan and of Dr. Warren's description of me. She has to be exaggerating or she has me on a pedestal of perfection I can't live up to. I am incapable of passing a mirror without stopping to look at my reflection, waiting for her version of me to be unveiled. I can see that I have grown another inch, giving my body a long and lanky awkwardness. My hips and breasts are continuing to round out, much to my horror.

Currently, I don't see "pretty" anything staring back at me in the dressing room at Von Maur. I squirm uncomfortably as Aunt Melissa ties the back of the bikini I am trying on.

"Quit fidgeting, Beth!" she protests. "I have never seen a girl hate shopping as much as you." I scowl at her as our eyes meet in the mirror. "We can't go to the lake this weekend unless you've got a suit, baby girl. That old one of yours can fuel the next bonfire."

"I like my old suit," I whine, "this shows too much skin, Aunt Melissa. I can't ski in this!" I face her and gesture toward the minuscule triangles of fabric she is calling a bikini. She cups my face in her hands and draws in a deep breath.

"Beth, you are a beautiful girl. You're going to be fifteen in a few days," her gentle tone softens the rough edge of my anxiety. "Let me buy you some new things. You can't hide behind your frumpy t-shirts forever. Trust me." As she speaks she runs her thumbs along my cheeks, soothing my frayed nerves. "Now turn around, but close your eyes until I tell you to open them." I am about to open my mouth in protest when she holds a finger up to my lips. "Trust me."

"Fine," I mutter. I close my eyes and allow Aunt Melissa to turn me toward the mirror.

"Now, stand up straight, shoulders back and smile like you mean it!" Even though I feel like an idiot, I follow her directive. "That's better, now open your eyes," she whispers.

Whoa.

I stare at my reflection in awe. My posture generates an air of confidence I don't have. It transforms my reflection and I finally see the "pretty" me. No longer the scrawny little girl, I am tall and lean with the soft curves of a woman's body. I run my hand across my flat stomach to where my hips flare, then across the fullness of my breasts. I am torn. Part of me loves the way this red bikini makes my pale skin look like creamy porcelain and the other part of me wants to hide anything feminine about my body. The image of Ryan sitting across the fire pops into my head. His lopsided smirk shifts as his lips begin to move, and then I hear it so clearly, I'd swear he was standing next to me, "Pretty." Thinking of him stamps out any lingering fear I have.

"Well," Aunt Melissa queries. "What do you think?"

"I don't recognize myself." My voice coming out of this girl's mouth sends goosebumps skating across my skin. "I love it! I can't believe this is me!" My excitement is uncontainable as I jump up and down.

"Whoa, there, baby girl. No jumping in the bikini unless you want all the boys to die of heart failure." Melissa puts her hands on my shoulders to keep me still. "Are you going to fight me on trying on a few more things? A dress? Some shorts that haven't been hacked at with kitchen shears?"

"No, ma'am," I giggle. "I'm sorry I was such a pain in the butt—you're a genius!" Aunt Melissa wastes no time dragging me around the mall, outfitting me in a new wardrobe.

Exhausted and starving, we stop in the food court for Tasty Tacos. "Are you excited about this weekend?" Aunt Melissa asks.

My mouth is full of spicy pork, giving me a minute to consider my answer when the realization hits me. I don't have anything I need to edit out. With most of the details of my life in Miami out in the open, there is nothing left to hide. Melissa grabs my hand, bringing me back from my wandering thoughts, "You all right, Beth?" Her forehead is wrinkled in concern, her eyes assessing.

"Yeah, I'm great. It just dawned on me that I don't have to filter every thought before I speak anymore. I'm just relieved, I guess." I squirm, suddenly feeling idiotic. "You know, about my parents and everything."

"That makes me so happy to hear! I love you so much, Beth, you're the daughter I never got to have." Aunt Melissa's eyes mist over with her emotions. "You can tell me anything, always."

I squeeze her hand back, wondering how I got so lucky to have a family as wonderful as mine. Warmth spreads through me as I think about spending the upcoming weekend with them.

"I was already looking forward to this weekend and now I can't wait for everyone to see the new me!" I bounce in my seat. "Just in time for my birthday, too."

This weekend marks our annual trip to Lake Panorama. Every summer, we spend the Fourth of July at Tommy's lake house. Lake house is a relative term—it is more like a small cabin consisting of two bedrooms, a bathroom and a kitchenette. Each bedroom is set up dormitory style, with three sets of bunk beds. The bathroom is nothing more than a pedestal sink, a toilet and a shower stall. It's very minimalistic, but none of us care, we only care about getting out on the lake and staying out there for as long as possible.

My birthday is July third so every year I celebrate it out on the water. We have certain traditions that are always followed: Tommy will take us water skiing and tubing, Gran will make my favorite chocolate cake and Pops will grill beer brats for dinner. I will open presents around the campfire and then we will set off a few celebratory fireworks.

It sounds simple, but it means the world to me. It makes me feel like I matter. I'm still getting accustomed to knowing I do.

"You are going to knock his socks off, baby girl." Aunt Melissa gives me a Cheshire grin.

I narrow my eyes at her as my face turns a deep shade of crimson. I am tempted to argue back, but I know acknowledging will only encourage her. I have already noticed her paying careful attention to my interactions with Ryan, staring a little too long or straining to listen in to our conversations. She thinks she is being subtle but it is glaringly obvious to me, hopefully it's not to anyone else. I shake my head and let out an exasperated sigh as we collect our bags and head home.

13

Gravel crunches under the tires on Pops' car as we pull through the gate at Panorama Lake. We wind our way around the shoreline toward the lake house and my heart starts to race. Tommy's truck and empty boat trailer are backed into the boat slip. My heart seizes just before it sinks.

They went out without me.

Pops' brows scrunch together as he surveys my disappointment. The moment the car is in park, I hop out and start unloading things from the backseat. He joins me, still dissecting my emotional state under a microscope; it makes me twitchy.

I need a little space to breathe so I grab my bag and turn to Pops, "I'm gonna go change." By the time he opens his mouth to reply, I'm already inside the house.

The familiar smell of pine and mothballs encircles me immediately. I glance into the first bedroom and find luggage already on two of the bottom bunks. Since the boys have clearly staked their claim, I continue to the next room. On a heavy sigh, I sit on one of the bunks and regard my bag. My fingers tremble as I pull my new things out and lay them across the bed.

It is early afternoon and there are still several viable hours left to spend on the lake so I grab my new bikini. I chew my lip as I hold it out in front of me, knowing that I am about to cross a line I have adamantly avoided. Embracing my femininity was hard but with Dr. Warren's wise and gentle encouragement, I did it. However, revealing my femininity still feels like a betrayal. It doesn't matter how many times she explains that being attractive isn't an invitation for men to behave poorly. I am still struggling with feeling guilty about my desire to strut my stuff in this bikini just to see the look on Ryan's face. I shake off the mental warfare and draw air deep into my lungs.

Don't be a coward, Beth.

I blow out the breath with force and slip out of my baggy clothes, into the much smaller swatches of fabric. There are no full-length mirrors in the house, just the mirror above the sink. As I tie the last string behind my back, I send up a prayer of thanks for that small blessing. There is nowhere for me to scrutinize myself into chickening out. I grab my flip-flops and a beach towel, carefully holding it in front of me.

You aren't hiding anything, dumbass. Get stepping!

Before I lose my nerve, I swing the front door open and step out into the sunlight. The first thing I notice is Tommy bent in half, tying up the jet boat in its slip. They're back from their cruise around the lake. My heartbeat vibrates through my body. I move my towel from in front of me to under my arm as I mentally force myself to follow Aunt Melissa's advice.

Back straight, shoulders back and smile like you mean it!

Forcing my feet forward, I pray I don't trip and make a fool of myself. I can vaguely hear someone whistle but the blood rushing through my head is so loud, it makes everything else sound like background noise. On reflex, I turn in the direction of the noise to find Uncle Rob and Aunt Melissa unloading their Cherokee. Melissa gives a quick thumbs-up and Rob mouths, "WOW." A sudden rush of shyness has me wavering, I giggle nervously but resist the urge to retreat back into the house.

You can do this, Beth.

Apparently, Uncle Rob's catcall has drawn more than just my attention. When I turn back to the lake, Ryan's head pops up from the back of the boat. The look on his face is *priceless*. Mouth hanging open, his eyes skim across my body, searching for a safe place to focus. I smirk in satisfaction, letting his appraisal fill me with confidence. When his eyes settle on mine, I raise an eyebrow in cocky awareness.

Who's hot under the collar now, Ry?

"How's the water?" I try to keep a straight face, but my body has other ideas as it begins shaking with laughter. Ryan's eyes immediately drop to my chest and his face flushes an adorable shade of red. My mouth goes dry at his boldness; a foreign fluttering begins in my belly.

Oh my.

From my peripheral, I catch a life vest soaring through the air just before it knocks Ryan in the head.

"Jesus Christ, kid, quit gawking!" Tommy's tone is meant to be teasing but the look on his face is anything but. My heart rate increases and I have a hard time breathing.

Wow, wow, wow.

I am unprepared for the physical response my body is having to Ryan. When I can't have control, I get scared; dictating how I react and detach from my feelings is how I survived my childhood. Ryan makes me feel things I have no control over and it's frightening. My brain recognizes the fear and wants to shift into defense mode but my heart is persistent and already addicted to this beautiful boy.

I am dizzy with my emotions so I focus on what is going on around us. Uncle Rob and Aunt Melissa are walking up behind me, Pops has disappeared inside the house. Tommy regards his nephew with a look I can only describe as overprotective. It frustrates me that Tommy is finding it necessary to shame Ryan. Even though

I feel conflicted and a little dirty, I like the way Ryan is looking at me and I fear that Tommy's outburst will hinder whatever this is cooking between us.

"Being a little hard on the kid, aren't you, T?" Uncle Rob's voice floats over my shoulder. Tommy turns his scowl to Rob. "Hey man, she's not our baby girl anymore. You can't chase off every guy that looks at her sideways, you've got to lighten up!" Tommy narrows his eyes at his best friend. I don't think he's buying it.

I try to be subtle as I glance over to Ryan hanging his head and rubbing his temple where the life vest hit him. Sensing my stare, his eyes lift to mine; the red staining his cheeks is a stunning contrast to the green of his irises. I give him a sheepish smile as I pull on my bottom lip with my teeth. He smirks back, his eyes dropping to my mouth. I suck in a short breath as the vision of Ryan's lips brushing against mine flashes in my head. His eyes find mine again, spreading goosebumps across my body. As if he can sense control shifting in his favor, he hops onto the dock and walks over to me. Praying my knees aren't knocking together, I hold my breath and close my eyes as Ryan brushes the hair off my shoulder and whispers in my ear.

"Pretty," his breath dances across my ear and it takes a concerted effort not to swoon.

I am a goner.

When I open my eyes, Ryan's face is barely an inch from mine. I can feel all of the color drain from my face and it is my turn to gawk openmouthed at a very pleased Ryan. I read his message loud and clear: I am playing way outside of my league. If I were smart, I would run for the hills but the feeling he pulls from me is addicting. I couldn't resist him even if I wanted to. He takes a step backward, chuckling as he reaches for something at his feet.

"If you are going to try and ski in that..." Very slowly, Ryan drinks in my bikini. His stare scorches my skin wherever it lands, "...you are going to want to wear this." He hands me the life vest that Tommy threw.

Shit or get off the pot, Beth. You wanted to play, so play, already! Ryan crosses his arms over his chest and cocks his head to the side. He thinks he's scared me off, but I'm not going to tuck my tail between my legs and run for cover. With as much confidence as I can fake, I take the vest and use it to smack Ryan in the gut.

"Perv," I snicker. Ryan's eyebrows shoot upward, and his surprise fuels my bravery. I am feeling smug that I defied his expectations. "Don't make me sic Tommy on you," I tease.

"Now that is just evil," he laughs, gesturing toward a still notably disgruntled Tommy. Tommy's mustache is twitching with irritation, his steely gaze shifting back and forth between Ryan and me.

Ryan throws his hands up in defeat, "I think he is plotting to lock you away in an ivory tower."

I smack him with the vest again as I step around him to get on the boat. "Who's driving this thing?" I ask Tommy who is still glaring at us. "For God's sake, Tommy, it's a bathing suit! Get over it already!" I huff.

"I've seen more material on one of those little rat dogs," Tommy mutters.

"Did you really just compare my bathing suit to a dog sweater?" I cringe. "Gross!" I slip my arms through my life vest and make sure to secure the buckles across my chest. Facing Tommy, I hold my hands out, displaying my aptly covered torso. "There, are you happy now?"

He doesn't answer me as he boards, he just points to the front bucket seat. When Aunt Melissa climbs on board with Ryan, Tommy points to the bench seat in the back.

For crying out loud!

Uncle Rob snickers under his breath as he unties the boat from the dock and joins us. I'm glad he finds this so entertaining. I'm thinking it's more of a buzzkill. Tommy looks over his shoulder as we reverse out of the boat slip, not wasting the opportunity to point his index and middle fingers at his eyes and then at Ryan.

This should be fun.

14

Once we are out on the lake, the tension is forgotten. The jet boat flies over the surface of the lake, spraying a thin mist across my face. I blink my eyes against the wind and hold back the tendrils of hair whipping my face. As we speed past the houses dotting the shoreline, I soak in the lake's magic. Wind and water bathe my senses, releasing all of my negative thoughts.

"You're up first, baby girl!" Tommy yells over the engine, "I brought the tube for you."

My heart surges with love for Tommy. Water skiing is as much a lake tradition as fireworks on the Fourth of July and I suck at it. On our lake trip a few years ago, I generated quite the scandal by announcing I was through with getting dragged around the lake on my face. Only Tommy would show up the following day with a bright yellow ski tube. It made me feel so special, knowing he'd gone into town to buy it and tote it back to the lake for me. The best feature on my ski tube is it has four handles for two riders. Tommy spent a lot time riding with me, until I was confident enough to go alone.

"Breathe, baby girl, I'm here," Tommy encourages. It's hard to stay nervous watching the way Tommy's face is lit up with excitement. I breathe deep into my lungs and smile back at my friend. "Now, grab the handle here and I will boost you up the rest of the way."

Once we are on the tube, Tommy instructs me to lay on my belly propped up on my elbows. "Don't let go, Beth. If your arms get tired

I want you to yell 'Hawkeye' so I know you're ready to let go, and I'll let go with you." Tommy puts his fingers in his mouth, whistling to signal Uncle Rob. The rope tethering us is pulled taut as the boat takes off.

Bouncing along in the wake of the jet boat, Tommy and I hold on for dear life. On the second lap around the lake, my arms begin burning in protest.

"Hawkeye!" I holler into the wind.

Tommy faces me and nods his head, "On three, ready? 1...2...3!" We let go and are dragged a few feet by the boat's momentum. Adrenaline is still racing through me as I swim toward Tommy.

"Oh my gosh, that was so much fun! Can we do it again?" My words come out with lightning speed, peppered with excited giggles.

Tommy's smile equals my own as we bob up and down in the water, waiting for Uncle Rob to circle back to us. He regards me with the warm tenderness he always does.

"You did great, Beth! I am so proud of you," he beams. "Happy Birthday."

The boat idles while Ryan grabs the ski tube. He turns to face me as he secures the towrope, "You know, I have never ridden this thing?" he notes. "Will you teach me, Beth?" He smiles innocently while I eye him suspiciously. His expression softens further and I am reminded of the boy who picked up cherries with me. The one I told I would trust. I struggle not to stumble as the boat rocks with our movement.

Uncle Rob and Aunt Melissa pretend to be in deep conversation, but I know they are listening carefully for my response. Aunt Melissa is practically levitating off her seat with anticipation.

"All you have to do is hold onto the handles, Ry. You don't need me for that." Suddenly feeling bashful, I look away. Ironically, I find myself better capable of handling flirty Ryan over friendly Ryan.

"Maybe not," he cocks his head as he contemplates, "it still looks like more fun with two people. You and Tommy always looked like you were having a blast out there together."

He looks at me with sheepish, pleading eyes. He's very deliberate with the way he's interacting with me, careful not to provoke defensiveness. He thinks he's "handling" me. I smile at my pink-pedicured toes, not wanting my pleasure to be obvious.

"No way, Casanova," Tommy chimes in from behind me. I sigh heavily.

Here we go again.

"What?" Ryan's face flushes slightly as he addresses his uncle.

"Do you think this is amateur hour?" Tommy turns all the way around in his seat facing Ryan, placing me directly between them. I lock eyes with Aunt Melissa, begging her silently. *Please, please stop them!*

"I was a seventeen year old boy once. I know..." Tommy doesn't have a chance to finish before Aunt Melissa jumps in.

"Enough, Tommy! You are embarrassing Beth," she scolds. "Back. Off." She crosses her arms across her chest giving Tommy the stink eye.

"But..." Tommy starts.

"But nothing! If you want to talk to Ryan about something, you should be doing it in private. You are making everyone uncomfortable with all your posturing," she continues.

"You two, in the water," Uncle Rob interrupts, signaling Ryan and I to get in the water and away from Tommy's grousing. In my desperation to get away from the argument brewing on board, I forget that I haven't actually agreed to this and jump in the water. Ryan follows suit, followed by the ski tube. I glance back at the boat where Melissa and Tommy are still going at it, and Uncle Rob has taken over the captain's seat. When I turn back to Ryan, he's watching the trio with the same skeptical reserve as I am.

"Quickest lesson, ever," I break the uncomfortable silence, smiling as Ryan turns his attention to me. "Hang on the handles. Don't let go," I crack myself up. Ryan rolls his eyes at me and splashes water at me.

"You're a dork," he laughs. We climb onto the ski tube and wiggle into position "You know you can trust me, right?" Ryan's question takes me off guard. I look at him blankly, my words failing me. "I meant it when I said it and I don't want you to doubt that because Tommy thinks I am a dirtbag." I jerk at his statement, reaching to grab his forearm.

"Tommy doesn't think you're a dirtbag, Ryan. Tommy doesn't want me to grow up and he's not handling it well. This has more to do with me outgrowing my pigtails than anything you've done. Don't believe for a second that he doesn't think you are anything less than wonderful." I squeeze his arm, hoping he believes me. I know how it feels to be thought of as less and it makes my heart ache for Ryan. He turns his face toward me and it steals my breath. The vulnerability I see there is as beautiful as it is shocking.

"Thanks," he whispers. The sweetness of the moment fades as Ryan's mouth draws up into his lopsided smirk. "You know, your pigtails aren't the only thing you've outgrown." My face flames and I squirm next to him. He laughs at the expression on my face. The towrope goes taut as Uncle Rob hits the throttle, leaving Ryan's statement to bounce around in my head as we fly across the water.

Uncle Rob is mercilessly steering the boat, swinging us in wide arcs that jump the wake. We hang on as tightly as we can, whooping madly as the ski tube catches air. Our landing reminds me of a stone skipping across the water. We howl with laughter as we skip along, making it hard to hold on. Uncle Rob makes another sharp turn shooting us into the air. My grip fails and I'm thrown off the tube. For a moment I am flying and then the surface of the lake rushes to greet me. I tuck my knees and head to my chest just as my body hits the water. Thanks to my life vest, I pop out of the water with the force of a champagne cork.

"Beth! Beth!" I wipe the water from my face and turn toward Ryan's voice. He is practically walking on water to catch up to me. "Woohoo! Wasn't that awesome?" I holler as he approaches. The closer he gets the more clearly I see the furrowed line of his brow. When he is close enough, he reaches for my arm. He pulls me toward him, grabbing my face in his hands. I forget how to breathe.

"Shit! Are you okay?" He is panting as his voice shakes with fear, "When you flew off the tube, you were so high up and then you hit the water," he swallows hard, shaking his head. "It scared me, I thought you were hurt." Without releasing my face, he leans forward pressing his forehead against mine. I am careful when I let out a shallow breath; afraid moving will break the spell of the moment. His eyelashes cling to the water on his face as he closes his eyes. His chest is rising and falling in quick succession under his life vest.

Without thinking, I wrap my arms around his neck and pull him into an embrace. Ryan responds by crushing me against him. The bulky life vest between us instantly irritates me. I lean my head against his shoulder and fight the urge to run my fingers through his hair. Enveloped in his arms, I feel safe.

"It's all right, Ry. I'm okay, I don't even have a scratch on me," my voice is a whisper against his shoulder. Any doubts I have about trusting Ryan, the lake washes away.

15

The ride back across the lake is surreal. Tommy doesn't complain when I sit next to Ryan but he does join us on the bench seat. Here I am stuck between two people that I care about deeply but who have very different ideas about me. I know that Tommy's need to protect me goes beyond my growing up. He wants to shelter me the way my parents should have. The problem is, I don't need protecting from Ryan. I needed it from Drew.

I pick at a string hanging from my life vest, shifting in my seat. Ryan doesn't know any of the details of what happened in Miami, he only knows that my parents are in rehab. If he does know about Drew, he's never let on that he does and has stayed true to his promise under the cherry tree. We don't talk about anything I don't want to talk about.

Once, Ryan was at the house when my mother called, and I really thought he would ask about her, but he didn't. He left me room to bring it up if I wanted but never pressured me to when I didn't. It's nice having someone around who doesn't know how damaged I really am. I hope that Tommy's tantrum doesn't raise a bunch of questions I don't want to answer.

Frustrated, I pinch the bridge of my nose and go over the ski tube caper again. I didn't think getting bucked off was that bad, but then I didn't see it like the others did. Being launched as high as I was made my subsequent landing appear pretty bad. Ryan wasn't the only one who was scared, Aunt Melissa clucked over me like a nervous hen, inspecting me for injuries when we got back on the boat. Tommy yelled at a white-faced Uncle Rob for being reckless, but poor Uncle Rob didn't need the ribbing, he was distraught enough.

Maybe it's the distress rolling off everyone or maybe it's just too much attention for me to handle, but I find myself slinking back into the quiet of my own world. It's been months since I've felt the need to detach myself from what's happening around me, and now I am flooded with the need to hide from the concerned faces around me. Tommy flanks my right and Ryan is to my left, the two people I have chosen to trust implicitly, and I am choosing to shut down like a coward.

My choice.

The thought slams into my head, stemming my impending retreat. I look back and forth between the two, reminding myself that I've made a good choice in trusting them and these are good men. They're not Drew, and it's not fair to allow his poison to affect the way I see them. Determined to prove a point to myself, I lean my head against Tommy's shoulder and clasp Ryan's hand in mine. With a resolute intention, I remind myself where I am and who I am with.

I. Am. Safe.

It surprises me when I don't have to repeat and play back those words a million times to convince myself of their value. Somewhere, not as deep down as I thought, I really do know that I am safe. I guess I have grown up in more than one way. Someday, I hope thoughts like these aren't secondary to thoughts of Drew. He stole every "first" from me. How do you get past that? I'll never know what it feels like to give the first piece of myself to someone I choose, someone I care about. Up until now, it's been hard to imagine caring for someone else enough to surpass the stain Drew left and that part of me will always believe shame is stronger than love.

"Only if you let it," Dr. Warren's advice rings in my head.

"It's how we put those pieces back together that matters." My mom's words of wisdom follow suit.

Ryan brushes his thumb across my hand, bringing me back to the present. It never fails, whenever my thoughts drift to heavy places, Ryan finds a way to reassure me. Whether it's his foot under the dining room table or the caress of his thumb across my skin, he knows what I need and it always makes me feel better. He cocks his head and gives me a warm smile. Maybe I am nuts, but I just can't imagine anyone else ever making me feel the way Ryan does. As overly dramatic as that may sound, it's true. Sure he can push my buttons, but he also makes me feel something no one has been able to—hope.

My cheeks flush with warmth when I squeeze his hand and return his smile. It's a day early, but I am powerless against my mind drifting to lit candles and birthday wishes. I look to where our fingers are interlaced and know what my wish will be—my first real kiss.

16

The next morning I wake on the cusp of a dream with sweat running down my spine. Disoriented, I blink at the rays of sun shining through the blinds and wonder where I am. My sigh of relief breaches the serene quiet when I realize I'm not in my bedroom in Miami and Drew isn't here. It takes me a moment to remind myself that I'm safe but my heart is still insistent as it pummels my ribcage. The last time I had a nightmare about Drew was right after I started to speak again. Every time I take a step forward with my life, Drew is there trying to derail me.

Only if you let him. Don't let him win.

There is no way I am going back to sleep, so I tiptoe to the kitchen to start a pot of coffee. As the grounds percolate and drip into the carafe, I try to set my mind to brighter things. Today is my fifteenth birthday and I have the whole day to look forward to, no sense in letting a dream get me down. Careful not to make any noise, I pour a cup of coffee and sneak out the front door.

The sun peeking over the horizon casts a hundred different shades of pink, orange and yellow across the lake. I walk gingerly across the gravel to the dock on my bare feet. The light dances across the surface of the water and beckons me with a siren's call. I find my spot at the dock's edge and hang my feet over the side. That is how Tommy finds me, savoring my coffee and drawing circles in the water with my toes.

"Hey baby girl, I thought I might find you out here," Tommy yawns, scratching his stomach through his Iowa Hawkeyes t-shirt. It doesn't surprise me to see him. We've been having early morning pow-wows on the dock for a long time. "Couldn't sleep?" He brushes his hand across the top of my head before joining me.

"Bad dream." I murmur into my mug. Tommy regards me with sleepy eyes, but the twitch of his mustache clues me in to his concern.

"Wanna talk about it?" He wraps his arm around me and squeezes my shoulder.

"No, but Dr. Warren says it's the only way I will ever get past it." I stare into my mug and try to gather the courage to continue.

"You know you can tell me anything, Beth. There is nothing I wouldn't do for you, baby girl." Tommy's warm baritone washes over me, giving me the boost that I need.

"It was about Drew," I start, "nothing specific, more like a mash-up of everything." My hair falls like a curtain, hiding my face from Tommy's reaction. I hear him blow out a breath as he takes in my statement.

"I have bad dreams too," his confession surprises me. Pulling my hair behind my ear, I turn toward him. His eyes are focused on the lake. "In my dream, I am back in your living room, pounding the living shit out of Drew, except this time I don't stop, Beth. I kill him with my bare hands," his voice trembles as he pinches the bridge of his nose. I reach over and lay my hand across the top of his. I don't want this pain for him. "The dream doesn't scare me as much as waking up wishing that I had."

I rest my head on Tommy's shoulder and let the weight of his words soak in. Knowing the extremes he would go to protect me makes me feel brave. As the sun continues its ascent into the sky, I lay out the whole story. I have to give Tommy credit, he masks his fury well when I tell him how Drew struck up a friendship with me when I was five and by my sixth birthday had me convinced that touching me meant he loved me. Tommy swallows audibly when I tell him how Drew encouraged me to show him how much I loved him by touching him, too. I close my eyes, not wanting to see Tommy's reaction when I explain it was two years before I realized Drew was doing something wrong and when I tried to stop it, he cried like I had broken his heart. After that, Drew made sure to remind me that no one would believe the word of a child over him. Once I have purged the last detail, Tommy cocoons me in his arms. The same arms that struck out to protect me, the arms that saved me.

"In my life, I have never known, nor will I ever know, someone as strong and courageous as you, Elizabeth Irene Bradshaw," Tommy whispers against my temple. I have no words, so I nod my head against his chest, hoping he understands my acceptance of his praise. "You honor me with your trust, baby girl. I am so very proud of you."

"Dr. Warren told me that I made a good choice when I told her that I trusted you, T." I hesitate for a moment, wondering if I should tell him the whole of what Dr. Warren said. "She told me that I did good choosing Ryan, too," Tommy's eyebrows nearly hit his hairline, "to trust, I mean." Tommy's face is frozen in surprise, so I continue, "I trust him to be careful with me. At the same time, he doesn't treat me any different than normal."

"I don't know about that, the way he was looking at you...." Tommy wiggles his eyebrows up and down, eliciting a mortified gasp from me.

"I mean, he doesn't act like he's afraid to be around me, like I'm going to fall apart if he says the wrong thing. It's nice to just feel normal." I shake my head, embarrassed by Tommy's candor but glad to have made my point. "He thinks you believe he's a dirtbag."

Tommy's face falls at those words. "Oh," Tommy whispers, "I never meant it that way. I just don't like boys ogling my baby girl."

I shove Tommy in the shoulder. "You mad at me for ogling him? Talk about a double standard!" I laugh.

"No! La-la-la-la-la-la-la!" Tommy sticks his fingers in his ears, "I am not listening!"

With the mood significantly lighter, we grab our mugs and return to the house to see who is ready for some lake time.

17

From the moment Tommy and I cross the threshold into the house, our day begins in a flurry. Gran is in the kitchenette frying up egg sandwiches and Uncle Rob and Ryan are at the card table scarfing down theirs. Pops is dancing around Gran, trying to pack a cooler to take fishing. As he reaches into a high cabinet, I catch him swatting Gran's butt.

Gross.

Aunt Melissa comes out of the bathroom with a towel wrapped around her head and pauses when she sees me. Her face breaks into a huge smile filled with her love for me. It makes me blush for some reason, and I feel a little sheepish when she holds her arms out for me. I step into her embrace and let the soapy scent of her shower wash over me.

"Happy Birthday, Elizabeth Irene!" She squeezes me until I grunt from the force, as she pushes me to arm's length, assessing me. "Well you look the same as yesterday, how do you feel?"

"I feel better than I have in a long time." I answer Melissa, but my smile is for Tommy. Yes, it's starting to feel like I am on my way to leaving Drew where he belongs, in the past.

"Saddle up, hanyaks! We are wasting precious lake time dilly-dallying in here." Uncle Rob pats the card table as he stands and clears the table. The promise of the lake is all the motivation I need—I am skipping to the bedroom when I feel eyes boring a hole in me. From the card table, Ryan is watching me with amusement. He stands and skips into the kitchen with over exaggerated movements.

Moron.

We all scatter to our rooms to ready ourselves for a day on the lake. I grab a pair of cutoffs and my Aerosmith t-shirt to wear over my bikini. While sunblock helps, unless I cover up, I will end the day with a gazillion more freckles I hate. I grab my bag, making sure to pack my towel with my SPF 85 and Walkman. I am anxious to listen to the mix tape I made for the trip. The pull of music and the lake almost has me skipping out the door before I remember Ryan poking fun at me. I sling my bag over my shoulder, lift my head high and remind myself that imitation is the sincerest form of flattery.

Ryan looks confused as I climb into the jet boat. "You aren't going out on the ski tube today?"

"I am," I reach into the neck of my t-shirt and pull the string from my bikini into view. "The sun is freckle fertilizer and I need more of those like I need another hole in my head." I mean to sound playful, but Ryan doesn't play along. He studies my face and cocks his head to the side.

"I like your freckles," he says nonchalantly, "they're you."

I blush at his compliment. He smiles warmly as he takes my bag and stows it under the bench seat as he continues readying the boat for the day.

"Hey, did you say something to Tommy?" his question pulls me back from my swooning.

"Huh?" I stall, trying to figure what he knows about my talk with Tommy. My stomach hits the floor of the boat at the thought of anyone overhearing my early morning confessions. Sweat beads on my top lip as I wait for Ryan to answer.

"About me?" he says. "Did you say something? Because he took me aside to tell me how proud he is of me." Ryan stops winding the towrope to look up at me through his long blond lashes.

Crap, I can't think when he looks at me like that.

"Umm…" I stutter, "No, he's just in a sentimental mood. He told me the same thing this morning when we were having coffee on the dock." There, that's part of the truth…minus the other nine-tenths of the conversation. Ryan raises an eyebrow at me and I shoot him a toothy smile.

"Uh-huh," Ryan mutters. "Well, since you didn't say anything, I won't thank you."

He goes back to winding the towrope, shaking his head at me. Even though he has turned his gaze back to his task, I can see the upturn of his lips and know that he is pleased. I smile, knowing how good it feels to hear those words from someone you respect and admire. I felt the same rush of pride when Tommy said them to me.

Pops and Uncle Rob take off with their fishing rods in the bass boat, determined to bring back a cooler full of Muskie and Catfish. They assure me that they will forfeit my traditional beer brat birthday dinner by opting for a Fourth of July fish fry. We wish them luck as we pull away from them and head toward the center of the lake.

"You think they'll catch anything?" I gesture in the direction of the bass boat. I am lounging on the bench seat with Aunt Melissa while Tommy and Ryan ride up front.

"God, I hope not," Aunt Melissa cringes, "I hate fish."

I snicker and nod my head in agreement.

Good, I'm not the only one.

I pull my Walkman out from beneath the seat and settle in for the ride. Strains of classic rock flow through my headphones as the boat picks up speed and we are flying.

I stare at the back of Tommy's head, thinking about all of the things he knows about me, now. I'm not sorry I told him everything. It feels good to know someone else knows my secret. Still, I worry that it's irrevocably changed the way he sees me. I close my eyes and tilt my face toward the sky, as the warmth of the sun chases the sudden chill away. The Stones are crooning on about wild horses when someone nudges my knee. I lift one eyelid, expecting to find Aunt Melissa, instead I find a grinning Ryan. Aunt Melissa looks over her shoulder from her new place in the front seat and winks. That minx, she is a shameless matchmaker. I love it.

"What's up, Ry?" I pull my headphones down around my neck, hoping I sound calmer than I am.

"You were sending me smoke signals up there," he gestures toward the front seat. I crinkle my brow in confusion so he continues, "The smoke coming off your head from thinking too hard. It spoke to me, 'Ryan come save me from myself before I think myself into a coma.'" I laugh at his observation and just like that, I'm relaxed again. We fall into easy conversation about life, music and talking Tommy into shaving his mustache.

"Tom Selleck called, he wants his 'stache back," Ryan chuckles.

"It *is* very Magnum P.I., circa 1981," I giggle.

The rest of the day, between our turns in the water, we whisper the names of famous mustaches.

"Groucho Marx," Ryan challenges.

"Charlie Chaplin," I shoot back.

"Burt Reynolds," he banters.

"Freddy Mercury." I smile—not only is Freddy's 'stache iconic, he's a musical genius.

"Ooo, that's a good one," Ryan cheers. I watch as his face lights up, "Geraldo Rivera!" he shouts.

"What the hell are you two talking about?" Tommy asks while we tie down the ski tube for the ride back.

Ryan and I shoot each other panicked looks and speak at the same time,

"Nothing."

I laugh so hard I have tears streaming down my face. Ryan is holding his stomach, trying to breathe between his guffaws. Tommy is looking at us like we are a couple of loons. He furrows his brow, shakes his head and goes back to securing our gear.

18

That evening, we gather around the card table where Gran has lit up her famous chocolate cake with fifteen candles that flicker like sparklers. My family belts out "Birthday" by The Beatles and chants for me to blow out the candles. Surrounded by the people I love most in the world, I have never been happier. Already having my wish in mind, I pull in a deep breath and blow.

"That was quick, did you make a wish?" Gran asks.

"I already knew what I was wishing for." I smirk but she doesn't see it, her attention is focused on serving us. She passes me a plate and kisses my forehead before going back to tending to the cake. I bite, savoring the rich chocolate while I try to think up a subtle way to get Ryan alone. Nerves start to kick around my self-doubt and when I am about to give into it, Ryan interrupts.

"Are you done with that?" he points to my plate.

"Yeah, I'm done," I sigh at the double meaning of my statement and push my plate toward him. "Have at it, it's all yours."

"No," Ryan chuckles, "I don't want your cake. I thought if you were done, you might want to go for a walk?"

Oh. My. God.

"Sure." I am certain I'm blushing head to toe but I am so excited, I don't care. I leap to my feet with too much enthusiasm, making Ryan laugh. As we slip out the front door, I don't look over my shoulder to see if anyone is watching us, but I'm pretty sure that Aunt Melissa has a big smile on her face.

We walk along the shoreline in silence awhile, until Ryan reaches into his pocket and pulls out a rumpled envelope.

"I got you something for your birthday, I just didn't want to give it to you in front of everybody." He holds it out for me to take. "Sorry, it got a little beat up in my pocket." He smiles shyly. I nibble at my bottom lip as I tear at the paper, inside are two tickets to see Brutal Strength at The Iowa State Fair. My eyes shoot from the tickets to Ryan's face.

"They are my favorite!" I gush, "Thank you, Ryan." I throw my arms around his neck and squeeze. He chuckles at my reaction and wraps his arms around my waist.

"You're welcome, Beth." His words dance across my ear, giving me goosebumps. He smells like something familiar and spicy, like the dock baking under the July sun.

Cedar, he smells like cedar.

I turn my head and my nose brushes against Ryan's cheek a moment before my lips. I let them linger against the warmth of his skin for a moment before leaning back but Ryan only tightens his arm around me, bringing us nose to nose. He cups my face with his hand and I am transfixed by the wonder in his expression, giddy that I put it there. He rubs his thumb across my cheek, releasing a swarm of butterflies in my stomach. I take in a shaky breath and close my eyes when he leans forward. I feel his warm breath and the promise of his mouth against mine but he hesitates. I open my eyes and when they meet Ryan's, he kisses me. There is nothing remotely familiar about this kiss. I can't believe I was ever worried about Drew spoiling this moment. He is a million miles away as Ryan's lips touch mine in a gentle caress, sending chills down my spine. My hands find their way into Ryan's hair and I lean into his chest, needing to be closer. Ryan pulls his mouth from mine, and he looks at me with a delicious mix of affection and want. No, there is nothing familiar about this at all—I don't want it to ever end.

When his lips meet mine again, they're more determined. His tongue sweeps the seam of my lips, luring me further into his spell. My lips part and a soft murmur escapes when Ryan's tongue brushes against mine. I am lost to the sensations that pulse through the places we touch. My skin hums where his hand touches my back, his fingers trail sparks against my cheek and his lips brand me.

"Wow," Ryan breathes as he breaks our kiss.

"Why did you stop?" I whisper as I press my lips to his neck. Being kissed senseless has made me rather daring.

"Hmm?" he mumbles as he trails kisses from my collarbone to my chin. My knees buckle, and Ryan grips me around the waist. God, everywhere he touches sends me falling further. He kisses the tip of my nose and makes sure I'm steady before he takes a step back. His hand laces with mine as he gestures for us to keep walking. I follow him blindly. I'd follow him anywhere.

"I don't want to screw things up with you, Beth," Ryan confesses. "You intimidate the hell out of me." I stare at him stunned for a moment before I start laughing.

"What? Why on earth would I intimidate you?" It sounds so absurd to me. I am the one who is out of her league—Ryan definitely has the upper hand.

"Don't laugh!" Ryan blushes. "You don't see it and that only makes it harder to resist. You're the coolest girl I know, you're so easy to hang with and you're so pretty." I smile at my favorite word. "You're strong, you're funny," he pauses, "you're everything."

"Oh." That's the only response I have. How lame. Ryan chuckles at my eloquence, and I can't help myself from joining him. I don't know what to say, so I let him steer the conversation wherever he wants.

"So, I was thinking for the concert that we could just make a day of it?" His suggestion ends on a question. My heart bounces in my chest at his uncertainty. Like I would ever pass up a chance to spend the day with him.

"It's a date." I try to sound casual, but the smile spreading across my face gives away my excitement. A first kiss and plans for a first date. I can't stop smiling.

Best. Birthday. Ever.

19
BETH

Life is full of lessons we either learn from or get bitter over. Currently, I'm a Bitter Bob. Life sucks. Hard. I don't care how melodramatic that sounds, it's the truth and I'm living it. Of all the things I allowed myself to believe in, happily ever whatever is the biggest farce of them all. I was stupid to think that I was destined to spend my summer with Ryan. Nothing good lasts. I should know that by now. Tears pool behind my eyes, and I fight not to cry as I watch our plane pull away from the gate. My mom's hand covers mine in a gesture meant to comfort, but I yank it away. I hate her.

"Beth, you're going to have to talk to us at some point," she pleads, "I know you don't understand right now, but this is for the best."

I turn from the window to give her the full brunt of my hatred. "When have you *ever* known what is best?" I spit out. "When did you ever *do* what was best? You know nothing about what is best for *me*. You only care about what is best for *you*." The tears I've been fighting spill angrily. I'm not in the mood to get into this with her again.

She hasn't listened once since she and my dad blew into town three days ago, and I don't expect she will start listening now. I turn back to the window, letting the ache in my chest bloom with hopelessness as we barrel down the runway for takeoff. As the plane's wheels leave the ground, my shoulders slump in final defeat. I'm going home.

Ryan and I are over before we even had a chance to begin. The roar of the jet engine drowns out my pitiful whimpering and any attempt my mom has for pleading her case. I pull one of Tommy's hankies from my pocket and blot my face. The scent of leather and cinnamon only makes me cry harder.

Once we are at cruising altitude, my mom turns in her seat to address me, "I'm sorry you feel that way, honey. We only have a handful of weeks before school starts to work on our family. We need this time for therapy. *We* need this, Beth. Not just your dad and I, all *three* of us need this. Your dad and I have been through so much...." Mom hesitates. She searches my face for understanding while she wipes a tear from my cheek, causing me to flinch.

"God, I was so stupid to think that I was getting anywhere with you," I scoff. "You'll never change. You'll always find a way to spin the story in your favor. You're not a victim; I am." My breath hiccups as I strain to keep composure. "I didn't have a hand in any of the decisions you made. Those were all yours, Mom, so don't tell me how much you and dad have been through. I've been trying to just survive my life for the last eight years while you've made one shitty decision after another."

I turn to the window where we're floating high above clouds that remind me of tufts of snow. The scene looks like a shot of heaven. What a crock. The reality is, out there it's freezing cold and the air is so thin you can't breathe. Sounds a lot like my life.

"I had something really good there. I had family who put me first, a therapist who really got me and I had Ryan. That might seem silly to you, Mom, but he's the only thing that ever made me forget what it felt like to forget. Good luck trying to convince me leaving that behind to join you and dad for part two of your rehab stint is in my best interest."

"You'll still get to talk to a therapist, Beth, and it's not like you will never see your family again." She leans in to make sure I can hear her clearly, "Let me get a couple of things straight with you, young lady, I may have made some terrible decisions, but I'm still your mother. I'm the only one you've got, so I suggest you find a way to show me a little respect. Another thing, you're four days past your *fifteenth* birthday, and if you're that hung up on a boy then it is a good thing we are leaving because it's not right, Beth. You're too young to be that emotionally attached to Ryan."

"Seeing your drug counselor will hardly replace my visits with Dr. Warren. I'm not an addict, Mother. I'm a survivor of sexual abuse. How do expect your counselor to help me?" I sneer.

How soon she forgets that I'm not one of her rehab buddies or counselors who hang on her every word, fawning over everything she says. I know the drill, I know how she operates and I've been conned one too many times to buy into anything she's trying to sell.

"Dave is a family therapist, Beth," she flips her hair over her shoulder and turns her gaze to my father across the aisle. "You can argue all you want, but it's done. You can make the best of it or you can make yourself miserable. You want to preach to me about choices, well, this one is all yours."

My family life has been one lesson in adapting after another— you either move or get run over. I watch with detached interest as my mom and dad lean across the aisle to whisper to one another. They pause to look my way and then continue their conversation, no doubt about how difficult I'm being. Tucking the pieces of my heart carefully back into its compartment, I think about Aunt Melissa and how hard she worked to get me to come out of my shell. The only piece I leave out is Ryan. I don't think the whole of my feelings for him will ever fit in that box. Still, there is no room for openness where I'm headed, so I do the only thing I know how to, survive. Rule number one in adapting—control the situation at hand before it has a chance to control you.

～

"Don't forget me," I whisper in Ryan's ear. *He squeezes my hand in his and smiles his lopsided grin. He's trying so hard but his smile doesn't reach his gaze.* It hurts my heart to see sadness in his beautiful green eyes, so I close my own and lay my head on his shoulder.

"Like I could ever forget you." The pad of Ryan's thumb brushes my cheek. *His words should fill me with warmth, but they break my heart for the chance we'll never get.* "Don't cry, Beth. You're killing me," he pleads, running his hands through my hair.

I look up at his profile and memorize my favorite parts of his handsome face—the slope of his nose, the way his mouth always tips to the left when he smiles, the thick blond eyelashes that frame his gorgeous green eyes. Every moment left is precious and I don't want to waste a single one.

"Come with me," I grab Ryan's hand and pull him toward the front steps. His brow crinkles as he tries to figure out my angle. "Come on." I give him a watery smile and my heart pounds when he lets me tug him along. I scamper down the front steps, dragging a laughing Ryan behind as I round the corner of the house. When we reach the backyard, I turn and face him. Still holding onto his hand, I step backward and give him a shy smile.

Once we are under the cherry tree, I wrap my arms around his neck and gently kiss his upturned lips. He hooks his thumbs in the belt loops of my cutoffs and pulls me closer, brushing my nose against his. The sweetness of his breath against my face sends chills along my arms and I bite my lip in anticipation. Ryan brings his thumb to my mouth and tugs, setting my lip free just before kissing it. He looks at me from half-closed eyes and says the word that I will never hear again without wishing for him.

"Pretty."

20
RYAN

Beth's got that look in her eye, the one that sends my heart into my stomach every time. She's got no clue the effect she has on me, which only makes her charm that much more lethal. Her big brown eyes are sparkling with mischief and that impish grin of hers turns my mouth dry. I let her drag me around to the back of the house, to the cherry tree. I know that's where she's headed, but I pretend to be clueless. It's far more fun to watch her scheming to get me alone. Like I need to be talked into that.

The only thing I need any help with is keeping my thoughts PG when I'm near her. Beth is trouble with a capital "T." She's gorgeous and has no idea. Most of the beautiful girls at my school walk around like the world owes them a great big favor for gracing us with their presence. Stuck up, snobby, high maintenance girls who look down at everyone else with their high and mighty attitudes. Not Beth. First of all, she puts every single one of those girls to shame.

Her beauty is something else—she has these warm brown eyes that can strip me bare with one look. She's beautiful anyway but when that girl smiles, it steals the air straight out of my lungs. As if I wasn't already crazy about her, she's the coolest girl I've ever met. She's so easy to hang out with and she even loves to go out on the lake to ski and tube. Most of the girls I've known would rather sunbathe on the dock than play in the water. Being around her is effortless—she's beautiful, she's perfect. She's also going back to

Miami. It's so damn unfair. The thought makes me want to punch something.

Beth turns to face me and the look on her face nearly brings me to my knees. Her cheeks are almost as red as the cherries in the tree, and she's smiling shyly as she backs under the cherry tree, towing me along with her. I can't help the smile tugging on my lips; she's so damn cute. When she reaches up to wrap her arms around my neck and presses her full lips against mine, I want to pinch myself. To stay as gentlemanly as possible, I hook my thumbs in her belt loops, keeping my itchy hands from roaming. What I really want to do is run my hand along the smooth skin of her stomach, peeking out from the bottom of her t-shirt. When she starts tugging on her bottom lip with her teeth, all gentlemanly thoughts hit the road. It takes every effort not to pin her against the tree and run my hands all over her sweet curves. *Pervert. She's only fifteen—that's what I keep reminding myself.* While I am only two years older than her, sometimes I feel like a dirty old man wanting all of her sweetness for myself.

I force myself to swallow the lump in my throat as I let go of her belt loop and let my hand travel to her mouth where I gently pry her lip free from her front teeth. When I kiss her, I swear my heart stops in my chest. I'm struck stupid by how much I want her and so frustrated that we're being cheated with bad timing. When her eyes lock on mine, I blurt out the first word that comes to mind every time I see her.

"Pretty."

∽

I stare at the concert tickets in my hand, wondering if this is really a good idea or not. I don't want them anymore, it just adds to the constant frustration of wishing Beth were here. It's been a month since she left and nothing I do can fill the hole she left. Tommy is eyeing me curiously; at least he hasn't been harassing me about my bad mood.

"You know for the Jedi Mind Trick to work '*Clear your mind must be,*'" Tommy snickers. "I assume that is what you are shooting for because I can't think of another reason you'd be staring at those tickets for the last fifteen minutes."

"O wise Yoda," I roll my eyes and laugh. "I'm gonna go see if Lori wants these tickets, I'm tired of hanging onto them. I'm not going to use them, anyway." The more I try to act like it's no big deal, the closer Tommy's eyebrows get to his hairline.

"You really want to bark up that tree? You know that girl's had the hots for you since you rescued her Frisbee from the roof," Tommy smirks.

"We were in sixth grade, T. I'm pretty sure she's over it by now," I grumble, walking away.

"All right, whatever you say, Ry," Tommy chuckles.

I roll my eyes as I open the front door and head across the street to Lori's house. I can't believe Tommy. I climbed the trellis five years ago when Lori's Frisbee got stuck. It's not like it was yesterday or even last year, it's over and I never gave Lori any reason to pine after me. I've been pretty clear that I'm not interested in her that way. I stare at her door when a sudden urge to run strikes me. I'm about to turn around and head back across the street when the door swings wide.

"Hey, Ryan," Lori smiles sweetly at me. She's a cute girl, petite with black, curly hair. Not hard on the eyes by any stretch, just not my type. Who am I kidding? If you aren't Beth, you're not my type. I should've run when I had the chance.

"Hey, Lori," I mumble," listen, I have a couple of tickets to the Brutal Strength concert this weekend, and I'm not using them so I thought maybe you'd like to have them." I shift nervously as Lori's eyes widen and her hands come up to cover her mouth.

"Ryan Cantwell, are you finally asking me out? I don't believe it," she beams. She bounds down the steps to where I stand, looking like she's about to throw her arms around me.

"*Whoa. Wait,*" I shout, throwing my hands out in front of me to stop her momentum. "I meant both tickets are yours to ask whomever you'd like. 'I'm not using them' means I don't want to go." I cringe when my words come out harsher than I intend. "I'm sorry, Lori. I didn't mean for you to think I was asking you out."

She stands in front of me with her arms across her chest and her hip jutted out to the side, all attitude. "It's because of Gran and Pops' granddaughter, right?" She narrows her eyes at me. "Beth?" The least I can do is offer up the truth.

"Yes, they were for Beth. Since she went back home, we can't use the tickets and I would rather not hang onto them." I sigh.

I should have never taken my eyes off of Lori, because an instant later her arms are latched tightly around my waist, her head pressed against my chest.

"Oh, Ry, that is so sad! You should go with me, I'll cheer you up," she croons.

I push at her shoulders to get her to release me and when she finally looks up at me, I swear she has stars in her eyes.

"You know, this was a bad idea. I'm sorry, Lori." Without another word, I turn and jog back across the street. Of all the stupid ideas I've had, this one takes the prize. As I make my way up to the house, I see Tommy watching from the front window. Great. All I need, a witness. When I walk through the front door, I walk past Tommy, refusing to acknowledge him.

"The force is strong in that one," Tommy laughs.

"Oh, bite me," I grumble.

21
BETH

A year sounds like a lot of time, but it's really not. It's a gateway between tenth and eleventh grade, it's time spent getting to know my parents for the first time, time to realize they aren't the monsters I want them to be. A year has taught me that really great people make stupid mistakes sometimes. My parents are good people. They aren't perfect, but they're mine. Despite everything, they love me. A year has shown me that just because my parents don't love me the way I need them to, doesn't mean they don't love me with everything they have.

Pops has always been the first to tell me—*you plant your own garden instead of waiting for someone to bring you flowers.* In other words, take responsibility for your own needs and your own happiness. Learning to do that has made it easier to forgive them and move on.

"*After a while you learn that even sunshine burns if you get too much, so you decorate your own soul and plant your own garden instead of waiting for someone to bring you flowers.*" I sigh, wistfully.

"Where did you hear that?" Dave stares at me in wonder.

"Pops." A smile creeps across my face as I think of my grandfather. "He quotes lines from that poem all the time."

"It's a poem? Would you share the whole thing with me?" Dave scoots to the edge of his seat and leans toward me.

I recite "After Awhile" by Veronica Shoffstall from memory. I never get tired of hearing the words and every time I do, it fills me with strength.

Dave blows out an audible breath and runs his hands through his hair. "Beth, you should really think about sharing that at Al-Anon. I think a lot of people in your group would identify with it."

Despite my best efforts, I really like Dave. He's been great with helping me and my folks develop a relationship, and he has been a great listener when it comes to my frustration with them. He even got me involved with Al-Anon, which I fought tooth and nail. He didn't let up, he even escorted me to the first few meetings until he felt I wouldn't bail. I hated the thought of spilling my guts to a bunch of kids I didn't know, but Dave was right, I got a lot out of going. It helped knowing that the feelings I was having weren't unusual and there were other kids my age struggling with newly sober parents. I even found my best friend, Charlie, there.

"I don't know, Dave," I waver, "that's a little too personal for a crowd."

"Just think about it, ok?" He pats my knee and is off to the next topic. That is one thing I really appreciate about Dave, he doesn't pressure me. He'll come back to the topic but he always gives me room to mull it over beforehand. "So, just one more week before you're off to Des Moines." He leaves the end of his statement hanging, unsure of what I'm willing to talk about today. I give him a non-committal grunt in response. "Beth, I think there are some things we need to talk about before you leave. You haven't seen Ryan in a year, and we should really talk about some safe boundaries with him. I don't want to see you get hurt."

This is one of those topics that never get easier to talk about. Eleven months of arguing with Dave and my parents over the place he has in my heart. Here we go again.

"Give it a rest, Dave," I grumble, "he's not even going to be there." I've known since the spring that Ryan was spending the summer in Iowa City, getting settled in and starting classes at The University of Iowa. Knowing it doesn't do squat for the disappointment that sends tears spilling down my cheeks. "You can rest assured, now. I won't see Ryan again." Dave hands me a box of Kleenex and waits quietly while I cry.

"You may not see him again, but we still need to talk about him. Ryan has become an unattainable ideal that has effectively kept all other boys at bay. You hold him up on a pedestal, Beth. It's not good for you or Ryan, not even he can live up to the expectation you've created."

Dave's words rip off the scabs of wounds that refuse to heal. It's hard to argue with his logic, I understand where he is coming from, but I wish he could see it through my eyes. I even understand my mother's initial concern—fifteen is too young to feel the way I do about Ryan, fifteen is too young to decide what you want for the rest of your life.

In most instances, I would agree with them but I'm not most instances. My story is unique and while I'm young, I'm more seasoned than most thirty year olds. I've seen enough and experienced enough to have a pretty good understanding of the world. I've got room to grow in my maturity but my view of the world and what I want out of it isn't going to change much. No matter how hard Dave and my parents press, I'll never stop wanting Ryan. He owns a piece of my heart and no amount of dating around can change that.

"Did my parents put you up to this?" I chuckle through my tears, "My mom was so pissed that she didn't get to dress me up for prom."

"Would that have been so bad? Why didn't you go to prom, Beth? I know Charlie asked you," Dave smirks at me and raises his eyebrow. I meet Dave's glare with annoyance: Charlie is my best friend.

"That was a pity date and I'm not some charity case, Dave."
I narrow my eyes at him. It pisses me off that he would taint my
friendship with Charlie with his innuendo. "Charlie is my best
friend and he didn't want me to miss out on prom if I wanted to
go, which I didn't. Prom is for couples not for buddies, and I especially don't want to muck up my friendship with him by making
him think that I'm interested in him like that. You know, Dave,"
I mock, "those pesky boundaries you harass me about all the time.
I would think you'd be proud of me." I fold my arms and wait for
his psychoanalysis.

"Beth, I know that Charlie is your friend and I know how
important that is to you. I'm not asking you to jeopardize that. I'm
only asking that you evaluate your motives. You care about him
more than you let on and I don't want you to ignore that because of
Ryan." Dave's statement feels like a sucker punch to the gut. It's so
insulting; I'm fighting back the urge to kick him in the shin.

"Who the hell do you think I am, Dave?" my anger punctuates
my question. "Ryan is not the reason I'm not dating Charlie. That
suggests that Charlie means nothing to me and only Ryan means
something to me. Do you really think I'm that shallow? Charlie is
the best friend I've ever had and he deserves someone who truly
cares about him, not someone who would use him for some meaningless date because her therapist is a pushy asshole. Charlie and
Ryan aren't in competition for my affection. They don't exist in
the same space in my heart. Ryan is my first love and no once can
replace him. Nothing will ever compare to him. Charlie is the first
friend I've ever had who knows everything about me and is still my
friend, despite how screwed up I am."

"But he doesn't, Beth. Neither of them does." Dave's voice is
soft compared to my angry shouting.

"What?" I'm so confused.

"Neither Ryan or Charlie really know all of you, do they? You say that no one gets you like Ryan does, but how can he possibly understand you so well when he doesn't know everything? Don't you see, Beth?" Dave circles me like a shark. In my fury, I walked right into his trap and now he's got me right where he wants me. "Until you can share all of the pieces of your past with someone, you can't possibly know what it means to love the way you say you love Ryan."

"Are we done yet?" my voice cracks with pent-up emotion. I'm not giving Dave one more tear today. I'm done. My mind is so clouded and confused right now, I just want to grab the headphones out of my purse and tune Dave out.

"Beth, look at me," Dave urges. I know I'll never be rid of him if I don't, so I look him in the eye. "I'm not trying to hurt you, I'm trying to show you that despite how deep your feelings reach right now, they will only become more powerful as you get older and you open up about everything to someone deserving. I'm not going to tell you that won't be Ryan, and I won't tell you it won't be Charlie, either." I open my mouth to protest, but Dave holds up his finger and continues, "I'm only saying that it would be a shame to force that decision right now. Keep yourself open to possibilities, Beth. Ryan isn't the only boy you'll love, and Charlie isn't the only friend you'll ever have."

Damn Dave, he looks so smug. Sure he makes perfect sense, but my heart isn't listening. It feels what it feels and the harder I push against that, the more miserable I become. Maybe Dave is right, maybe I just need to force myself to move on.

"You want me to let Ryan go, and I don't know if I can do that," I sob.

"Moving on doesn't erase the special place he has in your heart, but do you really think he would want you to hover in limbo on the chance you may or may not cross paths again? From everything you've told me about him, I think he'd agree—it's time to let go." Dave pats my knee and shifts nervously in his seat.

"You know, it could be considered an occupational hazard for you to squirm at tears," I giggle. The session is finally over, so I gather my things and head to the door.

"Just yours, kiddo," he sighs, "your tears break my heart."

Damn Dave, I can't ever stay mad at him. His hand is on the handle and just before he opens the door, I give him a fierce hug.

"I know you're just trying to help. You're still an asshole for that whole Charlie thing, though." I snicker.

"I can live with that," Dave laughs and ruffles my hair.

22
RYAN

The campus is a lot more crowded than I thought it would be during the summer, and for that, I'm grateful. My dorm is one of a few open to students who are spending the summer taking classes, so I'm surrounded by activity 24/7. Bring it on, the more distraction the better, as far as I'm concerned. Between classes, work and life in the coed Quadrangle Hall, you would think I could forget Beth. I thought doing the right thing would make it easier to be here and not at the lake. I thought loving her enough to stay away would grant me some cosmic pass on all this regret. No such luck. I miss her more than I should and it scares the crap out of me.

It's been a year since I saw her last and you'd think it was yesterday, the way she dominates my thoughts. The selfish part of me wants to jump in the car and drive the hour and a half and surprise her at the lake. The nobler part of me knows that she would be better off without my interference. If this year has taught me anything, it's that sometimes things just don't work out. No rhyme or reason, the best plans have a way of falling apart without warning. No matter how much I wish it could be different, the most Beth and I could have would be a few weeks before she'd go back to Miami and I'd go back to Iowa City. That's if she would still have me, for all I know this Charlie guy Tommy keeps mentioning is more than her "good friend." I wish I could say I would happily step aside for her to have a boyfriend who lives in the same city and state, but I'm human, not some freaking martyr. I still want her, I still dream about her and knowing she's so close is eating me alive. The real pisser is there is no one to blame for crappy timing so I just have to deal. It sucks.

"Yo, *Ry*," my roommate Jack hollers. "Disc golf, dude. Saddle up and quit mooning over that chick." I haven't said a word about Beth to Jack, but according to him, my aversion to hot chicks and overall grumpiness can only be the result of a girl. "Come on, you pussy," he scowls at me from the doorway.

"It's tough to be intimidated by a clown in a Dr. Who t-shirt," I snicker. Jack is pretty cool; I could do worse for a roommate.

"Do. Not. Diss. The. Tardis, asshole," Jack threatens. "Let's go, already. There are babes in the quad. Chop-chop, motherfucker."

"All right," I laugh. It actually sounds good to get out of this room for a while.

When we get downstairs, a group from our floor is gathered in the center of the quad and true to Jack's statement, several of them are female.

"Wassup, ladies?" Jack saunters up to the first girl he sets eyes on and drapes his arm across her shoulders, sending her and her friends into fits of giggles. You can say whatever you want about Jack, but the dude's got game. Anyone else would've gotten a punch to the balls for that move, but Jack's new friends lap it up like cream. "Who? That tool?" Jacks points over his shoulder at me and then I see her. Smiling shyly and nodding her head at Jack is a cute brunette with piercing blue eyes. "*Ry*, get your ass over here."

"Hey." That's the best I come up with when I walk up. I really am a tool.

"Ry, Elizabeth. Elizabeth, Ryan." Jack points his fingers back and forth between us.

Are you kidding me? I force a smile and stick out my hand. "Nice to meet you, Elizabeth." I hope I'm pulling off interest— it's not her fault. Her killer eyes take me in warily, I guess I'm not very convincing.

"Call me Liz," she shakes my hand, "nice to meet you too, Ryan." Jack is busy chatting up the remaining girls and I start to wonder if we're still disc golfing or whether we've scrapped our plan for our new friends.

"Jack, we still headed to Sugarbottom or what?" I ask.

Liz crinkles her nose and her friends don't look very enthusiastic either. That answers that question.

"Nah, the scenery is better here." Jacks little harem squeal with delight; I can't believe they fall for that shit. I notice that Liz is regarding them with the same disbelief, making me laugh. She smiles up at me and then squinting one eye she taps her chin.

"Something tells me I'm not the only Elizabeth you know," she smirks.

Crap.

"No, I know another Elizabeth. She goes by Beth, though," I shift back and forth. "What're the odds?"

Liz tips her head toward a bench on the edge of the quad, so we wander over and sit down. My gut is churning with nerves, wondering what she must think of me. Asshole? Wimp? Idiot? All of the above?

"She must be someone special because the look on your face when Jack introduced us was like someone had kicked your puppy." She chuckles at me, but her eyes are sympathetic. Taking a deep breath, I let the whole sordid tale flow.

"Beth and I grew up spending the summers together in Des Moines," I start and before I know it an hour has passed and I have totally chewed this poor girls' ear off. "God, I'm sorry, Liz. I can't believe I just spilled my guts to the first cute girl I met. What a dick move." I shake my head.

"Well, I *am* pretty cute," she laughs, "but don't apologize, that was the most romantic story I've ever heard. You give me hope, Ryan…" she accentuates the "n" and raises her eyebrow in question.

"Cantwell," I fill in.

"You give me hope for an epic romance, Ryan Cantwell," she smiles. The first cute girl also happens to be a super cool girl.

"Hey, thanks for listening. I guess I needed to get that off my chest," I mumble.

"Anytime, my friend. Anytime." She squeezes my shoulders, and I feel a huge weight lift from them. Friends are good. That means that I can keep Liz's company without it leading her on. There's something about her that reminds me a lot of Aunt Melissa and I'm reminded just how close the lake is. "Come on, I'll let you buy me dinner at The Fieldhouse. You need a distraction and I need a burger."

"Liz…" I hang on the "z" and look to her for help.

"Gaston," she fills in with a smirk on her face.

"Liz Gaston, you speak my language. Happy to buy you a burger so long as you let me kick your ass in pool." I laugh, and for the first time since I arrived in Iowa City, Beth is in the back of my mind instead of front and center.

23
BETH

Charlie turns in his seat a few rows back and smiles at me. His curly brown hair is smooshed underneath his cap, but he still looks great. The pale blue caps and gowns we're donning match his eyes. Go figure, the rest of us look frumpy and awkward in a sea of baby blue satin and Charlie looks like he belongs in a magazine spread. I blow the rogue piece of hair from my eyes for the millionth time and give him a quick wave.

When the principal announces the end of the ceremony, we all stand and throw our caps into the air. I close my eyes and fill my lungs with the hot, humid Miami air. It makes me smile knowing this is one of the last times I'll ever have to breathe the swampy nastiness that passes for oxygen in South Florida. When I make my way to the aisle, Charlie picks me up and swings me around, I laugh when the girls around me sigh audibly.

"We did it, Beth!" he yells. "We're finally out of here."

Charlie understands how badly I want out of Miami because he does, too. Charlie's mom is an alcoholic and he doesn't know his dad. While his mom is sober now for four years, he still wants a chance to leave all the bad memories behind. I get that, my parents have been sober for three years and we have come a long way with mending our relationship but I still don't want to see Miami again unless it's in my rearview mirror.

Charlie places me back on my feet and we make our way through the crowd to find our families. When we spot them, our moms are huddled in an embrace, sniffling and blotting their eyes with Kleenex. It makes me smile to see my mom wrapped up in a sentimental moment with Sarah. They're good for each other. When Charlie and I became friends at Al-Anon, our moms started hanging out and before long they were inseparable. Deep down, I know they wish Charlie and I would've dated but neither of us sees the other in that way. I would no sooner go out with Charlie than I would my own brother, if I had one.

"*Baby girl!*" I hear Tommy's voice, but I don't see him. Reaching up on my tiptoes, I scan the area around our parents and find him flagging us down.

"*Tommy,*" I squeal and take off running. When I reach him, he hugs me tight as he lifts my feet off the floor. Giggling, I plant a loud kiss on his cheek, "I did it, T!"

"I'm so proud of you." He sets me down and steps back to assess me, "Look at you, Ms. UNC Scholarship." His eyes crinkle at the corners and his mustache curls up on the ends with his smile. "My baby girl is all grown up." The pride in his voice takes root in my heart, filling it with love and gratitude.

"Tommy, I want you to meet my friend, Charlie." I reach behind me and haul Charlie forward by his sleeve. His face flushes as he wrings his hands. I grab onto one of them and give it a reassuring squeeze. He's been nervous about meeting Tommy ever since I told him about the night Tommy whupped Drew's ass. I didn't get into specifics, only that the fight was related to my parents' drug use. Tommy has been an enigma of sorts, ever since.

"Mr. Cantwell," Charlie reaches his hand out cautiously. Tommy takes his hand and pulls him into a "man hug." Part handshake, part chest bump with a slap on the back.

"Call me, Tommy, please, " he insists, "Beth has told me so much about you, it's good to finally meet you, son."

Charlie beams at Tommy's endearment and my heart melts. That's just Tommy's way—he wants everyone to feel comfortable and accepted. From our weekly conversations, he knows that Charlie doesn't have a very strong male role model in his life. I love Tommy for wanting to put him at ease so quickly.

"Good to finally meet you, too, Tommy," Charlie returns.

"So Beth tells me that you got yourself a full ride to the University of Georgia for swimming." Tommy puts his arm around Charlie as we walk out to the parking lot. "*Go Bulldogs.*"

"Well, I guess those two hit off." My mom comes up next to me and hugs me to her side.

"They sure did, one mention of college football and they were golden. I told Charlie he had nothing to worry about," I giggle, squeezing my mom back.

"Charlie knows how important Tommy is to you," she kisses my temple, "he's a good boy for wanting to make a good impression."

I smirk at her subtle nudge toward Charlie. I know she means well and if I thought there could be something between us, I would be the first to take that step. Charlie is a catch. He's tall and has the strong, lean definition of a swimmer's body. His eyes are the palest blue I've ever seen and when you combine them with his tan skin and shaggy brown curls, girls don't stand a chance. Charlie is all too happy to oblige them. He spent all of high school sampling girls from every clique except swim team. That was drama that he didn't want to invite. He flitted all the way through the cheerleaders, and even the mathletes, spreading his sunshine wherever he went.

Charlie has a gift for leaving things better off than when he found them and that goes for his girlfriends, too. He's totally a player, but he's a gentleman about it. He never kisses and tells; he's loyal, funny, charming. He's the total package. There just isn't that spark between us, not like what I felt with Ryan. For me, it always comes back to Ryan.

"Let's go eat," I sigh, "I'm starving." Tommy still has an arm draped across Charlie's back and they're laughing like old friends. Part of me wishes that Charlie and I had clicked as a couple because he fits in so well with my family. Selfishly, I want him to fit into my family just like Ryan does, but I can't replace Ryan with Charlie and I would be a selfish cow to try.

We pile into our cars and head to Christy's, my favorite "special occasion" restaurant in Coral Gables. Driving up Coral Way, I stare out the window and daydream, soaking in the one thing I'll miss from Miami—the historical architecture. There's a tangible history along these streets of Coral Gables; a story in every pane of glass and arched doorway, all of it preserved inside the city limits like a time capsule. It's a completely different world in here, insulated and untouched by the chaos of the city. It would be so nice if life worked like that and we could all have a beautiful place to go be buffered from the frantic pace of outside life, but life is messy and there's nowhere to hide from it for very long. Better to just roll with the punches and try not to get knocked out.

During dinner, Charlie is seated to my left, and Tommy is to my right. I'm sandwiched between my two favorite guys. Life is good. Charlie and I field questions about college and what we think we may want to study. All the talk is making me anxious to pack up and go right now. I eye Tommy and fuss with the linen napkin in my lap, I haven't told him or anyone else back home that I won't be going home to Iowa this summer. I wasn't sure if my scholarship conditions would allow for me to start this summer and once I found out that I could, it got harder and harder to tell them I wasn't coming home.

"That's an awfully long face for such a happy day, baby girl," Tommy interrupts my thoughts.

"Just a lot on my mind, I guess," I speak truthfully, "I'm anxious to start my new life." I sigh and lean my head on Tommy's shoulder. He kisses my forehead and puts his arm around the back of my chair.

"You want to tell me about it?" He cocks his head and smiles.

"I found out that my scholarship will allow me to start classes this summer," I start.

"So you aren't going to come home, are you?" Tommy asks.

I nod my head and pinch my eyes shut to stave off the flood of tears threatening to spill. I didn't have to say a word, Tommy just knows me that well. Guilt rips through my chest when Tommy pulls me into his side and kisses the top of my head. "Beth, I understand wanting to get out there and start living life. Honey, no one back home would ever begrudge you that. We'll miss you like crazy, but we'd never be mad at you for that."

"I feel like I'm letting everyone down," I whimper.

"Stop that, you're not letting anyone down. It's high time that you put yourself as priority number one. Gran, Pops, Uncle Rob and Aunt Melissa *would* be mad at you if you went home just because you thought they wanted you to. They are just as excited for you as I am. In fact, they're pretty damn jealous that I could get off of work to be here and they couldn't." Tommy chuckles, "It pays to be the boss."

I know that Tommy left a bunch of projects in the hands of his foreman to be here for my graduation. He makes it seem easy, but his construction business is booming and with it, his responsibilities have multiplied. Knowing how much he juggled to be here only makes me feel like more selfish.

"Thanks, T," I whisper.

He's just given me the reassurance to feel good about moving to Chapel Hill early, but I still want crawl under the table and curl into the fetal position. I remind myself that this is what I wanted. It is what I want. I excuse myself for the ladies room, thinking some cold water on my face will knock some spine back into me.

When the door closes behind me, I lean against it and try to breathe deep. The rich red hue of the walls and soft lighting cast the illusion of a dark corner to hide in. Sinking to the floor, I weep for Ryan. Bypassing my trip to Iowa this summer means more than just missing my family, it signifies the finality of letting go. For the last three years I have held out hope, even if only a tiny thread, that I would see him again. By skipping my annual trip to Iowa, I'm resigning myself to moving on completely. No more wishful thinking, no more holding out hope for something that just wasn't meant to be. There's a burning in my chest that threatens to engulf me and even though the odds are stacked against me, my heart still pleads for me to hang on.

"Beth?" My head snaps up when Charlie's voice comes through the door. I scoot away from the door, and Charlie's head peeks inside. When his eyes settle on me, he pushes all the way in and joins me on the floor. "Beth, what is it? What happened?" The tenderness of his concern only makes me cry harder. Charlie scoops me into his lap and rocks me gently while he shushes me. He runs his fingers through my hair and kisses my temple, waiting patiently until I'm calm enough to speak.

"It feels so final, Char. I didn't think it would be this hard," I whisper against his chest. "I mean, so much time has passed, why does it still hurt so much?"

Charlie's chest rises and falls with a heavy sigh. He has heard everything about Ryan. He's the only person who seems to care about what I'm feeling instead of trying to talk me out of it.

"Sometimes the right decision is the hardest one to make," Charlie murmurs into my hair. "It's not easy but it's time, Beth. You know it's time or you wouldn't have made the choice to start school early."

"I know," I sniffle into my Kleenex, "it just sucks. It really, really sucks." Charlie tips my chin up until our eyes meet. "You're going to make some UNC guy the luckiest bastard on the planet," he smiles sincerely, but it hints of a lingering sadness. My brows pinch together as Charlie looks away. "I'm so glad that you had a 'Ryan' in your life, Beth. I'm so sorry that you're hurting, but I'm glad that you got the chance to feel something big and wonderful with someone who felt the same way." I tilt my head and try to get him to look at me. Instead, he grabs my hand and focuses on our fingers as they lock together. "You're my best friend and I wouldn't trade that for anything, but I would be lying if I said I didn't have moments I wished it were me."

I force air in and out of my lungs as I stare at Charlie in shock. I never knew. I never ever knew. The closeness of our bodies and Charlie's candid confession makes for a long awkward silence. When he finally looks at me, the sheepish smile that crosses his face steals what's left of my breath. Charlie's been my lifeline for the last three years, my rock. His blue eyes confess a need that I can never give him. God, I wish I could. I cup his face in my hand, rubbing circles with the pad of my thumb. Charlie leans into my touch and closes his eyes.

My throat tightens when I think of all the times Charlie let me cry on his shoulder over Ryan. How could I have been so self important that I could miss this? The thought of him hurting from something I'd done, willingly or not, punches a hole in my gut. He's always been there to comfort me but I can't remember the last time I offered him any. Before I can think better of it, I wrap my arms around Charlie's neck, pulling him just close enough to brush my lips against his with as much tenderness as he's always shown me. The flutter of my heart doesn't feel anything like the erratic spasms I felt when I kissed Ryan. It feels strong and steady, just like Charlie. The urge to kiss him again surprises me almost as much as how good it felt. I start to breathe a little harder when an image of Charlie returning my kiss pops into my head. I can feel the blush creeping up my neck and the telltale heat burning my cheeks. He's my best friend. Rewind. Play. Repeat.

"Some Georgia peach is going to win the lottery with you, Charlie. You're going to fall in love and have it all with someone who feels the same way." I muster a big smile but am scared to death that I've just screwed up royally.

"Don't do that, Beth." Charlie's grip on my waist tightens, reminding me that I'm still sitting in his lap with my arms wrapped around his neck. A chocolate curl wraps around my index finger at the base of his neck as my mind and heart war over where my loyalties lie. Letting go of Ryan is the right decision, but whatever this is I'm feeling with Charlie, I won't use him to do it. My heart is stubborn in its yearning for Ryan, but it won't deny Charlie, either. Ever since my summer with Ryan, Charlie is the one who's been there for me. He's the one I turned to when I needed to vent about my parents, the one I leaned on when life was unbearable. He's always been there for me and I love him for it. I gasp as the thought ricochets between my head and heart. I need space. Now. I shift to move off of Charlie's lap, but sensing my retreat, he tightens his hold on me.

"Please, Beth. Don't," he pleads.

"Don't what, Char? I don't know what you want me to say," my voice shakes, betraying my feelings.

"Don't *run*." Those piercing blue eyes trap mine with their intensity. "Don't pretend like you didn't just kiss me, and don't you dare act like it didn't mean anything."

I'm pinned by his stare; I can't breathe when he brushes his fingers across my bottom lip. I close my eyes, trying to generate space any way I can, when I feel Charlie's lips brush my cheek. My eyelids flutter open in time to watch him lean in and kiss my other cheek. The gesture is so sweet, it takes the edge off my frayed nerves; I can breathe again. He knows me so well. It would be so easy. His mouth hovers in front of mine, so close, our noses touch.

"You're my best friend," I whisper.

Charlie silences me with a kiss filled with so much unspoken emotion it tears my heart in two pieces.

"Still am." His answer makes me smile, despite myself. "And I'm still the same guy who's been dreaming of kissing you since tenth grade. My feelings have always been there, Beth. I've just been waiting for you to realize that you're madly in love with me."

"Smartass," I laugh, poking him in the ribs. It feels good knowing that our playful banter is still alive and well. "We should probably get off the floor of the women's room," I suggest.

"Yeah, we should before they send out search and rescue," he laughs as we stand. I stop short when Charlie hesitates at the door. His tone turns serious, "Walking out this door doesn't erase what happened in here." He tips my chin up when my eyes drop to the floor. "We're talking about it and no matter what, no hiding. Okay?"

If I wasn't already freaking out about the shift in our relationship, now I have to deal with being in one with someone who already knows all my bad habits.

"Fine," I sigh, resigned, "but you've got to be patient with me, Charlie. I'm scared." Scared shitless is an understatement. I just made out with my best friend in the ladies room. Worse, I liked it. A lot. Then there's the small issue of moving to different states in a few weeks. What have I done?

He cups my face in his hand. "You don't ever have to be scared of me, Beth. Ever." I know Charlie would never hurt me. He doesn't have it in him.

"I'm not scared of *you*, I'm scared of *losing* you," I confess.

He pulls me against his chest and I let his warmth comfort me. Every time Charlie touches me, it becomes a little easier to let go of Ryan and let Charlie in.

"Not gonna happen," his voice reverberates against my cheek where I'm pressed against his chest, "you're stuck with me." With a quick peck to the top of my head, he lets me go and we walk out of the bathroom, into the real world.

24
RYAN

I step out onto the deck and check to make sure that no one can see me slinking outside by myself. Immediately, I am attacked by the stench of old beer and feet. Damn, these guys are high if they think I should give up my gig as a resident assistant and move into this animal house. Nasty.

The noise from the party is finally muffled with the click of a sliding glass door. The cordless phone from the kitchen feels like a boulder in my hand.

It's a phone call. Just a phone call, man.

The bones in my neck crack as I roll my head on my shoulders and blow out an anxious breath. I punch the numbers on the keypad and listen as the other line rings.

I can always ask for Tommy.

"You've reached the Bradshaw residence," Beth's voice fills my ear for the first time in three years, "we're sorry we missed you. . . ." The rest of her words trail off as I drink her in like some thirst-starved lunatic. I sigh, defeated as I hang up the phone and lean against the railing. What am I doing? I hang my head and kick the rail with the tip of my boot. What the hell am I doing? Alone in the dark, I let the frustration have control and launch the phone into the yard, cussing like Jack until I hear it crack against the patio stones.

"Feel better?" I jump at the sound of Liz's voice. She walks up the steps onto the deck. The sight of her eases some my anger. I give her a tight smile.

"Oh, hey." Crap. She just witnessed me murder the cordless over a botched call. "Sorry, I didn't you know you were out here."

I can only guess what she must be thinking. She hasn't said anything but I know she's aware Beth graduated from high school today. There are pros and cons to having a chick as a best friend. Pros: I can talk to her about anything. She's funny. She likes to watch football and play disc golf. She's hot. Cons: There's just one, there's no insight into what the hell girls are thinking. They are still every bit as confusing as they were before Liz and I became friends.

"Clearly," she chuckles as she saddles up next to me and leans her forearms on the railing. I huff out a breath and try to shake off my embarrassment.

"What are you doing out here?" I ask, when it occurs to me that she came from the yard. Apparently I'm not the only one in hiding.

"Grabby Gavin wouldn't keep his hands to himself," Liz mutters.

That fucker, I should kick his ass.

"It was either go for a walk or kick him in the balls the next time he put his hand on my ass."

That's my girl—she doesn't need me to fight for her. I'd pay good money to see her bring Gav to his knees. The thought makes me chuckle and from my peripheral I can see her turn her head toward me. Her eyes feel like a spotlight.

"Wanna talk about it?" She bumps her hip against mine.

The frustration from the phone call takes a back seat to the curvy hip brushed up against mine. I scoot down the railing a little, but not before I notice the way her hip curves around to her very nice ass.

Down, boy. Can't say I blame Gavin.

"Nah," I blow it off, "I'm good." Yeah, right. I'm an asshole who's spent three years tied up in knots over one girl and lusting after another who also happens to be my best friend.

Dick move, Ryan. Dick. Move.

"You need to get laid, my friend," Liz laughs. I choke on her words; coughing and sputtering like an idiot. "The frustration is rolling off of you, Ry. There's a long line of freshman eager to get their Felicity on and bone their R.A., it's just the truth."

"For chrissakes, Liz," I huff, "you know I'm not like that. Besides, I would feel like I was robbing the cradle or something." As soon as the words are spoken, I want to take them back. Beth will be a freshman this fall. Liz arches her eyebrow and I know she's thinking the same thing.

"Where did you say Beth got accepted?" She cocks her head to the side, challenging me.

Here we go.

"I didn't." I shift my weight to one elbow so I can face Liz. "Why are we going there, Liz?" I hate it when she talks about Beth. It always feels like she is baiting me, daring me to go toe to toe with her over a girl she'll never measure up to.

"It's pretty easy to figure out who you were calling, you've had her graduation marked on the calendar for months." Her eyes are slits as she scrutinizes me, "What exactly were you expecting to gain? Unless she's headed to Hawkeye country, what's the point?"

"I don't know," I snap at her, "she's not headed here, she's going to UNC–Chapel Hill."

I want to kick myself for letting Liz reel me into this conversation but I can't stand it when she uses that tone, the one that makes it sound like Beth's a disease she needs to rid me of. The protective streak in me draws up for a battle.

"Then what are you doing, Ryan? Is that why you broke up with Jordyn? So you could fantasize about hooking up with a girl you haven't seen or spoken to since you were seventeen? Or were you going to fly across the country to spend a few days with her and then come back here and pine for another three years?" Liz's voice gets louder as she finds her rhythm and goes in for the kill, "Grow up, Ryan. Who do you think you're kidding? Do you think no one notices how you'll date someone for a couple of months and move on but never stick around long enough to really get to know anyone? Do you think Jordyn didn't know she was just a fucking place holder until Beth magically reappeared in your life?"

"What the fuck, Liz?" I shout as my anger pulses through me, "If I'm such an asshole, then why are you here? Where I'm standing, you sound more like a jealous brat than my best friend." Liz purses her lips together and blinks rapidly.

Fuck me, I made her cry.

"Aw, Liz, I'm sorry...." I step toward her.

"No," she jerks away from me," I don't give a shit if you think I'm a brat. What's going to happen in ten years when you wake up and realize that you've wasted your whole life on the idea of a girl instead of a real one?"

"Liz," I warn. I won't go another round with her, but I'm not going to let her make me feel stupid, either. "I'll always love Beth, I'll always want her. I can't help how I feel. Maybe someday I'll meet someone who makes me feel more than she does, but right now, this is how it is."

She scoffs at me, "So let me get this straight, it's perfectly okay to date girls that you don't have an emotional attachment to, but it's not okay to date a girl you *are* emotionally attached to?"

I take a deep breath before I continue. "What kind of a dick would I be to stay in a relationship with someone when I can't stop thinking of someone else? There isn't a single thing wrong with Jordyn. She's beautiful, smart, and funny, but I don't feel it with her, Liz," I pound the center of my chest with my fist. "Do you know what I mean?" Liz's chin trembles as she holds back her tears. "Wait, what the hell are you talking about 'a girl I *am* emotionally attached to'?" The look she gives me says it all: I. Am. Such. A. Dick.

"Yeah, Ryan, I know," her voice shakes with her emotion. This time when I step toward her, she meets me in the middle, allowing me to hug her against my chest. I know she cares about me, just like she knows I care about her. We toyed with the idea of dating back in our freshman year but never went there. Not because I didn't care about her and definitely not because I'm not attracted to her. She knows enough about Beth to know that she could never have all of me, and she means too much to me to have the short and sweet relationships I'm used to.

"I'm sorry," I whisper, "I didn't mean to make you cry." The last thing I ever meant to do was hurt Liz with my anger or anything else. These are the moments when I wish things could be different between us.

"I'm sorry I was a brat," she laughs softly and looks up at me, "I just want you to be happy. It makes me sad to see you this way." She reaches up and plays with the hair that's fallen against my collar.

The heat that is buzzing between us feels way bigger than the phone carcass out in the yard. I swallow hard and try to back away from the ledge before I fully fall off.

Liz looks at me with her piercing blue eyes, pleading. She's my best friend, but she's also hot, and I'm a guy, not a saint. Like a freaking witch, she puts me under her spell, urging me to touch her. One of my hands hovers on the small of her back, while the other grips her tiny waist; she feels incredible. I shift from right to left, trying to adjust my shorts. My brain is screaming at me to walk away from my friend, but other key parts are reminding me that she's always been a little more than just a friend. When Liz presses her body against mine and wraps her arms around my neck, it feels natural; it feels good. When her boobs rub against my chest; I almost lose my shit. She weaves her hands into my hair and pulls me toward her.

"Kiss me, Ry," she whispers.

All logic flies out the window at her gentle pleading. I dive into the kiss, nipping and sucking at her soft lips. There is nothing gentlemanly about it when I grab her ass and press her against my raging hard-on. I groan into her mouth, when she grinds her hips against me. She matches my enthusiasm, kissing me like her life depends on it, and when she moans against my ear as she rakes her nails down my back, I come unglued. Grabbing her by the waist I hoist her up on the railing and suck in a breath when her long legs wrap around my waist.

Holy shit.

All of the moments I've been this close to Liz beat at my brain, making me crazy. I tug the hem of her tank top out of her shorts and run my hands along the warm smooth skin beneath. Everything about her feels amazing.

"Fuck, Liz." I pant against her mouth when my thumbs brush the undersides of her breasts, and she arches her back. Somewhere in my haze of lust, it registers when I kiss her jaw and it's wet. I pull back and force my eyes to focus on Liz's face. Her eyes are glassy with tears that haven't already spilled. It sobers me up instantly. She tries to lean into another kiss, but I pull away.

"Why don't you want to be with *me*, Ryan?" she whimpers.

Fuck.

"Liz," I help her down off the railing, feeling like a total ass. "I care about you so much. Don't ever think I don't want you, that's not it at all."

She tries to retreat but I hold her against me. She settles against my chest while I run my fingers through her hair. This is no time to dick around, I need to shit or get off the pot. It's not fair to her.

"Why not, Ry?" she whispers. "We're great together. We care about each other. Why not me?"

"I don't want to hurt you, Liz," I sigh. "You know better than anyone how bad I am at relationships."

"You're only bad at them because they're supposed to be between two people, not three." She lifts her head and cocks her eyebrow at me.

"I deserve that," I smirk.

"What do you want Ryan? I mean really, don't just say 'Beth' because it feels familiar. Really think about what you want." The absence of Liz's sarcasm where Beth is concerned hits me hard. This girl is amazing, smart, funny, and beautiful—and she wants me.

I will always want Beth.

Always.

But no matter how much I want Beth, life never brought us to the same place at the same time again. Liz searches my face, waiting for me to say something. What do I say?

I want you, just not as much as I want Beth.

I think you're great, but you'll never come first.

You deserve to be with someone who loves you, too. The words form a lump in my throat, but I can't say them, because I'm so damned lonely, it hurts. I already care about Liz. I can grow to love her. This is what I tell myself when I take her face in my hands, close my eyes and picture Beth as I kiss her.

25
BETH

There are certain rules, a code of conduct that my friends and I follow. The most important rule of them all is: Do one of us wrong; bear the wrath of all of us. Trent the Tool from down the hall is about to learn that lesson firsthand. I don't know how he thought he'd get away with it, because it took less than fifteen minutes for the news to filter down the hall that Trent was claiming to have "tapped Cyn's ass" over spring break. That creep didn't even go to Myrtle like we did. So we do what we girls do when the situation calls for it—revenge. Cyn, Les and I are well-known for our mischief and pranks, which only lends more credit to Trent's stupidity. Seriously? He had this coming.

I make eye contact with Cyn and Les and give them the signal to proceed. With the Mission Impossible soundtrack running through my mind, I stand lookout as they creep into the laundry room. My heart hammers against my chest as the minutes tick by.

How hard can it be, for chrissakes?

I'm just about to whistle the one-minute warning when they come barreling out of the laundry room holding a dingy pair of tidy whities up in victory. We've got a minute to get our asses back in our room before we're caught out here red handed.

"Save your laughter for the room or we're gonna get busted," I hiss at them. Cyn turns to me and slingshots Trent's underwear into my face. "Gross." I yelp, swatting them toward Les, who is laughing so hard she snorts.

We barely get through our door before we hear Trent's guffaws start to trail down the hall, toward the laundry room. Les and I fall onto the couch, cackling, while Cyn makes a beeline for the closet. She sifts through box after box until she digs out her weapon of choice.

"A-ha," she crows, "behold the almighty BeDazzler! Just four payments of $19.99, plus shipping and handling."

Les launches the underwear at her and she snatches it from the air in triumph.

"Somebody ate their Wheaties this morning," Les snickers as she ties her long blond hair up in a messy bun. I grab Tommy's hankie from my dresser, fold it into a triangle and tie my hair back, too. It's strictly business until our plan is carried out. Any horsing around can lead to campus security, and we haven't had a run-in with them since freshman year.

Cyn goes to work fastening colored jewels to the fabric. It's an improvement to the not-so-tidy-or-whities gray hue. We're carrying on, snickering when my phone buzzes. I know who it is, but I check the screen anyway. Charlie's smiling face comes into view and I press *ignore*.

"You're going to have to talk to him at some point," Cyn looks up at me from her bedazzling. With perfect timing, the room phone rings. "Now's as good a time as any." She gives me a sympathetic smile. I know I've got to talk to him, but we broke up and that ended my promise not to hide with him. Serves him right.

"Hi, Charlie," Les coos into the phone, "yep, she's right here." I shoot her the stink eye.

Traitor.

Charlie and I broke up over spring break a few weeks ago. I wish he would take that for what it is and stop calling. Technically he broke up with me, although it was mutual.

Blah, blah, blech.

Long distance relationships are a recipe for disaster. Starting a relationship a few weeks before you both move to different states was insane. We'd grown apart since Christmas and I was already planning on breaking up with him when he joined me in Myrtle Beach for spring break. What I was not counting on was him beating me to it and then telling me that he was interested in someone else.

Ouch.

Good ol' Charlie, ever the gentleman, waited to break it to me gently before he pursued a relationship with *Tina*. Whatever. I shouldn't feel betrayed because, technically, he didn't do anything wrong. The stinger is that over Christmas break, we had sex. That was supposed to bring us closer, but it only made growing apart that much more painful. I can't help but think that I wasn't good enough or that maybe Charlie could tell I wasn't a "real" virgin. A million insecurities bloomed from a person I'd counted on a lot for a long time. It sent everything spinning off its axis. I just want some space to hide and heal. I don't like showing any weakness and mine just seem to multiply every time we talk.

I grab the receiver from Les and take a deep breath before I put it up to my ear.

"Hello?" my voice is even weak.

"Hey, Beautiful." At the sound of Charlie's voice, my eyes fill with traitorous tears.

"You shouldn't call me that anymore, Charlie," I scold, "it's not appropriate."

He sighs heavily on the other line. I'm not in the mood to make it easy for him. He's the one who wanted to talk.

"Beth, I can't stand the way things are between us," he pleads. "You're my best friend."

I used to be his best friend, now I'm his ex-girlfriend. Les sits down next to me, silently hands me a Kleenex and wraps an arm around me. At least I'm not alone. The vacancy left from Charlie's friendship was already full to brimming with Cyn and Les. They're wonderful friends, and I would be miserable without them here to hold my hand. They get how I feel because they were there for the majority of my relationship with Charlie. They saw it all unfold and then fall apart.

"No, Charlie, I'm not. Things can't go back to how they were in high school. Too much has changed." I try to keep my tone even because if he suspects I'm crying, I'll never be able to get him off the phone.

"But, I miss you," he murmurs.

"I think I recall you telling me once that sometimes the right decisions are the most difficult to make." I know he remembers sitting with me on the floor at Christy's, pressing me to give Ryan up. I don't like throwing Ryan in his face, but I can't back down on this. Too much has transpired between us and I don't see how I can ever go back to confiding in someone who I loved and lost.

I don't want to get back together with Charlie, I don't hate him or wish him any ill will, but I mourn the piece of myself that I gave away and will never get back. I loved Charlie; I still do, but I was never in love with him. I wanted to be, so badly. If fact, I wanted to fall in love with him so badly, I kept giving more of myself away, thinking what I gave could force feelings that were never there.

I thought I could prove to myself how far forward I'd come by sleeping with Charlie. All it did was shine a light on how pathetic I'd become.

I should have never dated him. I should've cared about our friendship more than that, but I was so scared of being alone, I slipped into the most comfortable and safest place I knew—Charlie. I used him and I think he always knew it. I'm a terrible person and I deserve the world of hurt I've brought down on myself. For now, I need space to lick my wounds. Charlie would never let me be alone in any kind of grief, and he deserves to move on with his life without the weight of my crap holding him down.

"I need you to let me go, Charlie," my voice cracks, betraying my hurt.

"Beth," he breathes, "please."

"I'm not mad at you, Charlie," I hiccup. Cyn settles at my other side and joins Les in embracing me. "I'll always love you, but I'm not one of those people who can be friends with my exes. I can't do it." I probably sound like a total bitch but I *need* this and the truth would only hurt Charlie. "Please, Charlie," I beg. "Go be with Tina. Have some fun. You need to stop worrying over me and go live your life. It's not with me, it never has been. You were always going to the University of Georgia and I was always going to UNC–Chapel Hill, we were never supposed to end up together. It still hurts, though. The only thing that will help with that is time and space. Please try and understand. If you love me at all, please try."

There is deafening silence on the line while Charlie considers his answer, and I use it to pray that he won't press me any further.

"Please promise me one thing," his voice is thick with pain and it breaks my heart all over again. "If you ever need anything. Ever. Call me."

It takes me a minute before I can breathe again, let alone speak. "Okay, Char. I will," I whimper.

"Goodbye, Beth." The finality of his words slice through what is left of my wretched heart. I can't help but think I deserve every bit of the pain.

"Goodbye, Charlie," I whisper and hand the phone to Les before I can change my mind. When I look at her my own sadness reflects in her eyes. It's all the encouragement I need to give myself over to the sobs I've been choking back. Cyn and Les hover around me until my tears have run dry, cheering me on the whole time.

"Of course you're sad," Les says, "He was your first. It's a big deal."

"You going to really worry me if you say that you wish you'd waited for Ryan, because it's been almost five years, honey." I laugh at Cyn's bluntness. She's right, but that's not exactly how I feel.

"No, I made the decision to let him go so I'm not holding out hope," I sigh, "but with all of this heartache, I can't help but get nostalgic for what could've been. It doesn't mean I'm closing up shop and waiting for someone who's not coming."

"Thank God for that," Les hoots. "Hey, I hear there's this great guy who lives down the hall, maybe I can set you up. Let's just give Trent a call."

I howl with laughter. I would be an absolute mess without them.

"All right, ladies," I bounce off the couch and clap my hands together, "where are we at here?" I grab the BeDazzler and the underpants for inspection.

For the next few hours, Cyn finishes up her handiwork; while Les makes sure we have plenty of frozen Reese's mini cups and bottomless Frodkas. Whenever one of us is having a bad day, it's our ritual to break out the peanut butter cups, Fresca and vodka. Cures whatever ails you. Under the cloak of midnight, we steal across the quad and swap out the UNC–Chapel Hill flag for Cyn's colorful masterpiece.

You Wish. Love, Cyn.

We were too busy getting pictures and giving each other high fives to notice campus security pulling up on their golf cart.

Crap.

26
RYAN

The setting sun is shining through the windshield at that perfect angle that no sun visor can touch, adding to my already foul mood. At least the traffic on I-80 is bearable. It's a little relief for the nagging anxiety pounding in my skull. What do they say about the road to hell? Good intentions and all that crap? Shaking my head at my own stupidity, I take the exit off Eighth Street and cross Grand Avenue into Gran and Pops' neighborhood.

Tommy's Explorer is parked in their gravel driveway, no surprise there. Grabbing my backpack from the passenger seat, I head into the familiar comfort of home. Adopted home. Whatever, this place has always felt like home to me.

"Knock, knock," I call out as I open the front door.

"Ryan Cantwell? Is that you?" I hear Gran's voice just before she turns the corner. "I thought that was your voice! What a wonderful surprise," she coos as she walks toward me with open arms. The lines on her face deepen with the warm smile that spreads across her face as she hugs me to her. "What are you doing home? You're not on break, are you?"

"No, he's not," Tommy walks through the doorway wiping his hands on a dishtowel. His brows meet in the middle as his expression goes from surprised to concerned. "What's up, Ry? Everything okay?" When Gran steps aside, Tommy grabs me in a fierce hug, "What's going on, son?"

"I just needed to get away for a day or two, so I decided to take a long weekend," I try to brush it off.

"Hmmpph." Tommy grunts. His mustache twitches and I know he's not buying it. "You're just in time for dinner. Melissa and Rob should be here any minute."

"Where's Pops?" I ask.

"Band practice," Gran smiles. Pops has played the drums in a local band for as long as I've known him and probably longer than that. The girlish blush that crosses Gran's cheeks makes the problems I left in Iowa City seem a little further away.

What is it with girls and musicians?

"Is that Ry's car out front?" Melissa's voice carries in from the porch. When they walk through the front door, she lets out a squeal and comes in for a hug, "What are you doing here?"

"Yet to be determined," Tommy cocks a challenging eyebrow my way.

Uncle Rob sniffs the air. "Smells like girl trouble." Melissa swats his arm. "Ow, woman."

"Behave, you two," Melissa points back and forth between Rob and Tommy. "Leave Ry alone. He'll tell us what hussy has his knickers in a twist when he's ready." She gives me a smug wink. I'm thrilled to know that my visit is so transparent. So much for running away for a few days.

Uncle Rob slaps me on the back as we head to the dining room. "Ry, the best advice anyone ever gave me about women was this— smile and nod." He smiles a big cheesy smile and nods his head.

I lucked out on dinner tonight, Gran made pot roast. My favorite, and highly preferred over the cafeteria food at school. Everyone chats casually about their day and what's going on around town. Tommy gives me the look from the corner of his eye for the third time tonight. I squint my eyes at him. I only ever get that look when he's chewing on something really good to tell. He's been building up the suspense with these sideways glances all through dinner.

"Spill it, T," Gran chimes in.

I laugh out loud at her spot on observation.

"I got a call from the dean's office at UNC today," Tommy's starts. My chest tightens in anticipation of what he'll say next. "They called me because Casey and John are out of the country, and I'm Beth's next emergency contact. Apparently, our baby girl got caught red handed, hoisting a pair of jeweled skivvies up the flagpole in the quad, early this morning."

We sit in stunned silence as we all soak in Tommy's words. I blink once, twice, and then start laughing so hard, I can't breathe. Tommy and Rob lose it, too. Aunt Melissa and Gran try hard to keep serious faces, but even they're sucked in by the hoots and howls that fill the tiny dining room.

"She did what?" I laugh.

Tommy holds an index finger up until he can contain his laughter. "Apparently, some dumb ass kid on her floor started a rumor about her roommate, Cyn. So she, Cyn and their other roommate, Les, stole his drawers from the laundry room and gem-wazzled a message on them," he howls with another fit of laughter.

"Bedazzled you fool. It's bedazzle not gem-wazzle," Melissa giggles,

"Whatever," Tommy waves her off. "Anyway, they snuck across campus and took down the state flag and raised that boy's underwear up the flagpole."

Any hope for controlling my laughter is gone. I use my napkin to dab at the tears in my eyes as I try to picture Beth dressed up like a cat burglar, slinking across campus with bedazzled Fruit of the Looms waving around in her hand.

Damn, I miss that girl.

"The campus security caught them taking pictures of their handiwork. I don't think they would've bothered with calling if Beth hadn't been holding the state flag. According to the police report, it's state property, and that's where it could've gotten prickly."

My eyes nearly roll out of my head. "There's a police report?" I gasp. Aunt Melissa and Gran lean in for the details on this question, no doubt already planning a Free Elizabeth Bradshaw Defense Fund.

"Yep, but no charges were pressed, so everything is fine." Tommy is still chuckling and shaking his head.

"Did you talk to Beth?" I don't know why all eyes are on me all of a sudden. I would think that would be the natural progression of the conversation. Aunt Melissa smiles a Cheshire grin that's got me shifting in my seat.

"Yes, I did. She is fine, just disappointed that she got caught," Tommy huffs. "She's pissed that she put her scholarship in jeopardy, but she's fine and so is her scholarship, thank God. I think her days of mischief are over, though." He looks up at me and gives me a tight smile.

All of a sudden I feel like I'm under the microscope.

"Well, now that we are all caught up on Beth's latest hijinks, why don't you tell us what's brought you home, Ry." Gran gives him a warm smile and I know she means it. These other hanyaks are nothing but a bunch of gossip mongers.

"I broke up with my girlfriend," I mumble. A chorus of "what?" erupts around the table. "She wanted more than I did and it got ugly at the end, so I wanted to get away for couple a of days."

"Liz?" Tommy asks, his face pinched with worry.

"Yeah," I sigh.

"What a minute," Uncle Rob waves his hands in the air, "you had a girlfriend named 'Elizabeth'? Christ on a crutch what'd you do? Call her Beth by accident?" He chuckles until he sees the look on my face, "Shit, son. I'm sorry."

"Nah, it was dumb. We were in the cafeteria, and I was asking her to hand me a tray. I said 'Can you hand me a tray, Beth?' and all hell broke loose." I shake my head at the memory of Liz's face registering the horror of my mistake. I've never felt like a bigger asshole, ever.

"Aw, baby, I'm so sorry," Melissa pulls her chair up next to mine and rubs my back. "Were you together for a long time?"

"No, just a couple of months, but she was one of my closest friends for three years before that. Now she can't even look at me without screaming at me. We have the same friends and hang with the same group of people, so it's not like I can avoid her. The thought of dealing with that this weekend was too much," I grumble.

"Of course it is, that's just awful, Ry," Gran brushes my hair away from my forehead and kisses it. "I suppose the silver lining is that graduation is only a month away," she encourages.

She's right, thank God for that. I can't wait to get my degree and find a job here in Des Moines. If anything, this mess with Liz has taught me that friends are fleeting, family is forever.

27
BETH

5 Years Later…

We all have our own way of preserving memories. Whether it's journaling the details or recording them on film, everyone possesses a drive to capture certain moments and freeze them in sacred reverence. My own life is cataloged by a series of photographs and journals that are all pinpoints on a timeline spanning my twenty-five years. The memories dearest to me, I pontificate through music and lyrics bound in a series of music composition books in my hope chest. With them are the artifacts of my childhood—old vinyl records, mix tapes, and sheet music—my most prized possessions. Then again, my passion for music is why I work in the industry. I'm living the dream as the event coordinator at a music venue called The Edge in Charlotte. We cater to everyone from B.B. King to Jason Mraz, and they all get booked through me.

Tonight's show is bittersweet. We are hosting Brutal Strength who are filming an acoustic set for the TV show, *Stripped*. It's been ten years since Ryan gave me Brutal Strength tickets for my birthday, and today's concert makes me think of those tickets and whether he ever found someone else to take. No matter how much time passes, I still get sentimental when I think of that summer and wish I could've included those tickets with my other music treasures. Nothing I have experienced since can hold a candle to my fifteenth birthday and no boy has ever filled the vacancy left by Ryan.

In the last ten years, I have found that some plans are nothing more than an invitation to disaster. While Ryan and I were planning our day at the Iowa State Fair, my parents were on a plane to come take me home. The rest is history, as they say. I clung to the idea of Ryan, and the feelings he awakened in me for a long time, but as life went on without him, I resigned myself to the fact that he wasn't meant to be more than the precious memory of first love.

Aunt Melissa still offers updates when I ask for them, but it's too tempting to fall back into that fantasy. Funny, for all the lamenting I used to do about my parents' addictive behavior, it never occurred to me that I would have an addictive personality. It got easier to understand their struggle when I was faced with kicking my own addiction—Ryan. In fact, it still amazes me that they never relapsed and forged ahead without looking back at all. They say they did it for me and I believe them. We've come a long way and I'm grateful every day for our relationship. Nothing is perfect, though; too much time in their proximity peaks my bitterness. It's hard to be parented by people who opted out during your formative years. Nothing is ever going to erase the mistakes they made, but forgiveness has gone a long way toward learning to love them, warts and all.

Les, Cyn, and I moved into a renovated bungalow in Charlotte after graduation. While our focus is now on building our careers and not pranking Trent the Tool, we are still the same girls. After a crappy day, you'll still find us commiserating over frozen Reese's and Frodkas.

I have the world at my feet—my dream job, great friends and even a hot date for the show. Then why am I daydreaming about a boy I haven't seen since I was fifteen? I blow out a long breath and grab the Brutal Strength playlist out of the printer. I need to focus on getting this set list to our sound engineer, maybe a walk back-stage will help clear my head.

"Elizabeth," my boss interrupts. "There's an agent on line two looking to book an unknown." Gesturing towards my office, she tosses her long black hair over her shoulder. She is the embodiment of indie style; her crimson streaked hair falls to the middle of her vintage Cure t-shirt. When she turns back toward her office, her plaid skirt swishes against her purple tights. Her motorcycle boots eat up the hallway when she saunters away.

"Thanks, Andrea," I holler after her, "I'm on it." She raises her arm, giving me the peace sign and keeps walking. Hopefully, a nice distraction can shake me out of my funk.

28

The opening act is halfway through their set when I finally make my way out front. Between the camera crew and the patrons, we have a full house tonight. Andrea flags me down from the box seat above the main floor; I nod in acknowledgment and head toward the staircase that will lead me there. A brooding giant of a man guards the velvet rope sectioning off the staircase from the concertgoers. Standing at six-foot-four with hulking muscles, he takes up the entire doorway and scans the crowd with menacing eyes. If I didn't already know that he had a cat named Phoenix and a penchant for Gershwin, I'd be scared to death.

"S'up Fred!" I yell over the music.

"Hey! How's my best girl?" Fred's booming voice floats effortlessly over the noise. He pulls the rope back for me and bows in a grand gesture as I pass.

"Such a charmer." I giggle, "Is everyone up there?"

"Yep. Andrea, Cyn, Les, and some dude named Steve." When he mentions my date's name, Fred lifts a cynical eyebrow.

"Calm down, big daddy. I am sufficiently buffered by the rest of our group. No need to bust any balls tonight," I tease.

"That's all you, sister." Fred snickers.

"Hey!" I shove his arm, but the steely rope of muscle beneath my hand doesn't budge an inch. "That was harsh," I complain.

"Just tellin' it like it is. You love 'em and leave 'em broken-hearted," Fred pins me with his eyes, daring me to challenge him.

"Never been a boy around here long enough to stick. How can you play 'em that way, girl?" He shakes his head and holds his hand over his heart. The way he is giving me a hard time reminds me of the way Ryan used to tease me.

There he is again! I blame Brutal Strength.

"Maybe I just haven't found one worth keeping around," I shrug at Fred. He hates my three-date rule. Three dates is enough to have fun but not enough to get attached. By the third date, I give the "we make better friends than lovers" speech and move on. I have a lot of male friends.

"Besides, Fred, who can compare to you?" I blow him a kiss and head up the stairs to meet my friends and my date.

"Whassup, sexy?" Cyn practically tackles me when I come around the corner. She gives me a loud kiss on the cheek and takes a step back to regard my outfit. "That shirt does great things for your rack." She reaches out to cop a feel, but I swat her hand away.

"Have you been in the sauce, already? What's gotten into you?" I laugh. Cyn rolls her eyes at me and sticks out her tongue. We are nothing if not mature young professional women. Her short black curls bounce with the same energy she exudes as she skips over to the railing to watch the band. She is a dynamo, she's got Fred-sized energy packed into her tiny frame. Standing barely over five feet, she reminds me of a pixie.

"She's sober, she's just wound up for Marcus." Les laughs as she gives me a fierce hug. All three of us are fan girls when it comes to Brutal Strength. We know every song from every album and own every gossip mag detailing the relationship between the lead singer, Marcus Anthony, and the lead guitarist, Avery Jones. She nods her head toward Andrea and Steve who are elbow to elbow in deep conversation. "Those two have been arguing about what kind of guitars Avery prefers for the whole set," Les throws her head back, sending her rich velvety laughter into the air. She is the kind of girl that most women love to hate and all men want in their bed. Long-limbed and curvy in all the right places, her blond hair and bright smile convey a sense of innocence, but those of us who know her know better.

I look back and forth between my two friends and wonder what people see when they see the three of us together. There is Cyn with her raven hair, blue eyes, and petite frame and Les with her light hair, hazel eyes, and statuesque frame. I float somewhere in the middle of the two, I am of average height with brown hair and eyes. I have the type of body that went out of style with Rockabilly and Betty Page—all the curves that people say are great but pop out like a sore thumb against the stick thin trendsetters I'm around all day. Voluptuous. Curvaceous. Please, those are just nice ways of saying you've got big boobs and breeding hips. Whatever.

"Who am I to interrupt, then? I wouldn't know a Gibson from a Fender if my life depended on it," I joke.

It figures Andrea would charm the pants off my date before I even had a chance to say *hello*. I am not too bothered by it, he's just another guy. Nobody special. As if he can hear me, Steve looks up and gives me a friendly smile. When he starts to stand, I motion for him to stay put.

Despite Fred's ribbing, I am not the love them and leave them type, I just don't like to waste my time. I can usually tell by the third date whether or not the relationship is going anywhere, and most times it's headed straight to the friend zone. This is date one with Steve, and I already know that it's going nowhere fast. It's not like I've never had a boyfriend before, I've had one or two—just nothing that's lasted longer than six months, except Charlie and that was a disaster. Otherwise, nothing memorable. So I am a serial dater, it works for me. What can I say? When I meet someone who is worth a fourth date, I'll go on one.

"Why are you letting her bogart your date like that?" Cyn whispers.

"Because she clearly likes him more than I do," I laugh, "besides he doesn't seem put out in the least."

"You're never going to meet someone if you don't give anyone a chance. Steve may end up being the love of your life," Leslie lectures. My heart flutters, not because I think Steve is my soulmate, but because I'm painfully aware that I've already met him. I glance at Leslie, and for a moment, I wish I could talk about Ryan. She would think I'm nuts for still being hung up on a relationship that never happened when I was fifteen. Maybe I'm comparing everyone to Ryan because I know that nothing will measure up, self-fulfilling prophecy and all that crap. Someday I'll fall in love and go through the whole sordid tale of my life but not before then.

"I know, Les." I give her a tight smile, hoping we can drop it.

She lets out a heavy sigh and nods. I know she worries about me, and I love her for it, but it's much more complicated than she knows. When I came out here for college with a clean slate, I decided that the past was best left far behind. I don't talk about it with anyone except Tommy, and I only see him once or twice a year. My parents, wisely, avoid the issue. We do better if we focus on the future of our relationship and not dwell on the past. Gran and Pops have always been the strong and silent type. They're my North Star—the ones that remind me that no matter where I am or how much time passes, *they* are home. They've never pressed me about Drew, but I know they watched me diligently for a long time to make sure I was dealing with what happened and to make sure that I saw a therapist twice a week until I left Miami.

Hindsight is a remorseful wench. I wish I'd worked out a way to blend my family into my life here. By the time I got a clue and realized my mistake, I was already so engrossed in who I was without them, it was easier to just continue pretending. My friends know my parents from their visits but they only know them to be the sweet, if not slightly misguided, folks who love their daughter and drive her crazy. They know that I have family in Iowa that I visit a couple times a year, but they don't know who they are individually or how important they were to me when I was growing up. The stage crew is clearing the opener's gear off the stage when I feel my pocket vibrate. I ignore my cell; there is no one I need to talk to that badly in the middle of a concert. I take my seat between Cyn and Les to watch as the stage is transformed to accommodate filming. My pocket starts vibrating again, so I take out my phone to turn it off. I have two missed calls from Uncle Rob. I fidget in my seat, wondering if something has happened with Pops. Making a quick excuse, I dart into the hallway to call him back. Pops has been having some issues with his blood pressure, so I hope that everything is okay. I tap my foot impatiently as the phone rings.

Pick up, pick up, pick up!

"*Beth*!" My name shoots out of Uncle Rob's mouth as a panicked exclamation. His tone sends my stomach plummeting; I sit at the top of the staircase and brace myself for the bad news coming.

"What's wrong?" My voice shakes against my question. I hold my breath waiting for him to tell me that Pops has had a stroke or heart attack.

"Beth, it's Tommy." Uncle Rob's voice breaks on a sob, turning my blood to ice. "He's gone, baby girl, Tommy's gone."

My phone slips out of my hand and starts bouncing down the stairs. There is total silence as I block out everything around me to concentrate on what my uncle just said.

Tommy is dead.

29

"*Why the long face, baby girl?" Tommy asks as he joins me on the dock.*

"I don't want to go back to Miami," I confess, dragging my toes across the surface of the lake. "I wish my mom and dad would move back here. I miss you so much during the year," I sniffle. Tommy wraps a strong arm around me, pulling me into his chest. His mustache tickles my brow as he kisses my forehead.

"Don't waste your time missing me, silly. I am always with you." He smiles down at me when I lift my head. "There is a saying that goes— 'Together forever, never apart. Maybe in distance but never in heart.' You are with me, baby girl and I'm with you. Always."

⤢

I watch Fred glance down at the floor where my phone lands against his foot. He looks over his shoulder and when his eyes meet mine, his face drops. Taking the steps three at a time, I watch his mouth form words I don't hear. His hands grip my shoulders, shaking me gently.

"BETH," Leslie's voice floats over my shoulder, breaking through my fog. "What the fuck is going on, Fred?"

Fred looks past me to answer her, "This landed at my feet." Handing her my cracked phone, he continues, "When I turned around to pick it up, I found her sitting here like this."

Les sits down next to me and puts the cracked phone to her ear, "Hello? Who is this?" her tone is defensive if not rude. "No, this is her friend, Leslie." She is silent while Uncle Rob speaks on the other line. Her tone is notably kinder when she speaks again, "I will have her call you back or I will." Her brow furrowed in confusion, she ends the call.

❧

As I take my diploma from the principal and shake his hand, a shrill whistle overrides the polite golf claps that fill the high school gym. When I turn to face the crowd, I find Tommy waving a UNC pennant enthusiastically. While my parents clap and wave politely on one side of him, the people on the other side cheer him on. I wave my diploma at him and blow him an exaggerated kiss. When I am back in my seat, the girl next to me leans in and whispers, "Is that your Dad?"

"No," I sigh. There have been countless times I have wished he was. "He's just a really good family friend."

"Wow." The girl is surprised by my answer. "He must really love you a lot."

I look over my shoulder toward the area I know he's seated. I don't see him, but I find the pennant still swaying proudly among the rest of the families.

❧

In one swift motion, Fred wraps a beefy arm around me and shuffles me through the crowd, through the backstage door. No one hesitates when they see him coming, they just move out of the way. Once I am back in my office, Leslie and Cyn surround me. They are hovering over me, clucking like nervous hens.

"Where's Steve?" my voice stops their chattering instantly.

"Andrea's still with him," Cyn answers and squeezes my shoulder.

"Beth," Leslie speaks as she and Cyn squat before me. They look at one another and then Leslie addresses me again. "Who is Tommy?"

Hearing his name breaks something open inside me. The cry that pours out of me is feral. Tears burn my eyes as I weep for the man that mattered most. Cyn squeezes my hand and Les rubs my back; they have no idea. At the time, the evolution seemed natural. Once I moved to North Carolina, I stopped spending my summers in Iowa. When I have visited, the trips are short and Tommy never made it out east to see me. I think he understood that I needed the space to make my own life, and not wanting to impose, stayed away. So I used the space and built my life, leaving out the inconvenient parts. Guilt punches a whole in my gut at what I did, erasing my past essentially erased Tommy. I look at my friends and shake my head; I don't know where to start or if I even should.

"I want to go home," I sob.

I grab my wallet out of the top drawer of my desk and sit down at my computer. The longer I sit here under a microscope the worse I feel. My instinct to run has my knee jackhammering the floor.

Cyn lays her hand on top of the hand I have over the mouse. "Beth," she whispers, "honey, who is Tommy?"

I stare at the computer screen trying to think of answer that won't hurt her feelings.

"Someone important from back home," I choke out.

Someone important I couldn't share with you.

Cyn nudges me out of my seat, taking over at the computer.

"I will find you the first flight I can into Des Moines. Is there someone I can call to meet you at the airport?" Her forehead is creased with concern. I hurt her and her willingness to take care of me despite that only breaks my heart further.

"I need to call Uncle Rob back, I'll ask him," I mumble, staring at my phone's fractured screen. Another missed call from Uncle Rob and three from Pops and Gran. I touch Uncle Rob's name and hit send, and a moment later Aunt Melissa picks up the phone.

"Beth, honey, I'm so sorry. It's so awful," she sobs. She tells me how Tommy was on his way to his dad's in Cumming when a drunk driver ran a four way stop, broadsiding him on the driver's side. Killing him instantly. The words all make sense. It just feels like it's happening to someone else. I can't connect to what she is saying— my brain won't accept it.

"When are you coming home? What time does your flight get in?" She keeps asking me, but I just sit there in stunned silence. Cyn takes the phone from me and relays the flight information to Aunt Melissa along with her phone number. Cyn looks at Les and then eyes me warily. I don't blame them for not trusting me. We're best friends who're supposed to share everything, and I clearly have left out some critical pieces. A fresh wave of shame washes over me; I can't look them in the eye while we gather our things and head home.

30

Illusions can be very convincing. No one has any reason to suspect that I am anything less than what I appear. I don't fit the typical victim profile. I may have some intimacy issues but those could be caused by a lot of things. There's no telltale sign that would lead anyone to believe I was sexually abused for most of my childhood. With some smoke and mirrors, I've managed to evade the parts of myself that I wanted to hide. I convinced myself it wasn't lying but a lie by omission is no less deceptive.

Where only a fool would build a house on shifting sand, the same goes for those who would build their lives on a lie—eventually, it is going to crumble. I spent so much energy on cutting and pasting together the person I wanted to be that I forgot who I was. I neglected the person who knew me the best and loved me the most. Now he's gone, and I will never have the chance to tell him what he meant to me.

❦

"Do You Love Me" by The Contours streams through the speakers in Gran and Pops' basement and Tommy holds out his hand to me. He pulls me to the center of the makeshift dance floor and spins me around.

"Show me what you got, baby girl!" Tommy's blue eyes twinkle with anticipation. As the music cues us, we grind our feet into the floor and do The Mashed Potato. I laugh at Tommy who's lifted his foot in the air and is now dancing on one leg. When the lyrics change we swing

our hips in unison and do The Twist. "Tell me baby! Do you like it like this?" Tommy sings.

We go through several records as we practice each of the dances he's taught me—The Pony, The Monkey, The Jerk, and my favorite, The Hand Jive. Fighting to catch our breath, we flop down on the couch to rest. I love these impromptu dance lessons with Tommy. I still can't picture him being my age, dancing with my mom and Uncle Rob this way.

"Woo!" He cheers while wiping sweat from his brow. "Your mama ain't got nothin' on your moves, baby girl." He winks and gives me a warm smile, sending me into fits of giggles.

❧

Cyn and Leslie drive me to the airport the next morning. The ride is eerily silent, as they have given up talking to me. There isn't much to say when I won't answer them about Tommy. I know they just want to understand and help but I just can't. The words "Tommy" and "gone" are still battering my skull, I can't tell them why he has never been a part of conversation. They deserve an explanation. I know they can handle it—they're my friends. They deserve better. Tommy deserves better.

When we pull up to the terminal, I grab my suitcase and face my friends who are waiting for me on the curb. Their pained expressions are battery acid on my already broken heart.

"I love you guys." I whisper as I pull both of them into a hug. "I am so sorry." I give them a sad smile and head through the doors.

"Beth!" I look over my shoulder at Cyn's call. "We are here when you're ready to talk. We love you, too." Les nods her agreement and blows me a kiss. I don't deserve them, I really don't.

❧

Pops and Gran have a full house as they usually do on Saturday afternoons. In an unspoken rule, their home is where everyone flocks. One Saturday, as a joke, Gran said, "I don't mind the company as long as they bring something with them." So began Potluck Saturday. Friends and family descend on the house with covered dishes, cakes, and cookies while we catch up with each other.

I hold my breath and hope it keeps me from crying in front of Gran and her friend, Rose.

"You just don't look anything like Casey when she was twelve, it's uncanny." Rose comments, "Does she favor John's family, Ellen?" Gran gives Rose a stern look that goes unnoticed.

"She's a combination of them both. I think she's got all of their loveliest traits." Gran smiles at me apologetically.

Rose shrugs at her answer like she isn't quite buying it. I know I don't have my mother's stunning good looks, but having my face rubbed in it stings. I excuse myself and head out the front door before Rose can say something else about what a misfit I am. Once my feet hit the porch, the tears come. I cover my face and blindly turn toward the porch swing, hoping I can hide out here for a while.

"Hey there! Whose ass do I need to kick?" I jerk at the sound of Tommy's voice. My hands fall to my sides and I swipe at my tears. Tommy is perched on the porch swing with his guitar in his lap.

"I didn't know you were out here." I sniffle.

"Clearly." Tommy raises his eyebrow when I avoid his question. "So?" he draws out the word while he pats the seat.

I climb up next to him and rest my head on his shoulder. "Rose." I giggle. It's pretty funny picturing Tommy duking it out with a little, old blue haired old lady.

"What?" he laughs. "Rose? What did she say?" He rubs my back and hands me a hankie from his back pocket. He always has a handkerchief tucked in his back pocket. Not just any kind, he only carries the red ones that come in a 5-pack at Hy-Vee. The best thing about them is they are always baby soft and threadbare. I wipe my face and am comforted by Tommy's familiar scent of the leather seats in his pickup truck and cinnamon. He's addicted to Red Hots, so he always smells a little like cinnamon.

"She wouldn't shut up about how much I don't look like my mom when she was my age. She kept saying, 'Casey is just so lovely,'" I whimper.

Tommy lets out a frustrated sigh as he sets his guitar down. Turning to me, he lifts my chin from where it rests on my chest. "Just because your hair isn't blond and your eyes aren't hazel doesn't mean that you are not every bit as lovely as your mama." I try not to start crying again, but the harder I try, the more my chin trembles. "Rose is an old fool, I wouldn't put any weight behind what she says." Tommy squeezes me in a big bear hug before picking up his guitar.

"Thanks, Tommy." I give him a watery smile.

"Besides, you got the best of all of your mama's traits, baby girl," he strums his guitar as he talks, "her smile." He serenades me with Van Morrison and before I know it, my tears are dry and my hurt forgotten. "You'll always be my brown-eyed baby girl."

31

"**D**ear *Tommy*," I've been staring at those words for the last twenty minutes. They're mocking me.

I miss you. Too lame.

I'm sorry. Too little, too late.

I love you. Always.

I'm stalling. I know exactly what I need to say but I haven't been down that road in a long time. When you've spent all your time hiding from your past, the last thing you want to do is jump in and go for a swim. Reflecting on it won't bring Tommy back. It's tempting to just throw away my scribbling and pretend that it's okay. God knows I've gotten good at pretending; I hate the coward I've become.

The pen shakes as I force it to connect to the paper through my memories. I upend every emotion and lay it out in detail, how he believed me without ever doubting me and how he fought Drew to keep me safe. The way he confronted my parents for me. For eight years, I waited for someone to stand up for me, and Tommy was the one who finally did. As I seal the envelope a thought occurs to me—all this time, I never thanked him.

I have been through more in my life than most people, but I've never lost someone close to me. For all of the horrific things I was forced to deal with in my childhood, death was never one of them. I thought I knew pain. I thought I understood it. *Nothing* I have ever experienced can come close to this agony. Now

I understand "died of a broken heart." I'd welcome death to come swallow me whole.

The wheels touch down in Des Moines, shaking me from my reverie. Everything looks the same, but nothing feels the same. People are bustling around me as I drag myself through the concourse when my phone chirps in my pocket. A quick glance shows that it's my mom.

"Hello?"

"Elizabeth? Are you there? Are you ok?" she batters me with a hundred questions all at once, making my head spin.

"Mom, slow down," I say.

"Oh, honey. I wish I was there right now."

"When do you fly in?" I sniff.

"We'll be there later on today," her voice is tense with worry, "who's picking you up?"

"I don't know," I wince, knowing she'll lecture me on that next. "Uncle Rob or Aunt Melissa, I assume."

"Beth, really?" She chides. "I'm calling Pops."

"No, Mom, please don't. Everyone knows my flight information, someone will be here, and if not, I can catch a cab." I reassure her.

She scoffs in my ear, "I know that, I just don't like that you are there alone. Honey, I am so sorry. I know how much Tommy meant to you." Her words cause my throat to clench. "He was such an important part of your life, and the thought of you alone in that airport just breaks my heart." I hear shuffling in the background and then my dad's muffled voice. "She isn't even sure she has a ride from the airport, John," she tells him. "I know how old she is, I'm not hovering." She continues to argue with my dad who is grousing about how overbearing she can be. Today, it's kind of nice to have her fussing over me, and I'm grateful that our relationship is good because I need all of the moral support I can find.

"If you two need to work this out, I can talk to you later." I use the distraction to get off the phone before I start to cry again. "I love you, Mom."

"Love you, too, baby. I'll call you when we land," she promises.

I don't want to be here alone either, so the sooner I can grab my luggage, the sooner I can get to Gran and Pops.

When I reach the security checkpoint, I rush past the folks reuniting with their loved ones. The pain in my chest swells when I think about the last time I was here and how Tommy's face lit up when he saw me through the crowd. No matter where I turn, the memories are unavoidable. After all the years of Tommy picking me up whenever I'd fly home, his ghost is everywhere. I run down the stairs to Baggage Claim.

I take a deep cleansing breath through my nose and close my eyes. One foot in front of the other, I need to keep walking through the motions because I don't know what else to do. I blow the air out through my mouth and open my eyes. It doesn't help ease my regret, but I doubt anything will. In a fog, I grab my suitcase from the carousel only to pause in confusion when I forget what I'm supposed to do next. I've never felt so lost.

Standing outside the doors, watching the cars come and go, I can hear my mother nagging me about who's coming to pick me up. I've been in such a daze; I don't even know whose car I should look for. Cyn was the one who called Gran to let her know when I'd be home, thank God or I would've forgotten that, too. This is so unlike me, I'm always the one in charge. Losing control is not an option. I need to get it together and start functioning better than this.

I am rooting through my purse to find my cell phone when I hear my name. "*Beth.*" My head pops up and I start to search the faces around me for a familiar one. "*Beth, over here.*" I spin toward the voice coming up behind me. "I was waiting for you outside security and you walked right by me."

I stare blankly at the man standing before me as every coherent thought escapes me. My heart slams against my ribcage, while my initial confusion becomes recognition. He hooks his thumbs in the pockets of his jeans and looks up at me through familiar blond eyelashes. The corner of his mouth tips up, revealing a lopsided grin.

"Ryan," I whisper.

32

I stare at Ryan in shock. Memories of us at the lake play in my mind through the grainy frames of old home movies. The images flicker and come to life as the last ten years fade away. His face no longer holds the roundness of a boy's, but of an angular man. To look at him, I have to tilt my head up further than I used to. The blond hair that is tucked underneath his Hawkeyes cap matches the scruff covering his face. His green eyes study me with same affection they did when I was fifteen, but sadness simmers beneath.

"Ryan." Tears burst with renewed grief as I wrap my arms around him. I cling to him shamelessly, breathing in the familiar scent of cedar. I weep without restraint as I give myself over to the pain of our loss. Ryan's strong arms pull me tightly against his chest and his lips press against the top of my head.

"Beth," My name comes out on a sigh. "I'm so glad you are here." Ryan's body tenses a moment before he sucks in a shaky breath. He's crying, too. I didn't think my heart could hurt more. In my eagerness to comfort him, I squeeze him tighter. I'm surprised by how easy it is to fall back into this need to be close to him. I rub his back and murmur quiet words of comfort until his body relaxes and his breathing steadies.

We stay locked in our embrace, ignoring the people shooting us curious looks as they detour around us. Even after our tears have subsided, I'm hesitant to let Ryan go. I give him a sheepish smile and tuck my hair behind my ear. Despite our willingness to skip the normal

social niceties, there is still a gap ten years wide between us. No—
hello, it's so nice to see you again—we bypassed that and dove straight
into hanging on for dear life. He picks up my suitcase and holds his
hand out for me. His hand is rough and calloused, and it eclipses
mine when he entwines our fingers. He waits for me to look up at
him before he smiles back at me. Typical Ryan, always so self-assured.

∽

I try closing my eyes on the way to Gran and Pops' house, but I am
restless. Leaning my head on the window, I watch the corn fields fly
past in a blur. In the background, a random rock song is ending and
the beginning strains of a Brutal Strength song begins.

"You know, I was at their concert when Uncle Rob called," my
tone is flat. I don't even bother to turn toward Ryan. I just continue
staring out at nothing.

"No way," Ryan returns, "you finally made it to a show."

"Actually, I never saw them play." I chuckle and shake my
head, "I guess it wasn't meant to be." My face burns at my choice of
words. I was talking about my thwarted opportunities to see Brutal
Strength, but it sounds a lot like a reference to our ill-fated romance.
I clear my throat and shift in my seat, "You know what I mean."

Ryan's laughter fills the cab of his truck. God, I missed that
sound. "I should have known I could count on you to make me
laugh," he jokes.

"You mean you can count on me to say something painfully
awkward," I laugh.

"Some things never change." Ryan chuckles under his breath.

I perk up in my seat. "What's that supposed to mean?" I turn
away from the window to address him. I fold my arms over my
chest while I wait for his answer.

"It's not bad, you've just always been a little…" he hesitates.

"Well, don't stop now." I cock my eyebrow and wait.

"Uneasy." He glances at me from the corner of his eye.

"I don't think that's ambiguous enough." I counter.

"Sarcastic."

"Do I get to play? Let's think of a few words to describe Ryan." I narrow my eyes at him while I scrutinize.

"Defensive," he continues.

Ouch, that stings.

"Cocky."

"Anxious."

I squirm at the accuracy of Ryan's words. It unnerves me that he can expose me so easily after so long.

"Tormentor."

"Now, when did I ever torment you?" he asks. He's either got a really bad memory or he's baiting me.

"You teased me relentlessly," I bite.

"Tease and torment are two different things. I teased you because your reactions were hilarious." He laughs.

"I'm glad you were entertained." I let my snark out in full force.

"Don't take offense, it was endearing."

"To whom?"

"To me. I couldn't help myself. You're adorable when you're all flustered."

I blush at the sweetness of his statement. A smile creeps along the corners of my mouth at his use of present tense. He's right, some things never change—I'm still a sucker for his charm.

The truck slows down, and all too soon, we are pulling up to the curb near Gran and Pops' house. The burst of giddy excitement Ryan conjured evaporates. Cars line the street on both sides; people spill out of the house onto the porch. Another thing that hasn't changed, everyone still gathers here. Even in grief, they flock here seeking the comfort of being a part of something bigger—family.

"It doesn't seem real," I murmur. The air in the truck turns thick with despair. "My heart still expects to see him up on the porch with his guitar."

Ryan hangs his head and lets out a defeated sigh. I release my seatbelt and slide across the bench seat. Without lifting his head, he turns to gauge what I am doing. I tip my head to meet his gaze and rest my hand in the center of his back. He looks so weary.

"Hey." I move my hand in circles across the tension in his muscles. "It'll be all right."

Without taking his eyes off mine, he puts his hands on my hips and slides us back to the passenger's seat. Still holding my gaze, he slowly lays his head in my lap. I force myself to breathe as I watch tears spill across his cheeks onto my jeans. My fingers shake as I run them along his hairline; the intimacy of this scene is wreaking havoc on my already ragged emotions. His face contorts in pain as a sob wracks his body. I shift to accommodate more of him in my lap. Pulling him against me, I rock us gently and kiss his temple. He still feels like home.

"I just need a minute," he whispers.

"Hey, it's all right. Take as many as you need." I murmur. My own sorrow, demanding release, wraps around Ryan's. His grief is palpable. Mixed with my own, it's suffocating. I can't stand it.

"No one's seen us pull up yet," I choke, "let's drive down to the park awhile." Neither one of us seems ready to face the crowded house. Not waiting for Ryan's response, I jump out of the passenger side and rush around to hop in the driver's seat. I crank the keys and the engine roars to life. Ryan's managed to fasten his seatbelt, but he is slumped over with his face in his hands. I throw the gearshift into drive and check the rearview mirror to make sure no one sees us.

The familiar streets and houses that used to bring me comfort only magnify Tommy's absence. The cheery bungalows and picture perfect Craftsmans, with their well-manicured lawns and prized peony bushes, seem worn. There's peeling paint and cracks in the sidewalks where weeds have found safe haven. Nothing is as perfect as we want it to be.

I pull into the parking lot at Legion Park and find a secluded spot. The playground is full of parents with their children and the half pipe is bustling with skaters. It pisses me off that life is continuing as if nothing has changed. Suffused with a sudden burst of anger I want to scream at all of them. How dare they go on with their lives when Tommy can't! My hands ache from white knuckling the steering wheel and my head is pounding from crying. I startle when Ryan puts his hand on my shoulder.

"I'm sorry I lost it back there." He squeezes gently, sending relief up my neck into my throbbing head. "It's not fair, I know this is hard on you, too."

I rest my head on the steering wheel as his hand continues to knead the tension out of my shoulder. The seat gives when he shifts closer to me. I tense when his fingers brush the back of my neck and relax again when he resumes massaging my other shoulder.

"If this is how you say you're sorry then how does anyone stay mad at you?" I groan in relief. "Seriously, you don't need to apologize to me and you don't owe me any explanations."

"Do you want to go for a walk?" With my head still resting on the steering wheel, I turn to face his question. I can't help but smirk. The last time he asked me to go for a walk he unleashed those wicked lips on me and ruined me for every boy that came after him. Red creeps up his neck and into his cheeks when he sees the connection. He's right, there is something adorable about flustered.

"Come on," I open the door and step into the crisp fall air. I meet Ryan at the front of the truck and reach for his hand before my brain can tell me to slow down. I don't care. I need to feel connected to someone; I don't want to hurt like this on my own. We walk past the picnic shelters and settle under a shady tree. "I know I said you didn't owe me any explanations, but if you want to talk about it, you can trust me." Sitting here takes me back to the day under the cherry tree when Ryan told me I could trust him. I want so badly to return the favor.

"It's too much to take in," he starts. "I keep thinking if I keep myself busy enough it'll make it easier. I just want it to be easier." He shakes his head at the absurdity of what he's saying. "While the rest of the family just shut down, I made the funeral arrangements, took care of the police reports and..." he pauses to pinch the bridge of his nose, preparing himself, "...I went to the impound lot to get the rest of his things from his car." I squeeze his hand and his haunted eyes meet mine, sucking all of the air from my lungs. "There was so much blood. Tommy's blood. Everywhere. On everything."

My eyes don't leave his, even as tears blur his face. I blink, sending them spilling and bringing Ryan back into focus. I can't imagine what he must've seen. I don't want to know that Tommy's blood is splattered all over the carcass of his truck. I don't want to know, but then I doubt Ryan wants to know either. I cringe at the thought of him in the impound lot, at the scene of Tommy's death, alone. I roll onto my knees in front of him and place my palms against his scruff.

He leans into my touch and continues, "I was afraid if I started to cry, I'd never stop." He whispers, "I wanted to do everything, anything to keep from thinking." He leans in closer and rests his hands on my knees. "I came and met your plane after I left the lot.

Rob and Melissa were supposed to pick you up, but I called to tell them to stay with the Cantwells."

"You needed to keep going." I sigh. Ryan's brow relaxes in relief as he nods his head. "I get it."

"I couldn't wait to see you, to surprise you, and for a few minutes, I could forget. When I saw you and you looked at me, you saw right through me." I think about the airport and the affectionate look he gave me—the one that couldn't hide the sadness behind it.

Oh, Ryan.

He shudders on a heavy sigh; I think he's done purging for now. My arms ache from cradling his face, but I don't want to let go. Instead I lean forward and kiss his forehead. Sometimes it takes more than just pretty words but something tactile to remind you that you aren't alone. Ryan seems to understand my intent because he embraces me and pulls me forward into his lap. I don't bother feeling uneasy because, at this point, we both just need someone.

33

Of all the years I spent in therapy, the issue that seemed to dominate above all others was boundaries. In my counselor's defense, Dave was a psychologist that specialized in addiction not abuse. He was our family therapist and since two out of three of us were addicts, we stuck with him. He was great; he just wasn't equipped to help me navigate what happened with Drew. Apparently Dave thought I wouldn't have boundaries at all and turn into an insta-slut. I always found that comical because I have more boundaries than Eastern Europe.

For a long time I wouldn't let anyone close enough to touch me, let alone have sex with me. When I finally did have sex, it was out of curiousity. I didn't take much stock in what Dave said back then because it was offensive, he clearly didn't know me at all. Little did I know that one day, I would finally understand all his concern. If he could see me now, curled up in the lap of a man I haven't spent a day with in a decade, he'd have a stroke. I'm not thinking about the position I am in or how easily it could get out of hand. I hurt too much to think. Maybe it is naïve, but Ryan's arms feel like a sanctuary for my pain. A place where I can give into it and not have to answer for it. I still trust Ryan. I need to.

"He loved you more than anything else in this world. I hope you know that, Beth." Ryan's voice is gravel.

I turn my face into his chest and find more tears as I think of Tommy. No one could possibly deny me this comfort. I don't care what Dave would say.

Ryan's sudden shift tears me from my thoughts, lifting my head. He reaches into his pocket and retrieves a vibrating phone. "Hi Melissa," he answers, giving me an apologetic look. "We stopped at Legion to catch our breath before we headed to the house." He cringes as I hear Aunt Melissa's raised voice through the earpiece, "I'm sorry I didn't call. We'll head your way in a few." He pauses to let her reply, "I love you, too. I understand and I'm really sorry I didn't call... ok, bye." Running his hand through his hair, he looks frazzled.

"She was worried, huh?" I move out of Ryan's lap, my movements are as disjointed as I feel. Ryan looks like he wants to say something but hesitates. With our moment broken, I feel foolish for my emotional display. "We should probably get going," I suggest as I stand.

"Beth," Ryan grabs my hand. This is where I should probably employ one of those boundaries and take back some of the dignity I just gave away. "Thank you," he squeezes my hand, "I needed this."

As we walk back to the truck, I try to regain a little balance by getting my hand back but every time I relax my grip, Ryan strengthens his. He looks at me suspiciously, like he can sense I am trying to distance myself. I find it both irritating and comforting that Ryan can still read me like an emotional barometer.

We ride in silence back to Gran and Pops' house, giving me time to try and figure out how close is too close. I don't want to push Ryan away but I don't want to make a fool out of myself again. Damn boundaries, damn Dave. He was right after all.

As Ryan parks, I prepare for the onslaught we are about to enter. My fear is that I will let Ryan fall into the role of my emotional crutch. He needs his own room to process—he doesn't need me to distract him.

As we walk up the steps, I keep my hands busy fiddling with my purse. I can see Ryan studying me in my peripheral, probably using his Spidey sense to read my mind. If I thought making my hand unavailable was a solution, I was mistaken. When we walk through the front door, Ryan's arm finds its way around my waist. Frustration courses through me when my body relaxes into his side. I have no self-control. There are people covering every inch of space in the house, and they all turn to see who's walked through the front door.

Through the sea of bodies, Gran's slight frame appears, "Blossom!" She grabs my face in her hands and kisses my forehead. "Thank God you're here," she gives me a watery smile and wraps me tightly in her arms. When she lets me go, Pops is there to hug me against him and escort me through the crowd. Tension coils around me as we brush past the mourners gathered here for Tommy.

"Beth," Uncle Rob's voice is vacant. His face is pale. The dark circles under his eyes announce his exhaustion. He pulls me into a hug and my heart breaks all over again. Tommy and Uncle Rob were more than friends—they were an extension of one another. Losing Tommy means that he has irrevocably lost a part of himself. Aunt Melissa appears at his side, looking every bit as haggard as her husband. Her curly blond hair is pulled into a limp ponytail, and her eyes are red and swollen. She wraps herself around both Uncle Rob and me, sobbing quietly against my shoulder.

"Tommy loved you so much, baby girl," Uncle Rob cries, "you were his from the moment you were born. He thought of you as his own."

Anxiety crackles along my spine; I feel like a fraud. Tommy loved me like a daughter and I cut him out of my life. I didn't deserve his love. Uncle Rob's torment and my anxiety swirl around each other, generating a funnel cloud that threatened to suck me in and spit me out. My eyes dart around searching for an escape. I kiss Uncle Rob on the cheek and then Aunt Melissa before ducking under Pops' arm to head for the kitchen. Without slowing down, I rush down the kitchen steps and out the side door. The stucco digs at my back as I lean against the house trying to calm down.

My face is soaked with tears and I am breathing like I've just run a marathon. I haven't had a panic attack in years, and the fact that I am having one now only serves to infuriate me further. The doorknob rattles, sending me running around the back of the house. If anyone finds me out here hyperventilating, I'll die of humiliation.

The cherry tree is blooming with fall colors, its branches beckoning me like open arms. I put my hand against the rough bark of the trunk and hang my head, willing my heart rate to slow and my breathing to steady. Once the adrenaline is gone, my body sags and I drop to my knees. Exhaustion tempts me to curl up right here and let sleep take me far away from the agony.

A twig snaps behind me, sending me scrambling to my feet. Ryan stands a few feet away looking both guilty and concerned. "I didn't want to startle you. I just wanted to make sure you were all right."

"How long have you been standing there?" I accuse. He doesn't answer and I realize he's been there the whole time. I am mortified.

"Beth," Ryan begins, taking a step toward me.

"Don't." I hold my hand out and step back. I need to put my foot down and make my limits very clear. My outstretched hand shakes and I curse myself for the outward sign of weakness. I will be hard pressed to convince Ryan that I don't need him to hold me up when he keeps witnessing my meltdowns. His eyes bore into mine with a mix of fear and irritation. All of the clever things I was going to say dry up in my throat.

"No, you don't, Beth." Ryan furrows his brow and closes the distance between us with two steps. "Don't push me away because you think you shouldn't lean on me. You need me, Beth, and I need you." We are nose to nose and I hope he can feel the fury rolling off me.

"*I don't know you anymore, Ryan,*" I yell. "What kind of fool would I be to just assume that we are the same stupid kids we were ten years ago? I shouldn't trust you any more than you should trust me."

His mouth pulls into a thin line and fire flashes in his green eyes. "You know me, Beth. In your heart, you know me and you still trust me or you wouldn't have crawled into my lap and bared your soul." His voice is soft but the pinch of his brow gives away his anger, "You're just pissed off because you're thinking of what everyone else might think. *Screw them and what they think.*" He grabs me by the arms, pinning them to my sides. "You want to know what I think? In the last forty-eight hours I have been tortured over Tommy's death and the only time I have had any peace was getting to see you again." His accuracy scares me.

"Please let me go," I cry. Ryan releases my arms but makes no move to step away. Instead he sweeps the pad of his thumb across my cheek, catching my tears.

"Don't be afraid of me, please," he begs. "I won't hurt you." He leans his forehead against mine and closes his eyes.

A war of logic and emotion pulls me from both sides, one pulls me back and the other pushes me forward. Being tossed around the two makes my head spin. It's insane to encourage this level of intimacy with someone who is practically a stranger, no matter how much I've longed for him over the years. While that makes perfect sense, my heart is begging me to fill it with the comfort Ryan is offering. If Tommy's death has taught me anything, it's that life is fragile and nothing is certain. I brush my hand against Ryan's cheek and stretch up on my tiptoes to kiss it. He shudders at my touch and lets out a relieved sigh.

"I don't want to be afraid of you, Ryan. Let's be honest, it's been a really long time." I try to lighten the mood but neither of us is in the mindset to joke.

"It has been too long," he starts, "but we've known each other our whole lives, Beth. I'm not a stranger, no matter what you are kicking around in that lovely head of yours." He hits me with that irresistible lopsided smile.

Crap.

"That's easy to say, Ry, but we should still exercise a little restraint. I mean you really have an issue with personal space." I can't help but snicker. This is far from humorous, but the absurdity of it is making me slaphappy. He arches an eyebrow that only makes me laugh harder.

He steps close enough that our bodies barely touch. His eyes study me with such intensity, I am sure that I will spontaneously combust. He rubs his scruff against my cheek, and I have to will my legs not to buckle when kissing it sends his breath skittering across my ear. Leave it to me to get turned on at Tommy's wake.

"Ryan," I whisper, gathering all my courage, "this doesn't feel friendly. We are teetering on a line here that we haven't crossed since we were kids. I don't want to hurt anymore than I already do." Ryan's body tenses and I wait for him to start laughing at me for being presumptuous. I don't think I am. Being this close to him muddles my brain, making me want dangerous things. Pulling his head back to look at me, his expression stops my heart.

"Don't you think I remember? How could I ever forget how it felt to kiss you?" His eyes drift to my mouth and linger. "It's all I have dreamt about for years. But I also remember how good it felt to have your trust, and to have someone I could trust. We were kids, but it was special, Beth. You were always special." I am drunk with his confession and so confused. The back of Ryan's hand brushes across my cheek, wiping tears I didn't even know I was still shedding. "Don't push me away," he pleads as he replaces his hand with his lips.

"Please," I whimper. My body shakes with a fusion of desire, fear and sadness; it's overwhelming. I close my eyes to block out some of the sensory overload short-circuiting my nerves. "I can't think straight, Ryan. I can't do this." My libido is screaming profanities at me but the last burst of logic wins out. I force myself to let Ryan go and walk back to the house.

34

Once the last of the mourners have left and the food is packed away, I escape to the security of my childhood bedroom. The delicate lace curtains have yellowed over the years but everything looks the same. The four-poster bed is tucked into the corner where the ceiling slopes, and my dresser sits against the opposite wall. The turntable is still perched on the hope chest that holds my records. This day calls for some music therapy. I choose my favorite Nina Simone EP and strip off my clothes in favor of PJ bottoms and my favorite chicken t-shirt. If only stripping off layers of clothing could also strip off the layers of the day. Tommy permeates every thought, consciously or not. Nina Simone was a favorite of his, too.

༄

"Nina? How old are you, baby girl? 30?" Tommy laughs.

"Thirteen. Ha ha." I roll my eyes.

"Who got you hooked on this?" he asks.

"Pops gave me this album," I answer proudly. "Nobody else sounds like she does. Her voice casts a spell on me."

"You've got the oldest soul of any thirteen-year-old I know. You're right, though, Nina's voice is hypnotic." He smiles.

We sift through the rest of the jazz albums Pops gave me: Ella Fitzgerald, Miles Davis, Sarah Vaughn, and Dizzy Gillespie. Tommy teaches me the melodic and harmonic structures of jazz theory compared to classic music theory. His passion is intoxicating and my heart leaps when he goes downstairs to grab his guitar. I love the way Tommy really gets into it when he talks about music. It feels like he understands how music makes me feel.

"Check this out, Beth," he bursts back into the room with his guitar case and promptly joins me on the floor, tuning the strings. Soon he's showing me examples of common jazz chords like the minor seventh and how it's built from the major C scale. I listen closely to his lesson in music theory, and he gives me all his attention when I go over my latest lyrical analysis. The afternoon passes with the two of us discussing music, in between singing duets. Pops sticks his head in my door when Tommy and I are in the middle of "Cheek to Cheek" by way of Louis Armstrong and Ella Fitzgerald.

"You hanyaks need to take your act on the road," Pops smiles. "Why don't you come downstairs and sing for your Gran and I?"

We follow Pops to the living room where Tommy and I take song requests. We harmonize our way through song after song while Tommy accompanies us on the guitar. It fills me with a kind of joy that only music brings me.

"I think I have found my musical kindred, Pops," Tommy laughs, "and just when I was sure I couldn't love this baby girl more."

His praise makes my cheeks hot but I am not embarrassed, I am thrilled that he feels that way. Acceptance isn't something I have when I am home in Miami. Having Tommy's fills me to bursting with happiness.

"You get me." I giggle.

∾

Tommy's voice is still ringing in my ears when I open my eyes. Confused, I sit up on my bed to find myself on top of the covers with an afghan over me. Gran never stops taking care of me. I don't think I will ever outgrow being her "Blossom." The clock on the dresser has to be wrong because it's insisting on 6:00 A.M.—there is no way that I have been asleep for the last ten hours. I grab my phone from the nightstand and am shocked that it's in agreement. Wrapping the afghan around my shoulders, I pad downstairs to start coffee.

Today I am burying the best friend I ever had. The title sticks in my craw because he was more than a friend—he was a father, a confidant, a friend, and a kindred spirit. There is no title for the person Tommy was to me, but there is a word for me: ungrateful. While I watch the coffee grounds percolate, I think about all the times I should've told him how much I loved him. All the times I should have sent him a plane ticket to come visit or at the very least let him know that I wanted him to come for a visit. Instead, I acted like everything else was more important, and he faded into the background. The letter I wrote Tommy on the plane is a poor substitute for one of our early morning dock chats, but all of the opportunities for that have passed and I wasted every one. I pour coffee into a travel mug before heading upstairs to change and grab the letter.

Pops' keys jingle in my hand as I carefully close the door and jog toward his old Lincoln Town Car. It's a beast with pale grey paint and burgundy velvet seats. I am not looking forward to navigating this boat through traffic, but I want to make this trip on my own.

⁓

"Hey baby girl, I thought I might find you out here," Tommy yawns, scratching his stomach through his Iowa Hawkeyes t-shirt. It doesn't surprise me to see him. We've been having early morning pow-wows on

the dock for a long time. "Couldn't sleep?" He brushes his hand across the top of my head before joining me.

"Bad dream," I murmur into my mug. Tommy regards me with sleepy eyes, but the twitch of his mustache clues me in to his concern.

"Wanna talk about it?" He wraps his arm around me and squeezes my shoulder.

"No, but Dr. Warren says it's the only way I will ever get past it." I stare into my mug and try to gather the courage to continue.

"You know you can tell me anything, Beth. There is nothing I wouldn't do for you, baby girl." Tommy's warm baritone washes over me, giving me the boost that I need.

"It was about Drew," I start, "nothing specific, more like a mash-up of everything." My hair falls like a curtain, hiding my face from Tommy's reaction. I hear him blow out a breath as he takes in my statement.

"I have bad dreams too," his confession surprises me. Pulling my hair behind my ear, I turn toward him. His eyes are focused on the lake. "In my dream, I am back in your living room pounding the living shit out of Drew, except this time I don't stop, Beth. I kill him with my bare hands," his voice trembles as he pinches the bridge of his nose. I reach over and lay my hand across the top of his. I don't want this pain for him. "The dream doesn't scare me as much as waking up wishing that I had."

❧

The memory of our pow-wow at the lake beats regret against my skull. The envelope weighs heavy in my hands. I want to go. I *need* to go.

35

There is no mistaking where Tommy's life came to a violent end. The tire marks still mar the pavement where the drunk driver tried to stop at the last minute. They lead up to a corner of the intersection that is covered with tokens of memorial, a monument to his death. I pull to the side of the road and throw the Lincoln into park. My stomach roils as I force the door open. With every step, it becomes harder to breathe, and I find myself panting with the effort. My hands shake as I open the letter and stand on the spot Tommy drew his last breath.

                        ᏵᎧ

Dear Tommy,

When I was a little girl, you always had the right words to make me feel better. You always knew what to do to dry my tears and make me smile. You were magic. I need some of your magic today but you aren't here and no amount of magic could fix the hurt in my heart. I can't believe you are gone. I keep expecting to wake up and realize that it was just another bad dream.

Do you remember what you used to say to me when I missed you? "Together forever. Never apart. Maybe in distance but never in heart." I'm sorry I never told you that you're in my heart every day. Every. Day. I never told you, that of all the horrible things I went through, YOU made the biggest impression. Not Drew, not the drugs, none of it. You made me believe in goodness when all I knew was evil. You showed me what it meant to sacrifice yourself for someone else and you showed me that I was important enough to fight for. You risked going to jail to defend me when no one else would acknowledge what went on under their noses. Above all else, you believed me. You never wavered or doubted that I was being hurt and that it needed to stop. When you grow up in a house where you're preyed upon and no one believes you, it makes you feel like you deserve what you're getting. It makes you think that your word is useless. The world is an empty and hopeless place when you don't have anyone in your corner. You were my champion. You gave hope back to me. You are my hero.

I would sacrifice myself, without hesitation, to have another minute with you. Life is cruel and unjust that you should die while I can think of many people more deserving. I know that's terrible, and I am probably going to hell for that. I just miss you. There will never be a day that I don't ache with missing you, T. Never a day.

I Will Love You, Always,

B.

⤬

The gravel from the shoulder of the road digs into my hands and knees. My letter is crumpled in the grass. Screaming releases the desolation and anger coursing through me. I rock back and forth in a pitiful display of grief. I don't care that I probably look like a crazy person. My heart is in pieces that will never fit together again. A feral moan erupts from my mouth, sending wave after wave of tears.

I've lost track of the time I've spent kneeling by the side of the road, wailing for Tommy. I only know that my throat is raw and my knees are sore. The discomfort it causes can't come close to the pain Tommy's absence creates. Part of me wants to curl up and die right here, but Tommy would never forgive me for leaving our family behind. I know he would be here if he could. I pick up my crumpled letter and place it back in its envelope. There is a nook between a statue of an angel and a cross with Tommy's name. I tuck the letter there. When I get off my knees and walk back to the Lincoln, I don't feel any relief. I know this is only one of the many times I will be saying goodbye to Tommy today.

When I pull up to the house, Ryan is waiting on the porch swing. He stands when he sees me and walks to the front steps to greet me. My sore eyes linger on him. He's beautiful in a dark grey suit and navy blue tie. I brush the remaining dirt from my jeans and do my best to act like I was just out joyriding.

"Good morning," I croak, forgetting my raw throat. He watches me suspiciously from the top of the stairs. I know I must look like a wreck, but I don't want an interrogation, so I continue to play dumb.

"Where'd you run off to so early?" He places his hand in the small of my back as he opens the door for me. I give him a quick smile and pick up my pace toward the kitchen. Gran and Pops are at the dining room table and when they see me fly through with Ryan hot on my heels, Gran's hand freezes with her coffee cup half-way to her mouth. Her eyebrows shoot straight up and Pops' pinch together.

"What the hell?" Pops mutters.

"Beth, *wait*," Ryan stops in the kitchen doorway.

I continue on my quest, grabbing a glass from the cabinet and filling it with water from the sink. I gulp down the tepid water, letting it soothe the burning in my throat. I wasn't counting on having to face him already. My back is to Ryan and I can feel him boring holes into the back of my head. The glass in my hand shakes as I turn on the faucet to refill my glass. I am not above blatant stalling; I'm desperate. Ryan's hand shoots around me and turns the faucet off. I can feel the heat of his body against my back making my heart leap. Damn him!

"You're running again," he whispers, as he rests his hands on my shoulders. I tense, getting ready to play defense against whatever questions he's about to hurl at me. Ryan ignores my posture and rubs my shoulders with tender care.

"I don't want to talk about it." My voice is still hoarse. I place my glass in the sink and lean my hands on the countertop, trying to put a little distance between us. His hands go a long way to soothing the angst from my visit to the site of the crash. Instead of fighting, I comply when he turns me around and pulls me against his chest. My eyes close, and I let the comfort he's offering wash over me.

"You don't have to talk about it. You don't have to say a word, just let me be here," he whispers into my hair. I heave a heavy sigh, letting the rest of my apprehension go. Grateful for his patience, I hold him tight to my body. No, I don't want to talk about it, but I still want him to know that I care. I won't let another person in my life go on without showing how I feel about them.

36

After a hot shower, I almost feel human again. The turntable spins an old school James Taylor album while I get dressed for Tommy's funeral mass. I slip on a simple black wrap dress with high-heeled Mary Janes. I am smoothing out the front of my dress when there is a knock on my door.

Gran sticks her head in and smiles when she sees me. "Beautiful, Blossom. You look so beautiful." The creases around her eyes deepen with her smile.

"Will you braid my hair, Gran?" I hold out my hairbrush and sit on the edge of my bed. Ever since I was little, I have loved it when Gran braids my hair. It is something so simple but very calming to have her play with my hair. She takes the brush and runs the bristles from my crown down to the ends. "Tommy would be very happy that you and Ryan are leaning on each other," she minces no words and moves in straight for the kill. With her fingers interwoven with my hair, I can't exactly run for the hills.

"Gran," I warn.

"Don't you sass me with that tone, young lady. Tommy realized how much that boy adored you the second you were gone. He felt the fool for giving you two so much grief. Poor Ryan moped around here like a lost pup when you went back to Miami. He even tried to give your concert tickets to Lori across the street. She was ecstatic until she realized that he was trying to give her both tickets." Gran chuckles while she is twisting the strands of hair into a French braid. I don't think she notices my slack-jawed response to her statement. The image of Ryan at seventeen pops into my head, making me smile in reverie. "What are you grinning at?" Gran teases.

"It's just hard to imagine Ryan moping around anywhere. It goes against his nature," I laugh.

"Exactly," Gran emphasizes. "That's how Tommy knew. That's how we all knew." She takes the elastic from the dresser, fastening it to the bottom of my braid.

"Gran?" I ask tentatively.

"What is it, Blossom?" She sits next to me on the bed and grabs my hand.

"Was Tommy happy?" I whimper and suck in a ragged breath.

"Yes, he was," Gran sniffles, "he had a good life and was happy where he was."

"I'm so glad," I give her a weak smile and squeeze her hand. Gran and I both turn our heads at the soft knock on the door.

"Knock, knock." I hear my mom's voice, "Can I come in?" Her beautiful blond head peeks around the corner. I jump off the bed to go hug her.

"Mom," I smile, "I'm so sorry I missed you last night, I passed out early."

"I know, when I came upstairs you were out cold, so I covered you up and turned out your light." She brushes my cheek with her hand. She laughs softly at my surprise and kisses my forehead. I pull her into another embrace and drink in the smell of her perfume.

"I love you so much, Mom," I whisper, "I'm so glad you're here."

"Me too, Beth," she says. Her eyes are glassy as they assess me with maternal concern. She strokes my cheek as she says, "Your dad and I are headed out with Rob and Melissa."

"Pops and I are going to head over to the church to help out the Cantwells." Before I can question, Gran adds, "Ryan said he would give you a ride to the church." She gives me a wry smile and my mom gives her a conspiratorial glance. I get the feeling that I am walking directly into a trap.

♋

"Will you miss me?" I whisper against Ryan's mouth. Beneath the cherry tree, we are snuggled together in the grass.

"Every day," Ryan promises, rubbing his nose against mine. He props himself on his elbows, drawing his face away from mine. "You know that, right?" His brows pinch together as he searches my face. His eyes lull me into a trance. I could stare into them forever. Their green is a perfect match to the grass we're laying on. "Beth?" He cocks an eyebrow, waiting.

"You'll miss me until some hottie comes along and steals your heart." I tease. I don't want to be the girl whose head gets so wrapped up in the clouds she can't see straight. Some beautiful girl will come along and replace me before my plane hits the runway in Miami. This is the last afternoon I have to spend with him, so I push those thoughts far away. The only things I want to think about are Ryan's kisses and the way they make me tingle.

"I don't want another hottie," he teases back before leaning in to kiss me. His lips brush mine with the tender promises of his heart. I wrap my arms around his neck and pull him against me. His hair winds through my fingers as my tongue grazes his. I like how he shudders when I take control. The warmth of his breath washes over my face when he pulls his mouth away from mine. His lips are puffy from our kisses; the look on his face chases the air from my lungs. He's taking me in like I am a treasure he's found, pure adoration. He smiles down at

me, making those jade eyes twinkle, "You're unforgettable, Elizabeth Irene. I'd be a fool not to miss rolling around in the grass with you." He laughs, rolling onto his back. I smack his stomach playfully and cover my face with my hands. "Don't be embarrassed, that's a compliment," he chuckles.

"You're an ass." My voice is muffled from beneath my hands.

"Maybe, but this ass will miss you every day. Every day, Beth." He peels my hands back, pinning them outstretched and my breath catches in panic. Before it can bloom, he runs his nose along my jaw, peppering kisses as he makes his way to my mouth. I am lost to the sensations, my panic forgotten as his lips trace mine, memorizing every curve.

∽

Ryan sits in the armchair by the window, staring out at nothing. Forlorn, he sits bent at the waist with his forearms resting on his knees. The pain etched on his face is a reminder of why we're here and who isn't here with us. Tommy's vacancy looms in the living room as I walk near Ryan. His head swings toward me and the desolation becomes wistful as the corner of his mouth tips up. If I had any hope of keeping him at arms length, it's gone into hiding. My heart cries for the years wasted on pushing everyone away, for never coming back to the boy I could never forget. What stings the most is how easily I believed that living that way was living at all. If Gran is right, I'm not the only one who's been pining.

Ryan's eyes don't leave mine as he crosses the room. The intensity of his stare strips me bare. He wraps his arms tightly around my waist and kisses my forehead.

"Pretty." That word and the smile stretching across his face remind me of the boy I used to play with on the lake. It takes me back to the last time Tommy, Ryan, and I were together there on my fifteenth birthday. The first time I confessed the depths of the abuse I suffered. The first kiss I took back from Drew—I was so certain that it would be a struggle to separate the two. What I couldn't possibly understand until it happened was how kissing Ryan would make me feel. There was never a question after his lips touched mine for the first time. Kissing Ryan stirred an array of emotions in me from desire to contentment.

"Whenever I hear that word I can't help but think of you." I smile up at him.

"Well, it *is* a pretty common word, Ms. Bradshaw," his voice is a deep rumble that sends chills over my skin. "How often did you think of me, exactly?" His mouth is so close to mine, I can't tear my eyes away from it.

"All the time," my voice is barely a whisper as the confession pours out of me. "More than I want to admit." There, now it's all out there. I hold my breath never taking my eyes from his perfect lips, and hope I haven't just laid myself out for slaughter.

"What would happen if you admit it?" He tips my chin up, demanding me to face him. "I *always* thought about you. I *always* wondered what it could've been like if our timing had been different."

I close my eyes as tears tumble silently from the corners of my eyes as bittersweet relief washes over me. He never forgot me, but he never really knew me either.

"I tried so hard to let you go, but I never could. You were always with me, Ryan." Shame colors my cheeks as I weep. "There are so many things that you don't know that you could never accept about me. If you really knew me, you wouldn't have wanted me at all." I try to pull away from Ryan but he only holds onto me tighter.

"Beth, look at me," Ryan pleads. I peer at him through wet eyelashes. He locks his emerald gaze with mine as our lips meet in a feather light kiss that marks my heart as his forever. My eyes flutter closed as the sensation overtakes me. His breath tickles my face with his next words, "Losing Tommy the way we did is a wake up call, Beth. He wouldn't want us to waste time on things we can't change. He would want us to have each other."

Fear and sorrow ignite a desire in me that threatens to burn us both to the ground. The sweet smell of cedar engulfs my senses, as I run my fingers through Ryan's hair and pull his bottom lip into my mouth. A growl rumbles through Ryan's chest as his tongue sweeps into my mouth. His touch stokes a flame that reduces my grief to ashes. He splays a possessive hand across my lower back and presses me against him. My hands are skimming down the sinewy muscles of his back when I hear someone clear their throat.

I gasp in horror at being caught making out in Gran and Pops' living room. My back is to the intruder but the look on Ryan's face isn't guilty, it's irritated. I spin away from Ryan to face whomever has trespassed on our private moment. I stare in shock at Lori from across the street and stumble as Ryan pulls me to his side.

"I saw your car, Ry." She gives me a critical once over. "I was hoping to get a ride to the church." She completely ignores me to bat her eyelashes at Ryan. A surge of protectiveness comes out of nowhere.

"We have obligations with our family so I wouldn't be the best person to ride with." Ryan's tone is cool and dismissive. I almost feel sorry for the poor girl. Her long black curls frame her lovely face as her hazel eyes dart back and forth between Ryan and me.

"That's not what I hear," she purrs and raises a challenging eyebrow. The hairs on the back of my neck prickle at her tone. I'm not so stupid to allow myself to be baited by her but it pisses me off, nonetheless.

"Get over yourself, Lori. This isn't the time or place for your bullshit." Ryan spits. I'm taken aback by his lack of patience with her. "Oh and tonguing Beth in the living room on your way to Tommy's funeral is more appropriate?" She sneers at us. "Whatever, I'll see you there." As she storms off, I have a vision of her bending the ear of anyone who'll listen about how she caught us making out like teenagers.

"Oh, no you don't," Ryan murmurs. He cups my face in his hands and gives me a tender, chaste kiss. "Don't you let her jealousy get under your skin. She's been pouting ever since I wouldn't go to Brutal Strength with her." I chuckle as he repeats Gran's story back to me.

"There aren't going to be any more scorned women waiting to kick my ass in the parking lot at church, are there?" I tease but Ryan knows I am fishing and his smile is devilish as he tugs my braid.

"No, I don't have a girlfriend, if that's what you're asking," he laughs, "but I can't help it if the ladies pine after me."

"You smug ass," I scoff, disentangling myself from Ryan.

If we are late, we will never hear the end of it. When I pause to open the front door, Ryan's hand slips around my waist and pulls me back against his chest. He sweeps my braid over my shoulder and plants a tender kiss at the base of my neck.

"You were the only one I wanted pining after me, pretty girl," he whispers.

37

The parking lot is full at St. Louis Catholic Church. The community has come out in droves to mourn the loss of one of its sons. Ryan pulls his truck into the parking area marked off for family members. I don't feel like I deserve to be considered as such—I abandoned my relationship with Tommy when I should have cherished it. Ryan opens my door and holds out his hand, pulling me into a hug when I climb down from the truck's cab. Sensing my remorse, he cradles my head against his chest.

"Stop beating yourself up, sweetheart, he knew how much you loved him. Everyone grows up and moves away, it's a part of life. He never held it against you," he murmurs. Heartache rips my chest open as I cling to Ryan. I didn't deserve Tommy's adoration and I certainly don't deserve Ryan's understanding.

Ryan shuttles me through the front doors into the vestibule where people are slowly gathering in the sanctuary. Keeping a protective arm around me, he braces me against the crowd. I am so grateful for the steadiness of his strength because my own is fleeting. My gaze stays transfixed on the floor, unable to meet the faces of our friends and family members. We pause at the holy water font and I watch Ryan dip his finger and make the sign of the holy Trinity. His head is bowed in reverence and I envy the look of peace that washes over his face. Stepping aside, he makes room for me to move closer. I shake my head, keeping my feet cemented in place.

"I'm not a real Catholic, Ryan. I was never baptized," I whisper frantically, not wanting to make a scene.

"That's not true." He has the nerve to smile. I scowl in return. "Your baptism is *legendary*," he whispers.

"*Stop it*, Ryan." I gasp when Ryan dips his hand into the font and blesses me. To my surprise, the earth doesn't shake in protest. "I have never taken communion or been confirmed. That's not funny," I hiss.

"It's a blessing, Beth," he kisses the top of my head, "no confirmation required." He chuckles and I want to kick him; I feel like an idiot. "Tommy loved to tell the story of your baptism," Ryan sighs. "I could always picture Gran's ashen face when your parents told her and Pops that they weren't going to have you christened. Of course, the best part was when Gran took it upon herself to baptize you in the kitchen sink when she was babysitting." The memory of Tommy's face lit up with laughter flashes in my mind. His arms are thrown wide in an animated gesture while he tells his story. I would give anything to hear one more story.

"Beth," Ryan's voice carries a heaviness that has me reaching to touch his cheek. "My grandfather wanted me to ask if you would do the placement of the pall with me." My throat seals shut, preventing me from answering; Grandpa Cantwell's thoughtfulness skewers me. "It's the white linen cloth that symbolizes baptism…"

"I know what it is," I cut him off, "I am just…" A sob keeps me from finishing my words.

"I should've told you sooner, I just didn't want you to stress over it," Ryan sighs, "I'm sorry."

I nod my head weakly as I wipe my tears. "Of course, I will," I whisper. Being gifted the honor of a part in Tommy's mass is humbling and heartbreaking.

The sanctuary is eerily silent, considering the number of people that line the pews. Tommy's casket sits at the front, and knowing his lifeless body is inside rips a hole open in my soul. My body shakes with a violence that threatens to bring me to my knees but Ryan's steady hands hold me up until we reach our families. I place my purse on the pew next to my mom and dad. In the pew ahead of us, Aunt Melissa gently caresses the hair at the nape of Uncle Rob's neck, while he rubs his hands over his face. We walk across the aisle to Tommy's father, who is flanked by his living children.

"Beth," he croaks as his gnarled hand takes mine. "Well, aren't you a sight for sore eyes, baby girl." He stands and wraps me in a fierce hug.

"Grandpa Cantwell, I'm so sorry," I squeak. So sorry that Tommy is gone, so sorry that I never came back, so sorry that I acted so selfishly for so long.

"Oh, darlin'," he murmurs, "I'm sorry, too. His loss is as much yours as it is mine. You're a good girl for doing this for our family. Tommy wouldn't want it any other way." I look to Ryan who nods and shrugs his shoulders. Banking on me to do the right thing is a risky business and his faith in me incites my shame. The anguish surrounding us is palpable; I close my eyes and pray for it to be over soon. My heart can only shatter so many times before the pieces become nothing more than dust. Ryan takes my hand and leads me to the sacristy where we retrieve the pall.

Father Paul begins mass by blessing the casket with holy water while the cantor's angelic voice fills the air with *Ave Maria*. Ryan stands next to me, stoic; the only evidence of his pain is the ferocity in which he grips my hand. The priest gives us the signal to step forward and together we cover the black casket with snowy white linen. My hand shakes as I place it on the cloth where my tears have left wet spots, and I lay a gentle kiss where Tommy lays. I close my eyes and gather every ounce of strength I can muster to prepare myself to walk away, leaving him one last time. When I open my eyes, I don't see a church full of people watching me with rapt interest, I only see the unshed tears pooling in Ryan's eyes and the tortured crease in his brow. My feet carry me around the casket to where he stands frozen. Tears spill down his face as he watches me approach but his face stays rigid in its mask of pain. Refusing to leave him in any way, I keep my eyes focused on his when I place his arm around my neck and guide him to our seats. Aunt Melissa turns in the pew in front of us to pass me a tissue. It's only then that I realize I am weeping. Clutching the tissue, my hand falls limp in my lap until Ryan takes it from me and tenderly blots my face. While Father Paul gives the liturgy, I lean my cheek into Ryan's chest while he rests his chin on my head. The sounds of the mass continue around me, but my focus stays on the steady beat of Ryan's heart.

At the cemetery, the ceremony is restricted to only those closest to Tommy when they commit his body to the ground. Father Paul leads us in prayer before explaining the symbolism of tossing dirt into the open grave. One by one, people shovel loose earth across Tommy's casket, marking a final goodbye. When my turn comes, I kneel and dig my hands into the fresh dirt. My breath hitches deep from my diaphragm as I watch the black soil trickle through my fingers. The pain in my heart is so excruciating, I swear I will die from it. Ryan kneels and wraps his arms around me, I wail when he urges me away. Somewhere, the logical part in me is aware that I am making a fool of myself, but my heart demands the release of this lament. I pull against Ryan, begging him to leave me to mourn.

"I don't want you to go, Tommy." I cry as I throw my arms around his neck. Time passes so quickly when he visits and it never feels like he is here long enough. Hot tears splash my cheeks and I squeeze Tommy as tight as I can.

"Baby girl, you are breaking my heart," Tommy's voice cracks with emotion. "I will see you soon, I promise. There are only a couple of months before you'll be home." He kisses the top of my head.

"I'll miss you so much," I blubber.

"I know, honey," he soothes, "There isn't a day I won't miss you."

"Promise?"

"Never a day, baby girl. Not one," he whispers.

"Me too."

∽

There's vague comprehension of being lifted from the ground and thrashing against the force carrying me away from Tommy's grave. The sound of feral keening rumbles from the depths of my soul as I am moved further and further away.

"Tommy." I shriek. I'm aware of Ryan rocking me in his arms as I scream for Tommy.

38

The sound of tires crunching gravel rouses me from a dreamless sleep. My eyes scrape across my eyelids like coarse-grained sandpaper, protesting when I peel them open. I am splayed across the bench seat in Ryan's truck with my head resting on his thigh. "Hey," he whispers, stroking my cheek. I watch him from where I lay as he concentrates on the road ahead of him. He's absolutely stunning with his tie loosened and sleeves rolled up. My heart stutters in confusion as the pain of Tommy's death takes up space with the yearning I have for Ryan. He throws the gearshift into park and sets his green eyes on mine. "We're here."

The lake is spread out before me, exactly as it has always been, perfection in its sameness. My breaths come shallow and short as thousands of memories engulf me at once.

"I can't." My voice is thick and husky from the scene at the cemetery. Being here is too much to process after a day like this.

"We need this Beth, you and I both," he starts, "neither of us needs to be under a microscope right now, and that's all that's waiting for us back home." I open my mouth to protest, but Ryan places his index finger against my lips. "I need you. Stay with me tonight, please," his eyes lock with mine, pleading. The thought of facing the rest of the family after my meltdown at the cemetery makes my decision easy.

"Okay," I keep my voice smooth and even in an effort to disguise my sudden nerves. The thought of spending the night being comforted in Ryan's arms sends electricity down my spine. Pools of green hold me captive with the longing swimming in them.

"I don't ever want to see you hurt like that again, Beth. You were so lost and in so much pain, it nearly killed me." He pinches the bridge of his nose, "I've never felt that helpless. It was awful."

"I'm so sorry, Ryan." I take Ryan's hand from his face and replace it with my lips. A need to touch him hums along my skin, covering me in goosebumps. For the first time in my life, I want to bare my soul. Ryan deserves the kind of woman who would share everything with him because he's the kind of man who would carry the burden with her. He is so much like Tommy in that sense. He would walk through fire for me if I let him. The last few days have taught me that time is not a guarantee and right now it would be so nice to pretend to be everything he deserves. "Thank you for taking care of me, that hasn't happened a lot in my life," I am careful to tread lightly across my confession. One thing at a time. This day has been heavy enough without adding more weight.

I grab Ryan's hand and pull him toward the dock to my favorite soul-bearing spot. Sitting as demurely as I can in a dress, I dangle my feet over the end of the dock and dip my toes in the chilly water. Ryan plops down next to me and when his feet hit the water he lets out a yowl.

"*Shit, that's cold!*" His wide-eyed reaction makes me laugh and relax.

"There's something I want to tell you, Ryan. I need to. Of course, if you want to listen." I drop my gaze to my lap, afraid that he will say no. He pulls his feet from the water and scoots his body behind mine, pulling me against his chest.

"There's nothing you can't say to me. I'd never judge you," he whispers against the side of my neck. I lean my head against his chest as my thoughts spin madly. *Never* is a promise that no one is capable of keeping. Reminding myself that he has no idea what he asking, I start with the easy stuff.

"When my folks moved to Florida, they got tangled up in some pretty crazy shit," I sigh in frustration. This is supposed to be the simple part, but it's not, it's hard.

"How old were you?" he asks.

"Five years old," I answer. "My dad was a banker and my mom was a marketing executive, so they were fully immersed in the whole 'yuppie' scene. It took me awhile to understand what that meant. I didn't get it at all, until one of the kids in our neighborhood lost his dad to an overdose. That shook everything loose for me. I always knew that my parents used cocaine—I just never knew that it wasn't normal. We lived in a neighborhood where using drugs was a way of life, so it didn't seem odd to me, not until Liam's dad died."

Ryan's arms wrap around me, squeezing me in reassurance. "I'm sorry about your friend." He kisses the back of my head.

"One day Liam was there, and the next he was living with his grandparents. No explanation, just gone. Some of the older kids in the neighborhood were the ones that told me how the paramedics came, but it was too late to save Liam's dad. That lifted the naiveté lens from my eyes, right away. All of a sudden, my perfectly normal life was flipped on its ass. I lived in constant fear that I would wake up one day and find my parents OD'd in their bed." The more I share, the easier it becomes to let it out. Ryan lets me go on about my life during those years, how aloof and irritated my parents were when they were using, and how sweet and attentive they were when they were sober. I told him how hard it was to always wonder what version of them I would find, so I learned how to take care of myself. Once I've told him everything I can without eluding to Drew, I turn my head and pull his head closer to kiss his cheek. "Thank you for listening. I'm glad I told you."

"You and I are a lot alike."

I hold in my breath and wait for him to continue.

"Growing up with a single mom, you learn to take care of your-self quick. My mom was always working. In the beginning, we were in Idaho so I was on my own a lot."

"How old were you?" I picture Ryan when I first met him—when I was six and he was eight.

"I was four when my dad left," he murmurs. The image of a little blond headed boy with big green eyes pops into my mind, and the thought of him being on his own makes my chest ache.

"You were eight when you moved back to Des Moines," I observe, putting the pieces together in my mind.

"Yep, and that is when Tommy became my surrogate dad, so to speak. He was always there for me," Ryan's tone is pained with loss. I turn around, straddling Ryan's lap and cup his face in my hands.

"He loved you, Ry. I hope you know how very much he loved you." I hold his gaze, searching for his understanding.

"Well, he loved you, too. He would've slain dragons for you," Ryan smooths his hands over my hair. In time, he will know that Tommy did.

We stay tangled together on the dock until the sun starts to set and a chill creeps along the water. When we enter the house, the ghost of Tommy is everywhere. It's easy to fall into thinking that he'll come bounding through the door at any moment. Ryan senses my melancholy and gives me a sad smile. I know his thoughts must reflect mine.

We miss Tommy.

39

Dinner consists of the only thing left in the pantry from Tommy's last visit to the lake, a can of chicken noodle soup and stale saltine crackers. We sit at the card table, like we did a hundred times as kids and laugh at our makeshift meal. My mind wanders back to the last time I was here with Ryan, and I can't control the blush that creeps into my cheeks.

"Hey, Ry?" My tone is matter of fact, but my nerves are anything but.

"Hmm?"

"Do you ever wonder," I swallow hard, "you know, if I had stayed that summer?" I wonder all the time, I want to say.

"I wonder all the time," he looks down at his bowl and clears his throat. My head pops up; shocked that he has spoken my exact thought.

"Me too."

He looks up with his brows arched in surprise. I give him a shy smile and go back to nibbling my ancient saltine. The promise of our confession hangs in the air like an unspoken challenge. I lick the salt from my lips and catch Ryan watching.

I am in so much trouble.

Once we are done and our dinner dishes are put away, nervousness settles in my belly. The silence that fills the house and my proximity to Ryan make me twitch. The emotion of the day has left me drained, and all I can think of is losing myself in Ryan's arms.

My breath catches when I picture curling up in his arms, naked and writhing beneath him.

"I'm going to grab a shower." I wince, wanting to slap my forehead when I remember that we didn't bring clothes or towels or anything else we typically pack for the lake. Ryan chuckles at my discomfort and tugs my braid as he walks past me toward the bathroom.

"There's got to be a stash around here somewhere. Aha!" He calls out from the linen closet. He returns with a lone beach towel and some travel size soaps and shampoos. My heart hammers loudly when I take them from him. The thought of being naked with Ryan close by sets a swarm of butterflies free in my stomach. It doesn't help that Ryan is looking at me like the thought has occurred to him as well. I force myself to swallow and give him a shy smile as I walk past him to the bathroom. A flustered sigh bursts from my lungs. I need to get into that shower, preferably a cold one, before I embarrass myself and jump him.

Putting my things down, I grip the edge of the sink and try to will my self-control to hold out. My brain ignores the plea and continues the slow torture of flashing vivid images of my hands caressing the hard plains of Ryan's naked body. I splash cold water on my face and drink in handfuls to quell the dryness taking residence in my throat. When I look up, I see Ryan's reflection in the mirror. He is standing in the doorway behind me with his hands gripping the top of the doorjamb; his pose accentuates the sinewy lines of his arms and chest. His tie is begging me to grab it and pull him forward.

The desire I've been desperate to tamp down is making the bathroom even more cramped than usual. I grip the sink so hard, I am sure the porcelain will crumble like my resolve. Ryan steps forward and takes my braid in his hands, my eyes flutter closed as he pulls free the elastic on the end and slowly unravels the plait in my hair. Strong deft hands reach the base of my neck where he combs through the strands from root to tip, sending tingles along my scalp. My hair spills over my shoulders in waves left from the braid, and the stare that meets mine in the mirror makes me feel incredibly sexy.

"Pretty." The green in Ryan's eyes burns with so such intensity, I need to shift my weight and rub my thighs together for relief. He grips me at the waist and pulls me against his hips. I shiver when my back comes into contact with a very hard Ryan. I close my eyes and try not to collapse when his hand slides from my hip to my stomach, leaving a burning trail in its wake. The need to run my hands up his chest and into his hair beckons me to turn around, but Ryan grips my hands and pins them back against the edge of the sink. The motion brings the hard length of him in closer contact with my backside, and I arch my back for more friction. A moan trembles on my lips as he drags his tongue up the side of my neck, stopping to nip at my skin along the way.

With my hands pinned, all I can do is wiggle against him and hope he doesn't stop touching me. He releases one of his hands to slide up my thigh, sending sparks of need up my spine. When he reaches the top of my thigh and slips his finger under the seam of my panties, the moan rumbling from his throat has me circling my hips, urging his hand to where I want him to touch me.

"Ryan, please," I beg shamelessly. Tension coils from deep in my belly, leaving me desperate and panting for release. He turns me to face him and lifts me from my backside and carries me to the bedroom. I wrap my legs around his waist and marvel at his ease in holding me.

Ryan lays me down as gently as he can without letting me go, spreading me out on the bottom bunk. He nestles himself between my thighs, rolling his hips against mine in sensual torture. Frantic, I tug at the tie of my wrap dress, needing his hands on my skin. With the arch of my back, the fabric slides open and I am exposed to his gaze.

"God, Beth. You are so beautiful, it hurts," he groans. Tugging me upwards long enough to relieve me of my bra, I pull off his tie and fumble with the buttons on his shirt. We fall back against the bed and Ryan reaches over his shoulder and, in one swift move, pulls his shirt over his head. The feel of Ryan's bare chest against mine is so intimate, so delicious, I moan in ecstasy.

"So good. You feel so good." I toss my head back as Ryan fills his hands with my breasts; leaving openmouthed kisses across each one. I don't recognize my own body as it builds with insatiable hunger. "Mmm...I've dreamt about this for so long." Ryan's hands skim my thighs and I lift my hips so he can take my panties with them. My skin is flushed in anticipation as my hands work proficiently to release Ryan from his pants. I am drunk with want. "I'm on the pill," I can barely breathe, let alone speak, but Ryan's answering growl assures his understanding. He drags his mouth from my nipple to my mouth, and I feel the head of his swollen erection slide against me.

"Look at me, Beth, I want to see you," I drink in his husky voice and lock my eyes on his as he pushes his way into my body and my heart. The veins in his neck bulge with his restraint, his sensuous mouth pulled into a silent "O." He moves in slow languid strokes, filling me fuller with each thrust of his hips, penetrating all of my defenses with the burn of his stare. I fight wanting to close my eyes in pleasure, needing him to have me stripped bare in every way.

Ryan's body should be chiseled in marble; from the hard muscles that lay beneath the soft dusting of hair on his chest to the rigid muscles of his abdomen that flex every time his hips meet mine.

My tongue draws lazy circles around his pebbled nipples as my nails rake down his chest; a tightening pressure builds from deep inside me, pulling my whole body taut. My muscles clamp down on Ryan as the orgasm crashes over me in waves.

"Ohhh, Beth." He picks up his rhythm, thrusting into me with fervor. His face is pinched like he is pain, as he slams into me harder, building another wave of desire in me. My nerves, still lit up with pleasure, start to sing when Ryan throws his head back, crying out my name as he buries himself deep inside me one last time.

40

The weight of Ryan's body anchors my body to the bed, keeping me from floating away. I've never been so aware of my body or felt as alive as I do laying here with Ryan as we fight to catch our breath. He is still rock hard inside me; I wiggle my hips to make sure I'm not imagining it.

"Have mercy, woman," he groans into my neck before nipping my skin. "We are never leaving this bed, ever. I don't care if the damn place burns to the ground around us. Do you hear me?" I giggle as Ryan rocks gently in me.

"Um, should I be concerned?" My cheeks flush as I try to find the words to continue. He looks at me through hooded eyes and tips his mouth the side. Tormentor!

"What do you mean?" He feigns ignorance but slowly starts to thrust inside me again. Cupping my breast in his hand, he darts his tongue around my nipple while watching me through his impossibly long eyelashes. Every coherent thought vanishes from my brain as blood rushes to more key places.

"Did you? How did you?" I stutter.

"God, yes, I've never been more turned on in my life." His breath skitters across my neck. "You do this to me, Beth. No one else."

This time Ryan takes his time savoring my body with his hands and his mouth, leaving every inch of me thoroughly cherished. When he moves in me, we find a lazy rhythm that drives us over the edge together. The slow burn of his mouth tickles the recesses of my memory; making me remember how I felt the first time he kissed me in the moonlight on my fifteenth birthday. There aren't many times in life you get the opportunity to come full circle, and I can't help but feel like life is telling me to grab on this time and never let go.

"What are you thinking about?" Ryan whispers into my hair. I am nestled into the crook of his arm with my head on his chest, feeling like I finally have my shot at happily ever after.

"Us," I sigh with contentment, "and how good it feels to be here with you."

"Mmm...so good," he murmurs. "Can I ask you something?" He strokes his fingers down my back.

"Sure."

"It's okay if you don't want to answer." His arm tightens around me, like he is afraid I will flee. My heart hammers a nervous beat, waiting.

"You're scaring me, Ry. Just ask me."

"What did Tommy do? I know something happened in Miami the summer you came home early because he had to visit a defense attorney a few times when he got back. And then you came back with him and Rob." He pauses, giving me a chance to respond. Without any doubt, I know that I want to tell Ryan everything. However, I don't want to tell him tonight. Tommy's death is the hardest thing either of us has ever been through and his funeral damn near killed us both. I'm not about to add Drew drama to the mix, not after what we just shared so I tell him as much of the truth as I can.

"When Tommy and Uncle Rob came down for The Daytona 500, my parents planned a dinner party with them and a couple of their friends. They weren't sober back then and the friends they kept weren't good people. One of my parent's friends brought cocaine to the house and Tommy lost his mind when he found out. He was furious that they would use in front of me. Anyway, he punched my parent's friend, and the asshole called the cops. It was a big mess, and I came home with Tommy and Rob so my folks could check into rehab." I take a deep breath but the knot in my chest is still there.

"Wow. You really had a crazy childhood, didn't you?" He cradles me against him, tipping my face up to his. He looks at me with adoration. "You amaze me, Beth. You are so strong, so beautiful and full of love. Life could've broken you, but you didn't let it." Tears spill down my cheeks. I am so head over heels in love with this boy. "Shh...." He runs the pad of his thumb across my tears and kisses me with so much tenderness it breaks my heart. I want to deserve him so badly but until I come clean, I don't deserve him at all.

"Ryan?" My question carries the tone of my anxiety. Sensing my tension, he rubs a soothing hand down my back.

"Yeah, baby?" His endearment takes root in my soul, fueling my courage.

"I love you. I fell madly that day under the cherry tree." His heart jumps against my cheek and I continue while I'm still feeling brave, "I never stopped. I didn't realize how much until you came out of the crowd at the airport.... you don't have to say anything. I just wanted you to know."

In one swift movement, I am on my back and Ryan's face is hovering above me. "Say it again, Beth. I'm pretty sure I was just hallucinating." His eyes twinkle with mischief, easing the thrumming of my heart and pulling my lips into a shy smile.

"I love you, Ryan." My face flushes at my confession, and I fight the urge to hide my face in my hands. Ryan's expression turns smug and I cringe at what his response might be.

"Elizabeth," he starts with a kiss on the tip of my nose, "that's the best news I've had in a long time because I'm so crazy in love with you, it makes me question my sanity." I pull his face to mine and kiss him with everything I've got.

"I don't know what we're going to do, but I'm not walking away from you again. Never again, Ry."

"I wouldn't let you if you tried, so don't you worry about that. In fact," he gives me a devilish grin, "I'd go so far as to say that I would tie you to the bed to keep you from running."

I swat at his chest, playfully and laugh. For the first time in my life, I'm certain that everything will work out like it's supposed to. I can't help but wonder if Tommy somehow has a hand in this and is smiling down on us.

41

Light filters through the window, stirring me awake. The first thing I notice is the heaviness draped across my stomach and legs. Careful not to wake him, I peek through one puffy eye at Ryan, who has his arm draped across my waist and his leg thrown over mine. I can't help the smile that steals across my face. His six-foot frame is crammed into the bottom bunk with me. One false move and he'll be on the floor, flat on his butt. The hope in my heart blooms, remembering the way he touched me, and how it made me feel to make love to him. My experiences with sex have been complicated.

First, there was Charlie. Having sex with him only taught me how much there is to lose when you've let someone that close. After that, I decided that emotional attachments weren't for me. The other guys that came along were fun, but nothing special. That's not to say they were lacking—I was. Sex was something I thought if I kept casual, I could protect myself from interference with my past. Distance was my answer for everything and the fallout from Charlie was all the assurance I needed. I didn't understand that by not investing my heart with what my body was doing, the closer Drew was brought to the surface. Tears pool in my eyes as my brain fires off neurons of awareness like the Fourth of July. From the beginning, Ryan has always chased thoughts of Drew away because of how I feel about him. There is no room for Drew because everything between Ryan and me has been rooted in love.

"Good morning, gorgeous," Ryan grumbles.

"Good morning, indeed," I smile, running my fingers through his messy blond hair.

"Damn, I had the best dream," he yawns, "my fantasy girl professed her undying love for me in between several rounds of mind blowing sex." I giggle and cover my blush with my hands. Ryan chuckles as he peels my hands away and brushes my mouth with his, "I love you, Beth."

"I love you, too, Ry." I close my eyes and nuzzle his chest. The whole world is waiting for us outside the walls of our childhood sanctuary, and I'm afraid of what will happen when it beckons us back to our lives.

"What's floating around that beautiful mind of yours?" Ryan kisses my forehead and pulls me tightly against him.

"The real world," I sigh.

"We'll figure it out, Beth. One thing at a time, together," he whispers against my lips, kissing me with tenderness that curls my toes.

"My dad is going to kick your ass," I chuckle, "then he'll turn you over to Pops."

"I don't expect them to take it easy on me, but I did text Melissa yesterday afternoon so someone knew where we were." He grins sheepishly as my eyebrow shoots up in surprise.

"Afternoon? Really? You're pretty confident in your seduction skills, Cantwell," my tone drips with sarcasm.

"Seduction? Nah. Still, there was no way I was going to let you leave here without telling you that I'm in love with you." The reverence in his gaze steals my breath.

"I beat you to it," I smile, "but I like that you were willing to fight for me. I can be a real stubborn ass."

"What about your ass?" Ryan teases, rolling me onto my stomach and palming my rear, "It looks pretty damn good to me. Let me make sure." Playfully he nips me, the sting making me squeal. "Mmm...damn good." His hands knead my flesh while his mouth samples the dimples of my lower back. I moan when he licks his way up my spine and shiver when he peppers my shoulders with light kisses. "I love your freckles," he groans against my shoulders. The moment is sufficiently ruined when I burst out laughing at his comment. He flips me onto my back, pinning me with his body, "What?" he grins.

"Ryan Cantwell, you don't need to sweet talk me. I think we've established that I'm a sure thing," I giggle, running my fingers along the sharp angle of his jaw. He frowns at me and shakes his head; I freeze with my hand against his face.

"Elizabeth Irene, I'd never lie to you about anything, but especially the things about your body that drive me crazy." Through hooded eyes he drinks in my body, stopping to caress my breasts. "I love this one here." His knuckle drags along the underside of my sensitive flesh, making me shiver. Continuing down my body, he pauses to kiss the inside of my knee, "And the one here." My skin is on fire everywhere he touches me. "But this one is my favorite." My eyes open wide when he lifts my foot to his mouth. I almost yank it away from him, but when he presses a sweet kiss to the freckle peeking out from between my second and third toe, I melt. Releasing my foot, he prowls forward and kisses me senseless. "They're sexy, just like you so don't you forget it."

The rest of the morning we spend worshiping one another before we head back to Gran and Pops' house. When we pull into the driveway, I smooth invisible lines from my dress. I don't know who I think I am kidding, I'm wearing the same dress from the funeral yesterday and they're going to notice. Even if they didn't, there is always the fact that I didn't come home last night.

"I feel like a teenager getting busted for sneaking back in the house after curfew," I groan.

Ryan chuckles at me and squeezes my hand. "I'm not sending you in there to face the firing squad on your own," he reassures, "besides, you're a grown woman. It's not like they can ground you. Your dad does seems like a reasonable guy."

"Oh, you laugh now, but wait until Pops gets hold of you. You had his baby girl out all night, corrupting her, no less." It's my turn to laugh as the blood drains from Ryan's face.

"Shit."

"Shit, indeed," I agree. "Speak of the devil." I nod toward the porch. Pops is standing at the top of the stairs with his hands on his hips. "You hanyaks better get your asses in here, *now*." If he were a cartoon character, steam would be shooting out his ears. He points to us and then to the house before he stalks inside, slamming the door behind him.

Ryan holds tightly to my hand as we step into the living room where Pops, Gran, Uncle Rob, Aunt Melissa, and my parents are waiting. I shift from one foot to the other as I wait for someone to say something.

"Boy, I ought to take you out back and tan your hide." Pops' face is red with anger, and he's directing it all at Ryan.

My mouth drops open in shock; I've never seen Pops' behave this way.

"*James!*" Gran shouts. She must really be pissed because I don't think I have ever heard her call Pops by his first name. "You watch your mouth. There is no need to threaten Ryan."

Pops glares at Gran while Aunt Melissa watches slack-jawed and Uncle Rob shakes his head in disbelief. My parents watch from the sidelines, more than willing to let Pops have the limelight. My dad narrows his eyes at Ryan, and my mom chews the inside of her cheek, trying not to laugh.

"He had my baby girl out all night doing God knows what to her." Heat rises from my toes all the way to my scalp.

"*Stop it!*" I yell, sending every head turning to me, "I'm sorry if you were worried, but I'm twenty five-years old, Pops. It's a little late to be concerned about my virtue."

Hot humiliating tears streak down my face. This is not what I had pictured when I got home. Ryan wraps an arm around me and kisses the top of my head; I'm so glad he is here.

"You should know that 'doing God knows what' entailed telling your granddaughter that I'm in love with her. No disrespect, sir, but anything else is none of your business." Ryan squeezes my shoulder and clears his throat, waiting for the next onslaught. "We did let Melissa know where to find us—it's not like we disappeared." Ryan shoots Aunt Melissa the stink eye.

"I told them, sweetie. Everything is fine, Pops is just slower than the rest of us to warm up to you two finally being where you belong." Her smile is sweet and sentimental. "We just stopped by to check in and let Ryan know that we're headed out to Cumming to get some of Tommy's things after we drop off Casey and John at the airport. We thought it would be good for him to come with, that's all. We didn't mean for it to seem like an ambush."

"Oh." Dumbstruck, I don't know whether to laugh or cry. "You should know, Pops, I love him, too." Pops' mouth twitches and tears glisten in his eyes. "Let's go sit on the swing for a minute," I turn to Ryan and gesture toward the porch.

Once we are outside again, I let out the breath I've been hold-ing. Ryan pulls me into a hug and lets out his own ragged sigh. "That was intense," he exclaims. I snicker into his chest, "It's not funny. I thought he was gonna go get a shotgun."

"I should spend some time with him—he worries about me. You should go with Rob and Melissa. We'll catch up later on, okay?" I promise.

"Is it crazy that I don't want to go without you?" he murmurs against the shell of my ear.

"Me too, Ry, but I should talk to Pops and then I should call my roommates and check in. It's only a few hours, right?" I try to reassure him, but I don't want him to go either. Growing up with parents completely codependent on one another has taught me the value of being able to stand on my own two feet. If a little bit of healthy distance is a good thing, then why am I already missing him?

42

Pops has been one of the most influential men in my life. Tommy taught me about unconditional love through the way he showed it to me. Uncle Rob taught me integrity in the way he stood his ground and insisted that my parents get sober. Pops taught me the value of a family that sticks together, no matter what. He stood by all of us while we picked up the pieces. He made sure my mom knew how much he loved her without excusing what she did, and he held me up when I was certain that my life was over. He showered me with as much love as I could take, until I was strong enough to stand on my own again. I watch him thumbing through a photo album at the dining room table and I am overwhelmed with gratitude.

"What've you got there?" Before I join him at the table, I wrap my arms around him and kiss his wrinkled cheek. The smell of his tobacco and Irish Spring fills me with the familiar comfort of home.

"I've got *you*, baby girl," he smiles, deepening the lines around his eyes, "always will." The album is opened up to my school picture from Kindergarten. The little girl in the photograph has long brown ponytails and a sunny smile that doesn't meet her eyes; they're blank, lifeless orbs staring at the camera. I swallow a painful lump in my throat when I realize the most vivid memory of that year was meeting Drew. I eye Pops warily, wondering where exactly he's headed down memory lane. He flips back a few pages to a picture of me as chubby toddler. "You were the happiest baby." He strokes the photo reverently. "Your smile and sweetness were something else, you had everyone wrapped around your chubby little finger." He turns the page to a picture of me sitting on Tommy's shoulders laughing, "You were four in that picture, it was taken right before your mama told us you were moving to Miami."

A deep sigh rumbles through his chest as he turns the page back to the shot of me in Kindergarten. The difference is painfully obvious, gone is the joy that radiated from my face, and in its place a forced mask. Even at five years old, I was learning how to slap on a happy face and muddle through. Pops flips two pages ahead to my school picture from second grade. My ponytails are gone and a short bob cut replaces it. My smile is wide and toothless but still as hollow as the one before. "When your mama called Gran and told her that you had cut all your own hair off, we knew something was horribly wrong," his voice crackles over his statement, "we just never knew how wrong." I sit paralyzed in my chair as fear grips me by the throat. Pops and Gran never knew what Drew did. I was always so scared that Pops would go after him. I pull in a shaky breath and wait for him to continue, "Tommy told us, Beth." I shatter into a million pieces. "He knew it wasn't right for him to keep it from us, once you told him how Drew abused you." My lungs suck in air, but I can't breathe and sweat trickles down the center of my back, "That's why I was so angry when Melissa told me you were at the lake house with Ryan. Yesterday, you left the cemetery hysterical. You were out of your mind with grief and I only let Ryan take you because I thought he'd bring you back here. When I got home and you weren't, I was terrified. Then Melissa told me that you were with Ryan, and I blew a fuse. The thought of you being in a position to be taken advantage of broke my heart," he huffs, trying to hold back his tears.

"Pops, I have loved and trusted Ryan since I was fifteen years old. It could very well be the soundest decision I've ever made in my whole life. I've spent the years since Miami running from the past instead of dealing with it. I have a shiny new life with wonderful friends who have no idea who I am." My breath hiccups when Les and Cyn come to mind. "I've hurt a lot of people I care about, pretending and keeping them at a careful distance. Ryan is the one person I don't have to pretend with."

"Have you told him about Drew?" Pops' question hangs heavy in the air.

"No," I confess, "I'm going to, but I couldn't tell him on the day of Tommy's funeral." Pops gives me an uneasy look.

"Don't wait to talk to him, baby girl. There will never be a good time for that conversation, you'll wait forever on the perfect moment." He sighs, placing his hand over mine, "I love you, Beth. If he makes you happy then I'm happy, too." Pops' words resonate in my mind as I thumb through the rest of the photo album. At the back of the album, there is a picture of Tommy, Ryan and me at the lake. Ryan has his arm around Tommy on one side and I have mine wrapped around him on the other side. By the look of us, I'd guess I was around eleven years old, making Ryan thirteen years old. Pops' is right, there will never be the right time to tell him—I've just got to do it.

My phone chirps from inside my pocket. The display shows a text message from Cyn: *Thinking of you. Miss you. <3 C&L*

"Excuse me, Pops. There's a phone call I need to make." I stand, kissing his cheek and head out to the porch swing. Staring at the phone in my hand, I wonder where I should start. Just as there is no perfect time, there is no perfect conversational lead in. I flip through my contacts until I get to our home number, hoping both Cyn and Les will be home; I hold my breath while it's ringing.

"*Beth!*" Cyn answers on the second ring and the sound of her voice already has me choked up. "*Les*, Beth's on the phone." That answers my question about whether I'll catch them both.

"Can Les pick up the phone in the other room? I want to tell you about Tommy." When Les picks up the other phone, I tell them about the night Tommy rescued me from Drew's advances. They listen aptly as that story bleeds into the years that Drew abused me. When I am through, there is an awkward silence on the other line.

"Wow, babe. I can't believe you went through something that awful and turned out so well adjusted," Les's remark makes me laugh.

"Says the girl who tells me daily to stop closing myself off." I laugh.

"True story," Cyn chimes in.

"Don't laugh at me, you cows," Les teases. "It just always seems like people who are victimized like that end up pretty messed up."

"Are you surprised I'm not draped around a pole in panties?" I giggle.

"That's so cliché," Cyn adds.

"No, I'm not surprised. I'm in awe. Your strength is unreal." Les's voice thickens with emotion. I wish I was there to wrap an arm around her, like she's done for me so many times.

"Leave it to Bradshaw to break the mold. B, you are amazing. Seriously. Consider my mind blown," Cyn says.

"BOOM. There goes my mind too," Les adds.

"I'm still me," I insist. "Nothing's changed."

"Your past doesn't change who you are, you idiot," Cyn scolds. "Now, when are you coming home?"

"Well..." I trail off. "I'm not sure." I'm greeted with a chorus of shrieks.

"Spill it," Les shouts.

I'm overcome with a sudden case of shyness. I'm afraid they're going to rain on my Ryan parade.

"Remember Ryan?" I mumble.

"Are you kidding?" Cyn's voice peps up at his name.

"This is gonna be good," Les snickers.

"Umm...." I giggle nervously. I have no idea where to even start.

"For the love of Pete," Cyn complains. "Please tell me you got laid after all these years pining."

"*Cyn*" I squeal.

"Oh yeah! She totally got laid," she answers.

"And at a funeral," Les playfully scoffs. "Beth, you saucy minx!"

"Shut up, both of you," I laugh. "Seriously, I've loved him since I was fifteen. I don't want to hear any grief."

"Does he love you?" Cyn asks.

"Yes, he does and we're going to take things a day at a time, so no interrogations, okay?" I plead.

"We just want you to be happy, that's all," Les reassures. "So, is he a hottie? Send me a picture!" Les purrs into the phone. For a second, possessiveness over Ryan flares at the thought of my gorgeous friend near him but as much as I trust Les, I also trust Ryan's feelings for me.

"Mmm....I bet he is, corn-fed Iowa boy and all," Cyn coos. "So, tell us everything! Does he have a big...."

"*Cyn*!" I shriek. Cyn and Les cackle on the on the other line.

"What? You're the pervert, I was going to say 'heart.' Does he have a big heart?" She snickers.

"He's gorgeous, smart, funny." I smile as Ryan's truck pulls into the driveway. "Hey girlies, speak of the devil, he just pulled up. Call you back later." I hang up the phone with loud protests still coming through the earpiece. The smile on my face drops the second Ryan steps out of the car, holding an envelope in his hand. From the look on his face, I know exactly what it is.

43

Ryan's face is a mixture of rage and fear. I can't imagine what my face suggests but I am petrified. He stalks toward me, his eyes never leaving mine and leveling me with their intensity. My lips tremble as I struggle not to cry when Ryan holds out Tommy's letter.

"Who is Drew, Beth?" Ryan's voice is deceptively soft as his whole body radiates suppressed anger. "And before you accuse me of stealing your letter, I have been at the memorial to help pack up the things that people left for Tommy. I didn't even know it was from you until I was half done." His temper flashes, but he quickly reins it in when he sees my tears.

"Ry," my voice quivers as his eyes lock with mine. Any hint of affection is gone from his eyes, replaced with fury. "Let's go for a drive, and I'll tell you about Drew, all right?" He stomps down the stairs with long strides, making me scurry to keep up with him. We climb into the truck and anxiety flares up my spine when he won't look at me. My hands shake so badly, I struggle with my seatbelt. "Maybe we should go back to the park. It was so easy to talk there."

"Easy?" Ryan shoots me a mocking look and goes back to staring straight ahead. When he pulls out the driveway and heads toward Legion Park, my only thought is—I can't lose him.

Ryan parks in the same spot we did the other day and strides toward our tree without giving me a second glance. I have no choice but to dash after him. Tears already leak down my face as I beg him to slow down.

"Ryan, please wait," I whimper, "let me explain." He turns on me so quickly I bounce off his chest.

"Explain what, Beth? Explain who the fuck Drew is? He sounds awfully important in your confessional to Tommy. Are you in love with him?" Ryan's face contorts in pain when I laugh.

"No, Ryan." I am afraid but resolute when I catch his gaze and hold it. "I am not in love with Drew. Drew was the person Tommy beat the crap out of when he tried to molest me in our living room in Miami." Ryan's mouth hangs open, as he is struck stupid with my revelation. "Kristy and Drew were my parents' best friends and Drew had a penchant for young girls." Ryan's face turns green as he sinks to his knees in the grass; although I want to console him, if I don't keep going I'll lose my nerve before I can purge the last of it. "He sexually abused me from the time I was five until I was twelve and they moved away." With the words out of my mouth, my chest shakes as I start to hyperventilate. Ryan's arms are around me in a second.

"Breathe, Beth. Slow. Come on, breathe with me, baby."

I pace myself against his steady breathing, drawing air deep into my lungs. I slip my arms around his back and nestle my head against his chest.

"I thought Drew was someone back in Charlotte, I thought you were... Jesus, I feel like an asshole."

"Ry, please believe me. I was going to tell you when you came back to the house anyway. I never intended to keep this from you," I plead.

"Is that what you've been running from all this time?" He strokes my hair, "Why, Beth? When you know how much your family loves you. Why? We could've helped you."

"Tommy knew everything, so do Gran and Pops. My folks know to a point, but they couldn't handle all of it," I spill.

"Do I know everything, Beth? Do you trust me with all of it?" I can't control the way my body tenses with his question.

"Of course I trust you," I answer, taking a step away from him.

"Then why are you backing away? What are you holding back?" He looks at me with pained eyes.

"I don't know what you want me to say," I stare at my feet and wrap my arms around my stomach, trying to hold it together.

"I want everything, Beth. All of it. I love you, and I want to share your burden. You don't have to carry this one alone anymore." He reaches for me and I wince. His face falls along with the arm he extended.

"No, you don't. You don't know what you are saying." I whisper. My body shakes so violently, my knees buckle and I hit the ground.

"I know I love you, damn it," he kneels in front of me, "that means I want you, Beth, all of you, not just the fucking pieces you want me to see." His temper is back but it's no match for mine.

"What, Ryan? What exactly do you want to know? Well, let's see, there was that time when I was five that he told me I was beautiful when I accidentally flashed my underwear. Or the time when I was nine and he showed me that if I rubbed myself just right, I could make myself come. Only to be rivaled by the time he showed me how to rub him the right way to make *him* come." Ryan runs his hand through his hair, pulling it like he wants the pain. "Or do want to hear about when I was twelve, and he told me how much he loved me right before he raped me? Don't shy away now, Ryan. This is what you wanted, right? Do you know he tried to tell me that it was consensual because he made me have an orgasm? Do you have any idea how humiliating it is to have your body betray you like that?" I am shouting at this point, and tears are dripping down both of our faces. Ryan's shoulders shake as he sobs; I am ashamed. It's so ingrained to push people away. I scoot forward until our knees are touching and pull his head into my lap. "I'm sorry. I'm so sorry."

Ryan lifts his red-rimmed eyes to mine and stares at me in disbelief. "Don't ever be sorry, Beth. I'm not. The way I hurt right now has nothing on what you've been through. No wonder Tommy kicked his ass, he should have killed that motherfucker." I shudder at the déjà vu.

"He wanted to. He told me that he had dreams of killing Drew and always woke up wishing he had. It scared him that he felt that way."

"You're amazing, do you know that?" It's my turn to look disbelieving at Ryan's statement. "You're so damn strong it blows me away, but you're never carrying this alone again. Okay?" I look at him, incredulous. "Beth? Talk to me."

Images of Ryan poring over the letter I wrote Tommy flash in mind, inciting my anger.

Okay?

No. Not okay.

The wind picks up my hair and fans it across my face, hiding me from him. Betrayal rips through my chest as I stand and walk away. There are no words for how painful Ryan's duplicity hits me. I'm furious. I'm mortified. I'm heartbroken that he would read my letter in the first place. To read it and then jump to the most morally reprehensible conclusion is devastating.

"Beth, stop." Ryan runs in front of me and puts a hand out to stop me. I refuse to look at him and move to sidestep him. As soon as I move, he blocks me and when I try the other direction he blocks me again. In a rage of fury, I plant my hands against his chest to shove him out of my way. He grips my forearms, trapping me, "Damn it, Beth, stop." I rip my arms free and beat his chest with closed fists.

"*You fucking Judas.*" I yell, "How could you read it? What gave you the right? Did it even occur to you to ask me first, you asshole?" Ryan grabs my flailing arms, trying to pull me to his chest, "Let me go," I wail.

"I can't," his voice is thick with misery.

"Why? You clearly don't think very much of me if you think I could sleep with you while I was with someone else. And Drew? What the hell, Ryan? There was nothing about that letter that even remotely suggested that he was my boyfriend." I pant.

Ryan drops his hands as his chin hits his chest. The adrenaline coursing through my veins triggers my brain into action. Fight or flight? I turn away from Ryan and take off running.

44

The cold air chaps my cheeks as I dip and dodge between houses and back alleys to reach Gran and Pops. I don't dare run the five blocks along the sidewalk, knowing that Ryan is in hot pursuit. When I ran from the park, it took all my willpower to keep going when he yelled for me, begging me to stop. Tears sting against my reddened skin when the house comes into view. My legs burn as they hit the pavement in the final sprint across the street. Tires screech around the corner from the bottom of the hill. Without slowing, I glance to see Ryan's truck eating up the pavement toward Gran and Pops'. I take the front steps two at a time and slam the front door closed behind me.

"Gran?" I pant. "Pops?" I sag in relief when no one answers. My breath hiccups with my cries as I crawl up the stairs to my room. When I reach the top landing, I hear the front door.

"Beth?" Ryan shouts.

"Go away, Ryan." I attempt to sound stern, but I sound as dejected as I feel. Turning the corner, I head into my bedroom and close the door. I flatten my back against the wall and let my sobs consume me as I slide down the magnolia wallpaper and cradle my head against my knees.

"Beth, please," Ryan's stricken voice floats through the door. When I don't answer, he cracks the door. I can hear him shuffle into the room, but I don't lift my head. Whether it's exhaustion or avoidance, I just can't look at him, it hurts too much. He thought Drew was my lover. Bile rises in my throat, threatening to upend my stomach. I read my letter over and over in my mind, trying to find the words that suggested anything but contempt and loathing for Drew. Maybe I can't see it. Perhaps the damage is so deep-seeded that something obvious enough to hurt Ryan would be undetectable to me.

No. I'm not that damaged.

In this moment, I hate Ryan for making me doubt myself but the gnawing ache in my chest disagrees. I'm hurt and I'm angry because I love him. I bared it all, the ugliest parts of my past, and he ripped out my heart at the first hint of misunderstanding. Worse than that, he was so consumed with his own rage that he failed to see how reading something so deeply private would affect me. I guess it was just easier to believe I was a whore. It's true, what they say, the people we love the most hurt us the most. Humiliation swallows me whole as tears show my weakness, shaking my shoulders. All I want to do is walk away with my dignity intact, but I'm trapped between loving Ryan and fearing what loving him will do to me.

"I need you to hear me, please," Ryan begs, "when Rob and I went to the memorial, we packed everything into boxes and took it back to The Cantwells. We sorted through everything to make sure the things worth saving could go into a memory box. I went through several notes before I got to yours and when I started reading, it didn't connect. You didn't even sign your name, you signed it 'B.' I read it again and realized the little girl named 'B' was you. I was confused. I was a total prick. Yell at me. Hit me. *Something.* Just don't shut me out. Please, Beth. Please."

I try to block out his pleas and explanations because anger is easier than hurt. What he is saying makes sense and while I can understand why he was upset, it's hard to grasp just how quickly he had me spiraling to the bottom. There I stood circling the drain, ignoring his betrayal to make sure he felt better. The people pleaser in me is relentless, even during the most tumultuous times. I don't want to live my life constantly worried whether the next argument will destroy me. I lift my head high enough to rest my chin on my knees. Ryan is on his knees in front of me looking pitiful. His hair is a disheveled mess from him yanking at it. His eyebrows are stitched together above murky green eyes that slay me with their suffering. I can't articulate what is searing my soul; he'd never understand.

"The first time I saw you, I mean *really* saw you was in the foyer at Gran and Pops'." His eyes lock with mine as he continues, "I was so pissed off because Tommy was considering postponing our trip to the lake. When I saw you leaning against the wall, I thought you were just being nosy until I got a good look at your face. You were fourteen years old and you looked like you were a war veteran. Your face was pale and your eyes were empty, the only sign of life was this crinkle on the top of your nose." He brushes the bridge of my nose with his knuckle. "It was the only marker that you were still inside that shell and it was there because you were worried about Gran, Pops and Tommy. I never felt so small than I did in that moment, until now. I did what I always did when I wasn't sure what to do, I teased you. When you turned those eyes on me, you bowled me over. That broken little girl I saw knocked me on my ass with one look. You were fierce and determined not to let me best you. Hook, line and sinker, Beth. In that moment, I was already yours." He pauses to see if I'll say something, when I retain my silence, he continues, "You slammed the door in my face and I swear, I stood there like a moron with my jaw on the floor." He smiles at the memory, and despite myself, I feel the corner of my lips twitch. "I didn't know what to do, I only knew that I wanted to be the one you turned to. When I found you in the cherry tree talking to yourself, all I wanted was to climb up that tree to be near you."

"I wasn't talking to myself, I was cursing you," my voice is lower than a whisper, but Ryan's face lights up with hope, nonetheless.

"Do you remember what I said?" he prompts. I don't want to remember, I don't want a reason to back down. "I said you could trust me," his voice cracks on his words. "You still can, Beth. I screwed up, but I never meant to hurt you. I'm sorry I betrayed you. I had no right to read that letter."

"I can't do this, Ry. I'm sorry," I whimper.

"Do you love me?" his breath hitches.

"Yes," I sob, "I love you, and you made me doubt everything. You made me wonder what in the hell I said to make you think I was involved with someone who sexually abused me for eight years. Damn you, Ryan, you're the only person who's ever made me forget and you thought...." He cuts me off.

"*I didn't know.* There was no way I could've known what Drew did to you and when I saw his name in that letter I flipped out. I was a jealous asshole. If I had known, I would've never... I want to *murder* that son of a bitch for what he did to you, and it makes me *sick* that I made you question yourself. "He sweeps my hair behind my ear. "I fucked up, Beth. I'm so sorry." Tentatively, he leans forward and kisses my forehead, "I love you, all of you. Every scar, every freckle.... I love that you didn't let your past stop you from chasing your dreams. Hell bent and beautiful, you're my heart."

"You hurt me," I whisper, as I fight the urge to curl into his lap and drink in his comfort.

"If you let me, I'll prove that you can trust me. I'll do anything, Beth. Tell me what I can do to make you believe me." He cups my face in his hands; I need to believe him more than I need to breathe.

"Tell me the truth," I challenge.

"About what?" He looks at me curiously.

"The night of the bonfire, the last summer I was here," I lock my eyes on his, "what were you thinking when you said 'pretty'?"

He looks down at his hands and blushes the sweetest shade of red my heart can handle. "I was thinking that you were so pretty with your eyes closed, swaying to the music. You were so alive, so far away from the broken girl in the foyer. I was so caught up in you—my thought came spilling out of my mouth. I wanted to die because it was in front of Tommy."

He's more honest and open than I have ever been. After all the mistakes I've made, all the people I hurt, I could never believe this was a lost cause. The fear of knowing that Ryan is capable of hurting me so deeply is sobering. Now that I have him, the thought of living without him is even more terrifying. In the end, there really is not a choice. I have been his since our first encounter under the cherry tree and, no matter how frightening, I know Ryan is worth the risk.

"This won't be easy, you know. Just because we've wanted this doesn't mean it won't be hard. We're going to have to be willing to fight for each other. There's a lot we need to figure out and it's not going to work if we handle things the way we just did." I lean into his hands, savoring his touch.

"I'd do anything for you, baby." He pulls me into his arms, and I hold onto him as tight as I can. I'm never letting go.

"Do I need to repeat the rules of this house? There are no boys allowed in bedrooms," Pops bellows up the stairs. "Get your asses down here." I swear I can hear him chuckling.

Ryan and I walk into the living room and find Uncle Rob and Aunt Melissa sitting with Gran.

"Where's Pops?" I ask.

"Here," he calls from the kitchen.

"I'll go see if he needs some help," Ryan kisses my temple and joins Pops. I'm left standing in the middle of the living room with curious eyes assessing me.

"What?" I ask.

"Don't 'what' me, dammit. Must I always browbeat the details out of you?" Aunt Melissa taps her foot impatiently at me.

"I don't know what you're talking about," I snicker. The look on Aunt Melissa's face is somewhere between murderous and ecstatic.

"If she tells you a duck can pull a truck, then shut up and hook the sucker up." Uncle Rob's back on his game, clearly. We all stare at him blankly. "Damn, you guys are about as useless as a screen door on a submarine." He shakes his head at us. "Just spill, Beth."

"Don't you guys have anything better to do than pimp me for the details of my life? Y'all need to work on generating some details of your own." It feels good to tease them, nosy old coots.

"Y'all?" Uncle Rob looks at me confused and turns to Aunt Melissa. "Did she just say 'y'all'? I think we need to hold some kind of confederacy intervention before we lose her to Paula Deen and Nascar."

Aunt Melissa turns a steely stare my way, "Don't make me hurt you. Please tell me that you are putting that boy out of his misery. The two of you are hotter than a billy goat's ass in a pepper patch."

My mouth drops to the floor and Uncle Rob clutches his heart.

"This woman is my prize. I'm one lucky bastard." He gives her a goofy smile and kisses the back of her hand. Gran is laughing so hard her eyes water.

"I know the feeling," Ryan says as he comes to stand next to me, "I'm feeling pretty lucky myself." He leans in and kisses me sweetly and turns to Aunt Melissa. "Does that answer your question? Because I can do it again."

I swat his arm.

"Ryan Cantwell, you hush your mouth," I use my thickest southern drawl.

"Christ on a crutch, we've lost her." Uncle Rob slaps his forehead, eliciting fits of laughter from everyone.

"Mmm....I like your accent," Ryan whispers in my ear.

"That's not all you like," I smirk.

45

The flight attendant snaps her gum and looks down her nose at me. This is the bane of traveling as an "unaccompanied minor"— always being stuck with the airline employee who likes kids the least.

"So," she yawns as she reads my ticket, "Tommy Cantwell is picking you up. Is that your daddy?" I shake my head and hike my backpack up on my shoulder. The sooner we can deplane, the sooner I can get away from Gum-smacking Gilda. "Your uncle?" she continues.

"No, he's just a good friend," I say in my most annoyed and petulant voice.

"What are you, like, ten? A ten year old with adult friends?" she snorts.

"I'm twelve and he is a friend of my family and a great friend to me," I sneer. "Can we go or what? Everyone else is off the plane."

She gives me a haughty sniff and pulls her bag down from the overhead compartment. "Brat," she breathes under her breath.

As we walk through the concourse, all I can think of is giving this clown the slip and running for the security checkpoint where I know Tommy is waiting for me. Fortunately, she seems as eager to ditch me, so she makes a straight shot to security without stopping.

"There's my baby girl!" I hear the boom of Tommy's voice before I can see him. When my eyes find him, I take off running with Snobzilla hot on my heels.

"Tommy!" I squeal, throwing myself into his arms. "I've got an AFA closing in," I giggle in his ear. AFA or Annoying Flighty Attendant is what Tommy calls the people relegated to escort me each year I fly home.

"Uh-Oh," he whispers, setting me on my feet. "Incoming, eleven o'clock."

"Kid! You can't just take off like that." Ms. AFA is huffing from chasing me through the crowd. She is about to lay into me when she notices Tommy. She admires him from head to toe through overly made-up eyes. Ew. "Mr. Cantwell? Annie Sampson," she bats her eyelashes at Tommy and extends her hand. Tommy shakes her hand and gives her his megawatt smile. I snicker under my breath because Annie looks like she's about to faint.

"Ms. Sampson, I trust that Beth was well cared for by your airline," he winks at me.

"Dude, she called me a brat." I narrow my eyes at Annie AFA.

"W-w-what? Don't be silly," she stutters.

Tommy ignores her and turns a concerned look to me, "She called you a brat? No kidding?" I nod. "What the hell is the matter with you? Who's the grown-up and who's the child? You should be ashamed of yourself." Annie blanches and then turns bright red with embarrassment. "Come on, Beth."

As we walk away, I steal a look over my shoulder and catch Annie Sampson watching us walk away. She's probably still trying to process being told off by the guy she was macking on. Feeling the need to prove her point, I stick my tongue out in pure bratty fashion.

"I saw that," Tommy chides.

"What? I figure if she was going to call me a brat, I might as well act like one." I giggle.

"I missed you, baby girl. Life is entirely too dull without you around." He swings his arm around my shoulder and kisses me on the head. "Hungry? How about Tasty Taco on the way home?"

"I missed you, too, Tommy. I love Tasty Taco." I laugh.

"I know," he winks.

❧

Being around Tommy was so easy, I always felt at ease around him. I'm finding, as I let down my guard, his nephew possesses those same skills. Being around Ryan is effortless, even after our show-down in the park. The steady confidence he exudes relaxes me. He pays closer attention than I give him credit for, too. From the Brutal Strength tickets to the random freckle on my foot, he notices all the little details that make me feel treasured. Despite the brutal play-by-play of my life in Miami, he hasn't changed the way he acts around me. At first, I expected him to pull out the kid gloves, but he didn't. He didn't hesitate to show me that he wasn't afraid to touch me or kiss me without freaking out. A day later, I am assured that nothing I confessed changed how Ryan makes love to me. Thinking about it makes my cheeks heat.

"What are you thinking about over there?" We're stopped at a red light, and Ryan narrows his eyes at me. We're on our way back to Pops and Gran's from Tasty Taco. "You look like the cat that ate the canary." I giggle uncontrollably as the light turns green, and I am rescued from his interrogation. "I have ways of getting you to talk," Ryan's voice is low and seductive.

"Saying it that way isn't an encouragement to get me to talk, babe." I laugh as his eyes pop and his mouth drops open. I can't wait to get my hands underneath that shirt and rake my nails down his chest. My tongue darts out to moisten my lips as all the ways I'd like to touch Ryan creep through my mind.

"I saw that," he whispers.

"Saw what?"

"Your tongue...." He leaves his thought hanging as we pull into the driveway.

"Now that's talent. You must have amazing peripheral vision, Cantwell." I lean over and nip the shell of his ear when he turns the truck off.

"I've got several amazing talents I'd like to show you," he's back to using that sex voice and when he turns to take my mouth in a searing kiss, a small cry escapes my throat. "God, you are so damn sexy, you're killing my will power, baby." With perfect timing, my stomach growls loudly.

"How's that for, sexy?" I laugh. We grab our bag of food and head to the back yard. I grab a sheet from the clothesline and spread it beneath the cherry tree while Ryan unpacks our tacos. The scene is a simple one, but it strikes a chord from deep within. I never thought I'd be in a place where my past wasn't a secret, let alone be here with Ryan. I pinch my arm for good measure.

"So, Ms. Thing, how's the hotshot music booking business?" Ryan lays across the sheet, propping himself on his elbow. He's so unbelievably handsome, it takes my breath away. "Beth?" My name shakes me from my reverie.

"Hmm?"

"Work? How is work, dear?" he laughs.

"Sorry, space shot. I love my job, I have a great boss and work with great people." I smile thinking of Andrea and Fred.

"Sounds, great," he teases.

"Ha ha. What about you? Where are you now?" I smile.

"I'm a counselor at Fisher Middle School," his smile turns shy as he shrugs. The things that get past his cool confidence constantly surprise me. I consider how much more there is to discover about him and it thrills me. I can't wait to peel back all of his layers.

"You would make a great school counselor, Ry. I think it's perfect. General population or special needs?" I ask. He looks surprised by my question. "My best friend, Cyn, is a special education teacher in Charlotte so I'm familiar with how the system works. Don't look so shocked," I tease.

"Not shocked, just pleasantly surprised," he smiles. "Fisher is pretty small so I see both. They're great kids, I love being in the position to help them."

"What's your favorite part of the job?"

He thinks for a moment before he answers, and when he does, his smile lights up his face. "Social groups. Twice a week for each grade, I host social groups for the kids in our school with autism. They're amazing, so smart and so sincere. I really love working with them."

"I didn't think it was possible for you to be any sexier, Ry." I abandon my tacos and crawl over to where he's still lounging on his elbow. I cup his face in my hand and kiss him with all the tenderness he evokes in me. "I love you."

"I love you, too." He smiles, brushing my hair off my shoulder to kiss the freckles there. "So, I've been thinking," he stares at his hands. I love that I can make this very sexy man nervous.

"In the last five minutes or the last seventy-two hours?" I snicker and he gives me a stern look, "What? It is a little humorous, isn't it?"

"It is," he shoots me his lopsided grin, "but I feel like our whole lives have been leading up to this moment. I've known you since we were kids, I fell in love with you when I was seventeen years old and now we're finally here." He sits up and pulls me into his lap, straddling him. Nose to nose, the air around us hums. "It doesn't feel quick enough, and I've never been more certain about what I want." He catches my lower lip in his mouth, sucking gently and teasing with his tongue.

"You could talk me into just about anything, kissing me like that," I murmur. He smiles wickedly. "But you know that. You're bad."

"But you love me this way," he chuckles.

"I do."

"So are you going to let me tell you what I've been thinking?" He bites his lip. He is pulling out all the big guns.

"I wasn't aware that I was holding you up. The floor is yours, counselor."

"Wrong kind of counselor, silly." He shakes his head at me.

"But you love me this way," I bat my eyelashes.

"So damn much, it hurts." He runs his hand across my cheek and I plant a kiss in the center of his palm.

"Tell me."

"I want to look for a position in Charlotte for next fall." My head is spinning. "Hear me out, I would finish the school year here in Des Moines and move into my own apartment in North Carolina in June. It gives us some time to catch our bearings and still be together." His plan makes so much sense; it's irritating. There is no loophole to argue, no detail he hasn't considered. When my eyes meet his, he's patiently waiting for me to absorb everything. I love him. I trust him. What is the issue?

"I'm scared," I whisper.

"I'm scared, too, but I am more afraid of losing you than taking a leap of faith with you." He makes too much damn sense. It makes my lips twitch. Ryan takes this as a good sign because he lifts the corner of his mouth. I'm a goner.

"Okay."

"Okay?"

"Okay," I giggle when he tackles me, "let's leap together."

232

EPILOGUE

One Year Later...

Dear Tommy,

Time doesn't heal all wounds. Whoever said that was either in complete denial or had never suffered the kind of pain losing you brought. In time I've learned to recognize the pain for what it is and accept it, but I'll never get over it. How could I? For all the suffering I've endured in my life, you were my redemption. The one constant who never gave me a reason to doubt your love or your faith in me. So few people are blessed to have someone like that in their lives, and you were mine. I miss you.

You once told me that my story was important and that someday I would tell it to whomever I wanted, whenever I wanted. You were right, I found someone to tell and it has made all the difference. It was long overdue, but when I finally purged every detail, it was finally over. I'm not afraid anymore. The past no longer holds any power over me. I'm not "cured" by any stretch, but I've accepted the scars as a part of who I am and so does Ryan. Yes, Ryan. Who would've thought that we'd find our way back to each other after all these years? Besides, Aunt Melissa. I swear that woman has a sixth sense.

You helped raise a good man, Tommy. A good man who reminds me so much of you it's like having a piece of you still with me. They say that all little girls grow up to marry men like their fathers. Well, I am marrying a man that reminds me of you.

He asked me to marry him at the lake house, on my birthday. He was sneaky about it, too! He had our Brutal Strength concert tickets from my fifteenth birthday framed. When he asked me to turn it over, I found Grandma Cantwell's ring taped to the back. I've never been happier a day in my life.

Life goes on but your absence is felt every day. It's getting easier to tell stories about you without breaking down, but the memories are bittersweet. I would much rather have you here.

I'll love you forever and miss you always. There's never a day I don't feel you with me.

Always,
Beth

"Are you all right?" Wrapping his arms around me, Ryan pulls me against his chest and rests his chin on my head.

"I just miss him," I whisper. The crisp autumn wind flutters the letter in my hand, reminding me of the one I left for Tommy last year and the impact it's made on my life. Ryan reaches for my left hand and kisses the diamond and sapphire ring twinkling on my finger.

"I miss him, too," Ryan sighs. Turning, I link my arms around Ryan's neck and bury my head in his chest. There's no greater comfort than Ryan's arms.

"Do you have it?" I ask.

"Right here," Ryan pulls a weighted picture frame from his jacket. I tuck the letter in the back of the frame and hand it back to Ryan.

"You do the honors," I smile at him.

When he takes the frame from me, my breath catches. After a year, his beauty still steals my breath. The wind brushes his blond hair across his forehead and his long legs bend gracefully as he kneels in front of Tommy's grave. I kneel next to him, placing my hand in the center of his strong back. His eyes meet mine, revealing his heart in his emerald stare. God, I love this man so much it blows me away.

"Hey Tommy, Beth and I didn't like the idea of you being alone, so we brought this for you." Ryan leans the frame against the headstone. "We miss you, man. Every day." He stands, pulling me up with him and we step back to check our handiwork. In the frame is the picture from Pops' photo album, the one of the three of us at the lake when we were kids. Around the edge of the frame are words that say it all:

Together forever, never apart. Maybe in distance but never in heart.

"Goodbye, Tommy." I kiss my fingers and then place them on Tommy's grave. Never a day, T. Not. One. Ever.

ACKNOWLEDGMENTS

First and foremost, I want to thank Steve for his unending support in this process. Thank you for moving mountains to make sure I had all the time I needed to write. Thank you for turning a blind eye to a dirty house and an empty fridge. Thank you for taking care of me when I'd forget to come up for air. Thank you for your faith in me.

CJ and Cameron, my sweet monkeys, thank you for not firing me for shirking my duties. Your strength and courage inspire me everyday. I'm so blessed to be your mom.

I want to thank my grandparents for teaching me the importance of family. The richest memories I have are of Sixth Street surrounded by your love. Thank you for teaching me that our family is more than who we're related to and that the love of our family is rooted in acceptance, warts and all.

Grandpa, I miss you. We were a pair, you and I. Kindred spirits. We "got" each other and I miss that every day.

Gran, your strength of heart and spirit is something I aspire to every day. I'm so very proud to be your Blossom.

My hanyak clan: Sue, Jim, Cindy, Corey, Cortney, Diana, Brittany, Mike, Dick, Ronda, Angie, Nate, Corrie, Mom, Dad, Cyn, Scott,

Thompson, Linnea, Jamie, Jariya, Jay, Janny, Mary, Dick, Nick, Carrie, Sam, Charlie, Arin, Bob, Carolyn, Julie Ann, Steve, Josh, Joe, Kim and Austin.

Aunt Mary and Father John Ludwig, thank you for the Catechism review.

A special thank you to my beautiful sister, Cynthia, who has always listened to and encouraged me. I love you and am grateful every day for our relationship. James Taylor, parasailing on Key Biscayne, flea baths in the swimming pool, '80s music trivia in the middle of the ocean, epic late night pow-wows in Duck, sitting at the dining room table with you on Sixth Street... the memories are as endless as they are priceless.

Mom and Dad, thank you for teaching me about perseverance. You taught me that strength comes from holding each other up, not bearing the load on your own. Thank you for believing in me and loving me, even when you didn't understand me. I love you so much.

Cynthia McSwain, your friendship is a rare and precious gift. The depth of my love for you holds no bounds, woman. I would still be holed up in my house, hiding from the world, if you hadn't wooed me out of my comfort zone. Your persistence and patience changed my life. I love you, sessy....

Natlaie Coffey, Candise Owens, Aislynn Kiser, and Sierra Faulk: Thank you for supporting our family and thank you for your dedication to the monkeys. Without you, we would be lost. I'm blessed to call each of you family.

Thank you:

Michelle Mankin for allowing me to include Marcus, Avery, and their band Brutal Strength from the novel *Love Evolution*. Love to you, MM!

A huge thanks to my sounding board—Melissa Brown, Leslie Fear, Dave Newell, Melissa Perea, Andrea Randall, and Lori Sabin. Your input, critiques, and encouragement were invaluable to me. I adore each of you and had great fun using your names for my characters.

My beta readers: Melissa Brown, Andrea Randall, and Tosha Khoury.

Melissa Brown and Andrea Randall: Thank you for mentoring me and challenging me to grow as a writer. I love you both with all my heart and am blessed everyday by your friendship.

My editing goddess: Lori Sabin, thank you for making my story come to life. You are gifted in so many profound ways, but your gift of friendship means the most.

Tarryn Fisher, a little book called *The Opportunist* started me down the path to writing my own book. Thank you, Tarryn, for inspiring me, encouraging me, and making me squirm. My love and appreciation know no bounds.

Thank you for to the friends who cheer me on, get the word out and love my crazy ass: Happy, Paul, Kelley, Steveland, Fred, The lovely ladies of BA, 50 Authors and Owl and my Guttermates.

For all of the indie authors who've paved the way: Thank you for showing me the ropes and for encouraging me.

ABOUT THE AUTHOR

 Maggi was born in West Des Moines, Iowa, and raised in Miami, Florida. She has deep love for The Heartland and really good Cuban food. When she's not writing, you can find her reading or singing into the end of her hairbrush. She's a steel magnolia and mischief-maker, wrapped up and tied with a sarcasm bow.

Currently she lives in Annapolis, Maryland with her family. For more about Maggi and future projects you can follow her on Facebook (www.facebook.com/author.maggi.myers) and Twitter (@Magnolia_B_My).